Calling Time

Matador
9 Priory Business Park,
Wistow Road, Kibworth Beauchamp,
Leicestershire. LE8 0RX
Tel: 0116 279 2299
Email: books@troubador.co.uk
Web: www.troubador.co.uk/matador
Twitter: @matadorbooks

ISBN 978 1785893 155

British Library Cataloguing in Publication Data.
A catalogue record for this book is available from the British Library.

Printed and bound in the UK by TJ International, Padstow, Cornwall
Typeset in 11pt Aldine401 BT by Troubador Publishing Ltd, Leicester, UK

Matador is an imprint of Troubador Publishing Ltd

MIX
Paper from
responsible sources
FSC® C013056

To James, Mark and Henry for their enthusiastic encouragement, to the BSG who were in at the beginning, to Suzette my guiding star and to Hugh for his kind oversight.

PART ONE

New Zealand 1953

Matron

'Bugger!', Matron muttered. She could have sworn there was more sherry. She didn't remember having anyone in – other than Valerie and she didn't drink. Very prissy about drink, she was. Isobel Gardiner came to the reluctant conclusion that she must have drunk the sherry herself. Staring at the remains of the delicious golden liquid, she realized there was only enough for two drinks. A pity, but she supposed she shouldn't have any more when she was going back on duty. Isobel poured half the sherry into a glass and hobbled painfully over to her armchair. 'God', she needed to sit down. Her legs were killing her; she looked down at the swollen, purple veins that so disfigured her legs. It was no wonder they were painful. Ugly as sin too. Settling into her chair, Isobel took a large gulp from her glass and sighed with contentment as she surveyed her surroundings. She would miss this room, larger than many a Matron's quarters, with its view over the garden at the side of the building with a neat hedge beyond, screening the road. Having a fireplace for real fires was a treat, with a wide mantelshelf for one or two ornaments. Not that Isobel had many ornaments. She wasn't the type for knick-knacks that required dusting. She slowly sipped the remainder of the sherry to make it seem more, cursing that she had not bought another bottle when she was in town. It was unlike her to walk past a bottle store.

At fifty-eight, almost fifty-nine, Isobel was looking forward to retirement. She was fed up dealing with smelly beds, dirty bottoms, gungy false teeth and moaning patients. There was a time when she had enjoyed looking after the elderly but that had long passed. Still, she'd managed to please the Board that morning.

"Well done Matron, numbers are up to scratch. I don't know how you do it," a smiling Richard Cameron had said, and the Board had agreed.

They must think she was doing a good job. The Chairman was generally stingy with his praise. Nobody noticed Isobel's guilty blush. They were only interested in the legal requirements, staff ratio to patients, that sort of thing. They didn't know about the corners cut to mask the lack of staff, the fact that most of the patients were totally dependent, only a handful able to walk on their own. It was very heavy work and she felt the Board should recognize it with a pay rise.

Isobel's legs were aching unbearably. Her varicose veins had become much worse over the years and being overweight didn't help. Diet after diet had been tried but as soon as she stopped, the weight went back on. She arranged the footstool in front of her armchair and heaved a sigh of relief as she took the weight off her legs. The blocks would have to go under the foot of the bed again tonight.

She shouldn't have to be going back on duty in the evenings and she certainly shouldn't be helping to lift heavy patients who couldn't help themselves. It'd done for her shoulders again now. She knew she shouldn't do it, she should ask one of the others but they were always short handed, never enough staff. Sitting there, sipping her sherry, Isobel reflected on the latest murmurings in the Home. This time they were about Angela. Well, she had a certain sympathy with Angela. She'd overheard her asking Sister why, if God was so clever, he didn't put these old people out of their misery. Isobel had thought Sister's answer, "God has his reasons," was inadequate. It didn't explain anything. Why *did* we keep these people alive? Edith Nolan didn't have any quality of life. She couldn't say anything sensible, she was incontinent, had to be fed, had no visitors. She was just there, and that was it. Elsie Hammond was just one long moan. She could barely move her head and could only feed herself if the spoon and plate were put into her hands and about six inches from her face. She could talk all right, she never let up. It must be jolly miserable if you couldn't move and were in pain most of the time but her constant moaning was very tiresome for everyone else. "Can you get me this, can you pass that, why do the girls never put things where I can reach them?" On and on it goes. Maybe she feels that a misery shared is a misery halved but that was selfish in Isobel's opinion. Angela shouldn't slap the patients though, if she did. Isobel only had Bill's word for it and if he hadn't seen her do it, he might be imagining it. He was a sanctimonious old sod anyway. The girls were only young and they were at the sharp end. They couldn't be patient all the time.

Isobel couldn't resist a smile. What if she'd said, 'Well Mr Harkness, you may be surprised to know that I believe in euthanasia.' Isobel laughed out loud. He would have been more than surprised; he'd have been horrified. Just as well she hadn't. Knowing him he'd have reported her to the Board.

Damn! Why hadn't she put the bottle where she could reach it. Isobel struggled to her feet to refill her glass with the last of the sherry before gratefully sinking back into her chair. She wished she hadn't eaten all the chocolates. Queen Anne, dark ones. Delicious.

She continued to search her memory. Did she have Kristine's starry-eyed dedication forty years ago? If she did, she soon had it knocked out of her. Cancer you can't treat; TB, well they did have some drugs for that but patients were ill for years and some still died of it, Polio was a menace, the wretched Parkinson's ruined many lives. Isobel acknowledged that things had been far worse before the First World War, when most diseases had to run their course and the patient hoped for the best. After that war, there were many damaged lives and since the Second World War, there were many more. Even now, half way through the twentieth century, there was still no cure for many diseases, although with Penicillin, there was now hope for things like pneumonia which had previously killed so many, particularly the elderly; besides, did it matter, we were all going to die in the end.

She wondered how long it would be before Kristine lost her illusions, started cutting corners, pushing a bit here, shoving a bit there. Perhaps she wouldn't. She was booked in to do her training in January and seemed a dedicated type but Isobel felt that Kristine was too soft and wouldn't last the course. She'd been with them six weeks and whenever there was a problem with a patient or someone obviously in pain, her face crumpled up and Isobel kept expecting her to burst into tears. Still, they'd been lucky to get the extra pair of hands. Apparently when she'd applied to do her training she'd asked to start early but Matron Thompson had said that wasn't allowed. She'd suggested she might like to get some experience in one of their affiliated old peoples' homes around the district, and so she'd turned up at Mountain View.

Isobel couldn't believe she had run out of sherry. Of course she would prefer gin but it wasn't quite the thing for a woman living on her own. Her Mum had called it 'mother's ruin' as it was supposed to secure an abortion if you drank half a bottle and sat in a hot bath. It must have worked, as that's what most women of her Mum's age believed. She must have known somebody who'd tried it. A sudden thought crossed Isobel's mind. Perhaps her mother had terminated an unwanted pregnancy? You couldn't blame her if she had. After all, there was no contraception except abstinence fifty odd years ago. Not much better today. No, she dismissed the thought. Her mother had been much too strait-laced. In fact, neither of her parents had been of a romantic nature and she followed in that mould. Isobel felt it was quite respectable to have a bottle of sherry in the cupboard, even two if they were different kinds. You never knew when someone might drop in and sherry was always acceptable. She'd have to get more drink in for the weekend. It was the only thing that kept her going. She often drank gin when she was out but never kept it in the house.

How she hated the evenings, having to put all the old dears to bed. At least she was off duty tomorrow. Maureen, the closest friend she had, said there would be time for a gin or two at the Royal Oak. She was a right smart arse though when Isobel had suggested they skip the film.

"You can't, it's history," she'd said. "Not likely to be another Coronation in our lifetime." The old bossy boots. She'd even commented on the book Isobel was reading, "They Do it With Mirrors," she'd picked up the latest Agatha Christie from the sofa. "Why do you waste your time on this rubbish, and "what *do* they do with mirrors, that's the question?" She tossed it onto the table.

"I like Agatha Christie. I buy the new ones as they come out. She helps me relax when I come off duty."

"You should read something mind improving, like that new Samuel Beckett, 'Waiting for Godot.'"

"What ever else I read it won't be that. Two old fellows hanging about waiting for something to happen – and it doesn't. Nothing mind improving about that," Isobel had retorted.

Her mind went back to drink, as it tended to do more and more in recent months. Maybe they'd have time for another couple after the film if it didn't go on too long. Isobel was aware she was becoming dependent on alcohol to see her through the day but managed to convince herself that it was better than cigarettes, which she'd never fancied. Or drugs that addled your brain. A few drinks were harmless and she wouldn't need so much once she'd retired and didn't have the pressures.

She should just be supervising. If that was all she had to do there'd be none of the rumours about Angela. She'd be able to walk about and keep her eye on things. There was too much to do. Isobel couldn't remember seeing her old Matron, Martha Johnson, ever washing backsides and changing beds when she was training. Very much the Matron, she was. The rumour still rankled. Still, she didn't believe there was anything in it. Someone would have complained. She would have to try and watch them more closely. The girls worked jolly hard and Angela got through the work quicker than most, and did more of it.

It was true that old Edie was always wet and Angela was probably just giving her some encouragement to hold on a little longer. She hoped she didn't get bedsores, as it would be a bad mark on the home. They had very few and that was a miracle as so many of the patients were incontinent. She could get the Doctor to put a catheter in but then Edie could pull it out or get a urinary infection, which would add to her confusion. She couldn't win.

Hell's teeth! Isobel realized it was nearly six o'clock. She heaved herself out of the chair and quickly made herself a cheese sandwich to soak up the sherry. Her little flat was very convenient but she was looking forward to living in the house where she'd been brought up and having a little more space, particularly in the kitchen. She'd be able to grow a few vegetables and hang her washing outside for a change. It got so dried up in the drying room. Isobel finished dressing and noted that her uniform belt got shorter every day. She would have to put another notch in it. Retirement would bring the welcome relief of not having to wear her cap as the starch rash was back. But for now, Isobel longed for a quiet two hours so she could get off on time.

Agnes Thorwood

Agnes shifted uneasily in her chair. She would have to call the nurse soon but was determined to wait as long as possible. Another fifteen minutes would help but she mustn't have an accident, and please, God, don't let it be Angela, she'd been so horrible yesterday.

"What do you want now, you old cow?" Her voice coarse, spitting out the words, her face set and hard. Agnes thought the girl's mother must have been wildly optimistic to call her daughter Angela. Someone less like an Angel she couldn't imagine. She mustn't cry either, it only made the girl worse. The girls cleaned her up, but not properly, leaving her feeling dirty and smelly. The weekly bath was never enough; she wished she could have one every day like she used to at home. A bath to Agnes, was Heaven. To sink into the clean warm water and use the sweet smelling soap Sister had given her for Christmas, to wash away the stinking odours. Bliss. But sadly it didn't last. Sandra, who nearly always came with Angela, was less cruel but Agnes could feel her cringe when she had to touch her unclean body and she never looked directly at Agnes. It was not clear why either of them were there as the work obviously didn't appeal to them and the money was poor, or so she'd heard.

As always when she was under stress, Agnes' thoughts went to her husband. Dear, kind George. He would never have let the girls speak to her in that nasty manner. At least dying early had saved him the misery of old age and the embarrassment of an ugly, useless wife. She should have died soon after George and it would have all been over now. To think she'd once wanted to live to be a hundred. Now she'd be prepared to throw in the towel at fifty-nine, today, this minute. It was the Parkinson's that had ruined her life. It had crept up on her. She first noticed it in church when she was trying to read the lesson. Her hands were shaking so much she couldn't turn the pages. Agnes had put it down to nerves but knew in her heart that it couldn't be. She was a teacher, used to standing in front of a class. That was sixteen years ago and it had been downhill to her present sorry state.

It was bad luck to get it early, as everyone said Parkinson's was an old peoples' disease. Agnes guessed she was the exception that proved the rule. Even walking was an embarrassment. The tottering, tiptoeing gait, the staggering, drunken appearance Agnes cried inside when people backed away during bouts of involuntary jerking and flaying of her arms. She supposed they thought she was violent. But the very worst thing was the wretched saliva. She could swear there were cupfuls of it, sometimes rivers of it, or thready, cobwebby streams of it. The good days produced only trickles of the stuff. Agnes couldn't imagine where it all came from. Only God knew. Bill didn't dribble as much as Agnes or she didn't think so, and yet he had the same disease. "You shouldn't worry about what you look like Agnes," he often said, trying to cheer her up, "Everyone's ugly in here." It was all right for him. Appearances didn't seem to matter so much for a man. She could put up with a skinny body; most people would rather be slim than fat, but she couldn't bear the face and the straggly, thinning hair which was seldom washed. The girls should treat her better but they didn't seem to care. It was up to Matron to teach them how to behave towards the patients and care for them properly. She walked around occasionally but never seemed to say or do anything constructive. Rumour had it that Matron Gardiner was due for retirement so Agnes guessed she had lost interest in the Home and was just serving out her time. Agnes knew she wouldn't have accidents if she was helped to the toilet more often. She always asked in time but the girls would say, "I'm coming," then they'd forget or deliberately ignore her.

It was a relief that she didn't have any visitors, as she couldn't have borne anyone seeing her in her present condition. Considering she had been one of the brightest teachers at the college, teaching Chemistry to future doctors and engineers, Agnes found it hard to believe how she'd ended up. She was treated like an imbecile by most of the people in the Home. Bill was the exception. Oh and Elsie was always kind. But Bill understood because he was bright too, a scientist, like she was. He had written two books on mathematics and still spent his time working out theories and formulae although she didn't know what for or what about. To keep his brain active, was all he would say when she asked him. Agnes still had all her faculties but nobody knew what she was capable of because she couldn't get it out. She didn't feel any different inside and felt she too could write a book if only someone could understand what she was saying. She'd never realised Parkinson's affected the voice but then she'd never known anyone with the disease before coming into this place. Your voice became slow and hesitant because you couldn't think of the word, then you couldn't pronounce it. It was so frustrating she could scream.

Reason told Agnes that she needed to be where she was. She'd been falling over, burning herself on the electric fire and narrowly missing her feet with a pot of boiling water. Full time care had been considered inevitable. It would have been unreasonable to expect her wonderful neighbours to do her shopping and keep an eye on her indefinitely. Besides, she'd heard Tom had had a transfer to Wellington soon after she'd left so she would have had to make new friends and possibly different arrangements. The doctor had said she was a danger to herself but Agnes felt she should have been allowed to take the risk, if only for a few more months. She would have done if she could have afforded to pay a companion to live in but then would she ever have found one willing to mop up incontinent accidents from every orifice, however infrequent? Agnes had only been in the Home two years but it felt like twenty. If she'd got a better price for the house, maybe she could have been in a better place. There must be better places, with more caring people.

Agnes leant forward and turned on the radio. It needed new batteries but she might hear something of interest... "congratulations still continue to pour in for Edmund Hillary...first man to reach the top of the world..." What a thrill! It was especially so, to have achieved it just a few days before the Coronation. Fancy someone from this tiny country with so few people being the first to conquer Everest. We are not so insignificant after all, thought Agnes with pride, sitting up straighter in her chair. George would have been thrilled with the achievement. She picked up the photo of her husband. Dear, handsome George, with his strong determined chin, lovely soft brown eyes and thick, wavy brown hair. She put her lips to the glass, in what had become a daily ritual. She knew it was ridiculous but if she didn't kiss George's photo everyday, something bad would happen. A stupid compulsion, as everything that happened in the Home was bad. How she missed her dear George.

Agnes wrinkled her nose in disgust. The stink wafting into the room made her feel sick. It was bad enough when she had an accident but the constant smell from the sluice two doors from her room, was overpowering. She knew she was welcome to sit in Bill's room at the other end of the corridor where she wouldn't smell it, but she'd have to get someone to take her and the girls might pass crude comments about her sitting in a man's room. At least Mountain View was all on one floor so with help, she could walk to the lounge and the dining room, but she seldom did. Whoever had called the home Mountain View, was either wildly optimistic or paid scant observance to the truth. There were only two or three rooms that had a view of Mount Egmont and even then, it was often covered in cloud.

Agnes congratulated herself. Sheer will power and concentration had enabled her to wait another half hour before calling the nurse. Maybe she could manage a little longer. Another half hour. As long as she thought of other things, she did not have the urge to go.

How she missed her lovely house. A beautiful garden, fashionable area; well it was now. Fitzroy had come up in the world since she and George had bought the house. Three bedrooms so they could have friends to stay and one for a study. Best of all there was a lovely glassed-in veranda at the back facing the sea, with dunes of gun-metal coloured sand studded with coarse tussock, right up to the fence. Agnes adored the sea. Never the same two days running; its incessant movement was quite hypnotic and always different. Sometimes crashing waves, often gentle, almost silent, ripples. One day peacock blue, the next summer green, but frequently scowling grey when the winter came. The magazines all said living by the sea was good for you, helped you live longer, but Agnes refuted that. George had died at fifty and she had become a disabled crock. She had to admit the sand was a nuisance sometimes. Into everything; in your hair, traipsed in the house, the way it stuck to the washing on windy days, but to her, it was worth it. The smell of ozone, of salt, of seaweed. She loved it. Anything was better than stale urine and faeces. Agnes didn't think the staff at the home knew how to do the washing. Her clothes came back from the laundry, stiff and dingy, smelling of disinfectant. They probably boiled them to kill the germs and she accepted it would be hard to get faeces out without soaking and boiling, but it was no wonder nothing fitted for long.

Oh. She mustn't think of wee, or she'd want to go. Then there was the spittle, which she could feel now, wet on her chest. The rash would be back and they wouldn't put the cream on. Even putting the waterproof bib on helped. It was ugly and made her feel like a baby, but it did keep her dry. Sister Johansen would do it but Agnes had forgotten to ask her. She did seem to understand and was kind too. Agnes couldn't comprehend why Sister came out to New Zealand. It was a long way to come to another empty country like her own, and she wished she wouldn't speak out the corner of her mouth. The words seem to come out sideways and her strong foreign accent made it worse. It distressed Agnes that she couldn't understand half of what she said and that she herself couldn't be understood properly by anyone. If only she could explain how she felt, what hurt, what was uncomfortable, what was unpleasant, how much she hated the smells. She damned the shaking; the hands were getting worse, the legs too. Friends had said she was pretty when she married. George always said so. His gorgeous scientist, he'd called her. They'd met at University in Dunedin and he'd proposed the second time he'd taken her out. "I can't have someone else getting their hands on you. Let's get married as soon as we graduate." And that is what they did. Agnes' parents were well into middle age and she had no siblings so they were glad a nice, steady young man wanted to look after their daughter. Agnes was relieved they had died before George so they never knew she was now completely alone in the world. She always felt that George's father had given up the ghost shortly after his son had died. He had been a widower for many years and the effort of carrying on was just too much. With no grandchildren, what was there to live for? Where did this beautiful girl go? She was still there inside looking out. Well, maybe, not the gorgeous bit, but people only saw the outside, looking in, a hideous spectre. They never used their imagination to see the real Agnes.

Suddenly, the urge was too strong. She would have to ring the bell. It was no good, she couldn't wait any longer.

'I suppose you've kacked your pants again you dirty old thing.' Angela's crude comment was typical of her. Accusing Agnes without question. No Mrs Thorwood either. In fact Angela hardly ever addressed her as anything, although occasionally she called her 'Old Aggy' which Agnes hated.

Sandra just giggled, always supportive of her friend, but nervous. She seemed to live in thrall of Angela's every word. A weak character, with never anyone to teach her differently, to set her own standards. She was pretty in a blonde, babyish way, doll-like and as empty-headed. Sandra reminded Agnes of Marcia Russell, one of her students. She had been known as the blonde bombshell, always flirting with the boys. It was no surprise to anyone when she dropped out of college. Pity. She had a good brain.

Agnes concluded it must be a slack afternoon as three of the girls had come to deal with her. Kristine was the third one. She was new, had only been at the home about four or five weeks. She had a lovely face and a gentle manner. The three girls stood in front of Agnes. Angela pulled her roughly to her feet and that did it. 'OH GOD!' thought Agnes. She could not control the shaking. Tottering forward, all the taps opened; the tears, the saliva spilling out, the urine flowing down her legs, warm at first, quickly cold, nasty.

Agnes cursed silently. 'Damn! Damn! Damn!' Her pants were wet, her slippers, the hem of her dress. Worst than that, some of her saliva dribbled onto Angela's hand.

Letting out a yell, her face contorted with fury, she pushed Agnes roughly onto the commode.

'You bloody filthy woman, I don't want your stinking muck on me.'

Kristine was horrified. 'You can't speak to anyone like that, and don't push her around.' There is definite strength in her soft voice. Angela; a name couldn't be more inappropriate.

'If you feel so much for her you can deal with her yourself,' said Angela, as she flounced out with the faithful Sandra.

Left to herself, Kristine spoke gently to Agnes, telling her not to worry. She said she would clean her up but she'd have to leave her for a minute to get a bowl of water. Agnes sat trembling in her chair fearful of what would happen next. Kristine returned with hot water, soap and a clean towel. She went out again to get a mop and bucket to clean the floor. She found some clean clothes in the bedside locker and laid them on the bed. Then she removed Agnes' wet clothes, draping her dressing-gown around her shoulders so she wouldn't be cold, all the while telling her what she was going to do. She carefully washed Agnes' face and chest before drying her and putting on a clean vest and blouse. Agnes had never had much of a bosom and she was now so thin she no longer bothered with a bra. Kristine helped her stand while she washed and dried her bottom then sat her on the bed to do her legs and feet. She found some talc in the drawer and gave it to Agnes to sprinkle liberally around her private parts and on her feet. Kristine finished dressing her and sat her back in her chair. Agnes felt like a different woman, fresh and sweet smelling. It was a struggle for one person to change her but Agnes had helped as much as she was able, anything to avoid calling the others back. Sister was the only other person who was so kind and gentle to the patients. Agnes struggled to thank Kristine for her kindness.

'Ith th, thos thorry. Icanth tell uth howh muth I ahath cawthing throuble.' She so wanted her to understand; to make her realise what kind of person she was. That she was really quite intelligent, had finer feelings like everyone else and that she was very lonely with no family or friends to visit. God only knew whether this new young girl with the lovely face, could understand what she was saying. Agnes found it so difficult to explain but she believed Kristine did understand as she nodded and smiled and patted her hand. Agnes prayed that Kristine would remain at the home. Life might then become more bearable if she stayed. *Her* sname should be Angela.

Angela

'Phew, what a stink! Gee she's an old cow. Why do we have to put up with these people? They're no use to anyone.' Angela marched up the passage and flung the door open into the yard. 'I've gotta get some fresh air.' She walked down the path past the dustbins and out onto the grass where there were a couple of cheap garden chairs. The striped canvas was worn with a spring or two missing but they were OK to sit and have a smoke. Sandra followed her outside but she was uneasy, standing first on one foot then the other.

'Shouldn't we help her change Agnes? It's bloody difficult on your own.'

'Tough, she thinks she knows it all, so she can get on with it herself.' Angela was just relieved to get outside. Having to look at Agnes, standing there dribbling from her deformed lip, shaking, stinking of pee, it was disgusting. They were all the same. Unable to control their bodies, or what came out of them. Old Joe Patterson threw shit at anyone who went into his room and even smeared it on the wall when he felt like it. At least Agnes didn't do that, but God knows what use she was. Angela knew that if it was her, she'd want to die and she said as much to Sandra.

'She doesn't have any fun, go anywhere or have anyone to visit. She sits there gazing at a picture of some bloke she said was her husband. God who'd marry her?'

'She probably wasn't always dribbly and shaky like now, Angela. She has got a picture of when she was younger. She showed me once. She looked quite pretty.'

'Well she's not pretty now. Dead ugly if you ask me.' Angela thought Sandra was rather pathetic and didn't have much of a mind of her own. She was fun to go out with though. She was pretty, and slim, apart from the big boobs, and attracted the fellas. They'd had a lot of laughs lately, joy riding down the beach, plenty of beer, but this Kristine, could spoil things. No way could she see her joining in any snogging sessions. She'd probably start screaming she was so prissy.

Angela had privately named her "Goody, Goody two shoes," but she was forced to admit that she was a good looker, beautiful rather than pretty, but so bloody prim and proper. It narked Angela that Kristine had been prepared to butt in and tell her what she couldn't do. She'd only been there five minutes, straight from school. It was none of her business how she spoke to the patients, or anyone else. She'd have to learn to mind her own bloody business.

'Come on, Angela, we'd better go back, it's nearly tea time and they'll all be wanting to spend a penny, or worse.'

'God! You're an old woman. You go in if you want. I'm going to finish my fag.' Angela was still seething about the way Kristine had butted in with Agnes. She'd speak to people how she bloody well liked. She got up from her chair and moved over to lean on the hand-rail leading up to the door. She took long drags on her cigarette in an effort to calm down. Finally, she stubbed out the butt on the path and went back inside. For a change, nobody was calling out for a bedpan or a drink or just being a damn nuisance. Angela felt she would be doing the world a favour if she helped some of these 'has beens' pass on. They were worse than children. A lot worse, in her opinion. Most children were OK. At least there was a chance that they would grow into someone interesting but old people were useless. Angela secretly believed it would be easy to finish some of them off. She'd given it quite a lot of thought recently. A pillow over the face while they slept? It would be dead easy.

They'd never know and it would be put down as a natural death. In a place like this, someone was always popping off. They were too weak to struggle, well at least against someone strong like her.

All the patients were ancient, a waste of space. Everyone expected them to die, sooner or later. The relatives, if they had any, and someone like Agnes didn't, would be glad to stop paying, stop coming on boring visits. Angela remembered how relieved her Mum was when her grandfather died. She was weepy at the funeral of course, she had to be, for the neighbours, but she was quite cheerful later. He probably had his heart attack from drinking. He put away enough of the stuff. For her mother it had meant no more washing, cooking, cleaning for him. And the shopping. That had been a right bore and he was always coughing and spluttering all over everyone and not always using a handkerchief. Ugh. Angela never wanted to get old.

She had heard about nurses knocking their patients off, usually for money. Well there was no chance of that in Mountain View. The patients were all pretty hard up or they wouldn't be in a dump like this. It was better if there was no money – less chance of anyone suspecting they'd been done in. Angela concluded she'd be doing quite a few people a favour, if she put some of these people out of their misery. She was sure Agnes and old Bill Harkness would be happy to pop off. She wouldn't try anything on him though. He'd fight like hell, and yell the bloody place down. Then there were the ones who didn't say anything, just mumbled rubbish, mucked their beds and spat out their food. They should definitely go. What use were they? The plan needed more thought. She'd have to choose the right time. It would be best to try one and see what happened. She'd pick one of the really daft ones first, so if it didn't work and they tried to complain, nobody would believe them. Angela knew there were some people, quite smart people, who believed in it. Youfinasia or something like that, they called it. When they'd had enough and wanted to 'pack it in' they got an injection. It was a jolly good idea, but if they went 'off it' before they'd had the chance to make their wishes known, then the relatives would have to do it – or people like Angela, if they didn't have family. If it was normal practise then there wouldn't be any places like Mountain View for people like her to work in. Not many people went in for it yet but when there were too many old people, maybe they'd come round to it.

Angela wished for the hundredth time she didn't have to work in such a place but jobs were in short supply in Oakune where her family lived. The pay wasn't great but it was better than the local dairy or the hardware shop she'd tried in Stratford.

Joe Patterson

Joe Patterson was rummaging round in his bed muttering to himself.

'Gotta find it, gotta find it. They'll be here soon. Bloody nuisance, always running out of ammo. Shouldn't 'ave used so much yesterday.' But he'd had to. There had been so many of them.

Joe had had a bad war. In his mind, he was still fighting it, still in the throes of battle, still amongst the enemy. His severe head injuries had stopped the clock in his mind and he was still in Gallipoli. Anyone who came in was 'coming over the top' and had to be stopped. Whatever he did he couldn't get rid of them. He needed reinforcements but all his mates were dead, Teddy, Bob, Billy, all of them, gone. He'd known them all his life, been to school with them. Now he had nobody. Tears welled up but he took no notice. It was the Turks he was fighting now but it was the bloody Germans that started it. Joe had heard that the Americans would be coming to help but where were they? Bloody Yanks. They were useless. There was no sign of them. But one thing was really puzzling Joe. All the people who came 'over the top,' all those attacking him, were women. All of them. He'd not seen any men for weeks. This added to his confusion. He had not realised the Turks, or the Germans, used so many women and for a while he wondered if they were in disguise but didn't really think they'd be able to keep it up for so long. Perhaps they were 'Ruskies'? He had heard that the Russians had whole battalions of women.

But they were supposed to be on our side, weren't they? Just then Joe heard someone outside the door and he fell to muttering again.

'Bugger! Someone's trying to break in. I've got no ammo.' He put his head down the bed pulling everything about in his agitation. 'Where is it? Where is it? Damn! Still no bloody ammo.'

At that moment, Kristine entered the room. She had her hand over the cup she was carrying and was prepared to duck, as the girls had warned her that Joe Patterson was likely to throw faeces at her. Luckily for her, Joe was constipated and had run out of ammunition.

Joe was disgusted. Here was another bloody woman, all smiles, trying to trick him, bringing him tea. It might be poisoned.

'How are you feeling, Mr Patterson? Can I get you anything?' she asked as she put the cup on the locker. 'My name is Kristine and I'm new here.'

Smarmy as you like, thought Joe. It was all a trick. She couldn't be an officer if she used her Christian name. She was a smashing looker too and not all smart-alecky like the others. Maybe she was their new weapon. Perhaps they'd run out of ammo too? If he could hang on till tomorrow he should be able to get some more.

'I'll bring you some clean sheets and we'll change your bed, shall we? You could do with a wash too, make you feel better.' Kristine spoke softly and smiled at Joe, hoping to gain his confidence. But he was too confused. He wasn't in bed so what was she bloody talking about? It didn't make sense. She was trying to trick him. There was no way he was going to leave his 'dugout'. It had taken him a long time to get the position right so he wasn't about to give it up. She was only after his guns but she would have to kill him first.

'Get off, get OUT, GET OUT. Don't come back.

Next time I'll shoot. Ahrr,' he shouted. But Joe was outnumbered. Angela and Sandra had joined Kristine. Sandra had an armful of clean linen and Angela moved the tea to the windowsill and put a bowl of hot water on the locker. Kristine made a mental note to get Joe some fresh tea when they had finished cleaning him up. The three of them managed to lift the struggling patient into a chair and stripped the sheets off the bed, relieved that they were not as foul smelling as usual. Angela and Sandra grasped Joe under the arms, pulling him to his feet and dropping his pyjama trousers around his ankles. They had given Kristine the unenviable job of cleaning his backside, which was smeared with stale faeces. It was obvious to Kristine that nobody had washed him properly yesterday, or possibly not in the last week. The stuff was caked on and took masses of soap and the use of the hot flannel like a poultice, to loosen it.

'Get a move on, can't you, his bum must be clean enough by now.' Angela wanted out of this smelly room and hanging on to this crazy patient. 'He's bloody heavy too.'

Kristine continued to clean Joe up, replying mildly, 'I'm going to do it properly or he'll have bedsores and then that will mean more work.'

The three women thoroughly confused Joe. Where did they all come from? How many more of them were out there, in no-man's land? He laughed hysterically at his own joke – all women in no-man's land. There were too many of them.

He made himself go limp in an effort to make it harder for his 'captors' and he reasoned it wouldn't hurt so much if he didn't fight them. He'd resisted last time, fought like a bloody tiger he had, but all he got for his pains were some nasty bruises and another wound on his leg. At least the hot water would stop the frostbite and get the mud off. It did some good, but for the life of him he couldn't see where they got it from. This Kristine seemed more careful than the others. She didn't slap or pinch. Probably trying to kill him with kindness. Ha! Ha!

Kristine

It was only ten o'clock. She didn't have to get up yet. She'd have another half an hour. Kristine turned over and went back to sleep.

Heavens! Sitting up quickly, she reached for her watch. It was eleven forty-five. How could she have slept so long? She'd better get up, not lie in bed all day. But what was there to get up for? Kristine sank back on the pillows. It was time she found a picture or two to put up, something to cheer her up. The room was quite bare apart from the bed, the dressing table and a small desk and plain chair in the corner by the window. She quite liked the green flowered curtains and the sludge green rug by the bed, but the walls were bare.

She continued to lie there, her thought immediately turning to the two girls she lived and worked with. They were not that much older than she was but they couldn't be more different. Sandra had told her she was twenty and Angela was a little older than her but she didn't know by how much. Why were they like that? Drinking and smoking and going out with boys; not ones they knew, just anyone who would take them. Picked up off the street. It was horrible. Was it her that was wrong. No. No, she told herself, I know I'm not. Everyone knew it was wrong to drink and drive, even if a lot of people did it. Not that they drove of course. They didn't have a car, but they went with people who did.

She would have to get up if she wanted anything to eat. She'd not bothered with food the night before and now she'd slept so long, her throat felt like sand paper. She desperately

26

needed something to drink and if the others had left any milk and bread she could have some cereal and toast. Then, maybe she'd feel better. Perhaps she needn't get dressed. She could nip to the kitchen in her dressing gown. Nobody would see her. Kristine swung her legs out of the bed and sat there deep in thought. Sandra might be all right by herself but she did everything Angela told her. What did they do yesterday when she'd left them, when they got in the car? She couldn't believe they'd get in a car with boys they'd never met before. Kristine didn't know where they went or what they did but she'd smelt the beer when they'd opened the door. "Come on girls, this is your lucky day," they laughed. "Come with us and we'll give you a great time." She couldn't ask them what they did; she didn't really want to know. She only knew they'd woken her up when they came in late trying to be quiet but giggling and banging into things. Kristine wondered if Matron had heard them but probably not as her flat was at the other end of the building.

Kristine pulled on her dressing gown and slipping her feet into her slippers, she carefully opened the door. There was nobody in the passage and she couldn't hear any movement. The girls must be still asleep. Quietly she went to the little staff kitchen at the end of the passage. She put the kettle on and plugged in the toaster.

It had been a relief to find everything was electric. She wasn't used to gas and she was slightly afraid of it. She'd have to ask Matron for more coffee, it wouldn't last the weekend. Damn, they'd eaten all the honey. Kristine resolved to put her name on it next time or perhaps she'd keep it in her room. Angela would be unlikely to leave it alone, name or no name. Toast and Marmite wasn't the same. Kristine washed a mug and made herself some coffee. That was another annoyance; the others never bothered to wash up after themselves.

A door slammed. Kristine jumped. Were the others getting

up? Hurriedly, she buttered her toast and put a scraping of Marmite on it. She'd never been that keen on Marmite. What was she scared of? It was them. She had to admit it, she was rather scared of them, although that wasn't really the right word. They made her feel uncomfortable, excluded, as if they were talking in a foreign language and yet she didn't wish to join in. Why did Angela have to swear all the time? Perhaps her family did? Kristine's parents threatened to wash their mouths out with soap if they ever swore at home. She couldn't wait to tell her friends Alison and Bridget about Angela, not that they'd believe her. She put her coffee and toast on a tray and crept back to her room, softly closing the door so if the others were awake they wouldn't know she was there. Kristine wondered what she should do? She'd have to stay. It was she that had insisted on coming half way up the North Island to do her training because it was supposed to be the best training hospital in the country, when she'd always preferred the South, where her family lived. But once she'd made that decision, it made sense to get a job in the area before she started. She'd hoped Matron would let her start training earlier but it wasn't allowed, you had to be eighteen. She'd offered her this job and if she left now she'd start her training in Matron's bad books. Even worse, she may not be accepted if she couldn't handle this job. It was her own fault, she'd just have to get on with it. Seven more months and one more week. Not so long really.

The sensible thing would be to get dressed and go for a walk but Kristine decided she wasn't going to. It would be warmer in bed and there was nothing to get up for. It was as well her mother couldn't see her eating her breakfast-cum-lunch in bed. She'd think her eldest daughter very slovenly! Kristine was tired of reading. It was probably that which was giving her headaches, that and sleeping all the time and not enough fresh air. She wished Monday would hurry up, as working was something positive and useful to do. The sensible patients were interesting to talk to but she couldn't work all the time or she would become tired and impatient and start behaving like Angela and Sandra. Anyway, there was no danger of working all the time as you wouldn't be allowed and it was probably against the law. Kristine got out of bed to put the remains of her breakfast on the small table under the window. Should she get up, or have some more sleep. Finding the bed full of crumbs, she decided to get up. She wouldn't have to talk to the others. They had to be out or still in bed as she hadn't heard a sound and they usually crashed about slamming doors and shouting to each other when they were in.

Oh God. What a mess. Kristine examined her face in the mirror. Shiny red cheeks, puffy, bloodshot eyes from sleeping too much. Some powder might cover the cheeks but what could she do about the eyes? Thank Heavens for the basin in her room. Perhaps bathing her eyes in cold water would help? Slices of cucumber were supposed to refresh tired eyes but Kristine knew there was no hope of finding cucumber in Mountain View. Damn, her hair was all knotted. Too much lying about. Her hair was quite thick but it was agony to try and comb it in its present state. She set to with the brush and ten minutes later, at least her hair was more like its normal, glossy self. Her face still looked as if she'd been crying; Angela and Sandra would love that. Kristine put on some navy trousers and a red shirt. She pulled back the curtains and the sun flooded in but it didn't look all that warm so if she was going for a walk she would need a jumper too. The red one would do. Where would she go? It didn't matter. Round the block or up to the park and back. The park would be a couple of miles but it would do her good. She had to get out, even if she did look a mess. Who cared? She did. She hated it, but she needed to get out. OUT, OUT, OUT. Anxious not to disturb the others if they were there, Kristine quietly left her room and checking she had her key, carefully shut the front door of the nurses' quarters.

She walked quickly along the pavement towards the park. It was quite a distance but she would have a good view from there. From the small hill in the centre, it was possible to see the port and part of the city, and the mountain, if the cloud ever lifted. It was cold but fine and apart from the cloud covering the mountain, which she had yet to see, the sky was blue and there was hardly any wind. Kristine hated the wind.

She'd come out for a walk to blow the cobwebs away but Kristine couldn't put Angela and Sandra or Mountain View out of her mind. Why did the girls stay? They were so unkind, even cruel. It was a shock to find so many of the patients wet their pants, even dirtied them sometimes – just like children. Second childhood the elderly, some people say, and to a certain extent it was true. And that Mr. Patterson threw – pooh at you when you went into his room. Kristine couldn't even bring herself to say 'shit' in her mind, she found the word so repulsive. The others used it all the time. He hadn't thrown anything at her yesterday but Angela said that was because he's constipated. He was so dirty when they'd managed to bath him and he'd smelt bad, so bad that Kristine had felt like retching. She'd noticed that he did have a lot of bruises though. Angela had dismissed her concern, saying he fell about but Kristine didn't believe her. Not the way he was cowering away from her. She probably hit him when nobody was looking. Quite a few of them have bruises and they're scared of her.

Kristine had arrived at her vantage point via the footpath and she was relieved to find nobody else there. There was also a one-way road that went around the hill and visitors often went up to look at the map or just to sit on the seats or in their cars, to admire the view. For a few minutes Kristine was distracted by the view but it was not long before her mind was wrestling with her situation in the Home, and as always, it revolved around Angela; what she said and what she did. It was only last week when Angela had told her, "don't put any pants on them, you can deal with them quicker and there's one less thing to change." But how can you? No pants! How can you let people go about without any pants? Krisitine found it disgusting. It wasn't decent and would be horribly cold. She wouldn't like it. Her mother would never believe it. Kristine felt she should do something about it, but what? Who should she tell? Matron wouldn't want to know. She might even agree with it and she certainly wouldn't take any notice of her, a new girl. Angela even said that if her own mother peed the bed she would smack her. No. She decided that the best thing she could do was to be as kind to the patients as possible and treat them all as if they were her mother.

Tears came to her eyes just thinking about the poor old people in the Home. Most of them were already suffering so much with their aches and pains and then having to put up with such rotten treatment, made her want to cry. Kristine got to thinking that perhaps she wasn't cut out to be a nurse. Maybe she was too soft? She pulled out her handkerchief to wipe her eyes and blow her nose. Poor Mrs Hammond suffered so with her pain and the rough treatment she got. It must be agony. If Mrs Hammond was prepared to complain then Kristine could back her up? That might be a solution. She wouldn't want to because if nothing was done then Angela would treat her even worse and give Kristine hell off duty. Perhaps Mrs Hammond's niece would say something? It was irritating, her ringing the bell all the time, but if she couldn't move, what else could she do? Hardly anyone at the Home had relatives, or if they did, they never came near. Just plonked their parents, their granny or uncle or aunt, in the Home and forgot about them. Kristine believed that if there were relatives, they should come regularly; make them feel loved, just as she would if it was her parents. But then she wouldn't put them in a home. She'd look after them herself.

It was a pity she couldn't go home in her spare time. She

mustn't go through all that again. It was her fault she had come so far away. It had been her choice even though her Mum and Dad had advised against it on the grounds that she didn't know anyone and she'd be homesick. Well, she wasn't really homesick in that she didn't physically want to go home. She just wanted someone who thought like she did, to talk to and go about with. She'd been desperate to get away from home, to do her own thing. Not to have to do kids stuff all the time, always say where she was going, when she was coming back. Now she had her own money to spend she could buy some more clothes, something she hadn't made herself. Now that would be nice. She'd like a pretty party dress but couldn't decide on the colour or style. She never seemed to see what she'd like but knew she would know if she saw it. If she was honest she would admit that some of these shop assistants in the smarter dress shops intimidated her and she didn't want them pressurizing her into buying something she wasn't a hundred per cent sure of. She never seemed to get it right. If she was smart, others were casual and if she was casual then everyone else was 'dressed up to the nines', as her Mother would say. She supposed it didn't matter if she never went out. Kristine consoled herself with the thought that once she started training everything would be OK. At least all the other girls would have the same objective and they would be given proper instruction. After all, it was supposed to be the best training hospital in the country. With that comforting thought, Kristine made her way back to the Home, still lost in thought but feeling better for getting some fresh air.

It was a pity Philip had gone away. He used to take her everywhere. Not that he always wanted to have his younger sister with him. He did moan a lot about having to take her places. Said it was a bore always having to take his little sister with him. She supposed it cramped his style, thought she'd tell on him if he had a smoke. No way. He wouldn't have taken her again. She was only two years younger which wasn't much but maybe he thought of her as a baby. Why should he worry? What about her, always having to go about with her brother? Still, if she didn't go with him she would have had to take one or two of her sisters along with her and that would have been much worse. They were so babyish. Safety in numbers was her mother's motto so they all had to put up with it or stay at home.

Kristine wouldn't tell her parents in her weekly letter how awful she was finding it. They would only worry and tell her to come home again until January when her nursing course proper started. She was made of sterner stuff than that. Besides, there was no way she would let on that she'd made the wrong decision. She would stick it out and find something interesting to do in her spare time.

Elsie Hammond

Elsie Hammond lay in bed, as she had done for the last two years. Well 'lay' was not strictly correct. She was unable to lie down properly. Her knees were permanently bent up and she couldn't raise her arms above her face. Elsie was thinking. She did a lot of thinking as she could do little else. Why was Angela so horrid to her? All Elsie had said was, "Please be careful, you hurt me so," but she had shouted at her in her usual rough way. Elsie couldn't see why Angela needed to push the bedpan under her so hard and then to let her body drop onto the bed when she removed it. She didn't weigh much and there was no reason why Angela and Sandra couldn't support her back while they eased the pan out. Sister did and so did Matron. Why didn't they teach the girls to do it properly?

Elsie was in pain, all day and every day. It nagged at her like toothache, niggling away, sapping her strength and her humour. She needed kind, sympathetic, caring people. If they couldn't be that then they shouldn't be employed. It was no good complaining to Matron.

"Yes dear, I understand dear but she's only young, they have to learn you know." That was the only response she got. It wasn't good enough. They shouldn't practice on her. Soothing noises was all she got from Dr. Forrest when she mentioned it. They were all useless as far as Elsie was concerned. Angela took a malicious delight in making Elsie wait for the bedpan or to be moved and turned. She even made her wait for her food. She always served her last even though she had to pass Elsie's room to get to all the others. It was far more work to change Elsie's bed than to get her a bedpan when she asked for it. Angela's actions showed limited intelligence but no doubt it created a feeling of power to have Elsie so dependent on her. That must outweigh the extra chore. Seeing Elsie humiliated and uncomfortable in a wet bed probably amused her too. Angela definitely had a cruel streak.

Elsie got to wondering, for what must have been the hundredth time, why she had to get her particular disease? It didn't run in her family or not that she knew of; arthritis yes, everyone had some when they got old, she knew that, but not this foul version of it. It was so hateful having other people attending to all her bodily functions. It wouldn't be so bad if they were kind caring people but maybe only people like Angela were prepared to do such demeaning tasks for strangers?

Elsie thought Angela an odd girl. She couldn't be very old, 21 or 22 at the most. What was her mother thinking of, calling her Angela? Devila would be more appropriate. She may have been angelic as a baby, but Elsie doubted it as that small sharp nose and those tiny cruel eyes, set too close together, told against it. Bill had told Elsie that Angela hit people.

"I was out in the garden one day and the girls were on the veranda changing poor Edie Nolan. They hadn't pulled the curtains across the window and I saw Angela slap Edie's bottom because she'd wet the bed. I couldn't say anything or they'd accuse me of being a peeping Tom," he had said

He seemed to find out most of what went on in the Home. Elsie wouldn't be surprised. Bill's presence in the home saved Elsie's sanity. He often called by her room as he was able to propel his own wheelchair. He talked to her about all kinds of things, took her mind off her pain and her complaints. He seemed quite a good judge of character, clever too in a rough sort of way. Third generation New Zealander he told her, which probably accounted for his strong, pioneering spirit, not refined like she was. Not that Elsie thought of herself in that way, well not until Bill had told her,

'You're more refined than some of the others here, which comes of having better class parents.' Elsie was thrilled. More refined, fancy that. Her mother would have been so proud. Bill continued, 'My Grandfather was a miner and he came out here for a better life. He'd got that too because he married a governess and their son, my Father, married a governess so they'd made sure 1 had a good education.'

Somebody should complain. Matron might listen to Joyce when she came next. She was presentable and intelligent and she was a relation after all, and she paid the bills. It was no good Elsie doing it. Nobody listened to her. Sister Johansen was kind enough but being a foreigner, she probably saw things differently. She said she came from Norway. Elsie couldn't understand why she had come all the way down to New Zealand. She would have liked to ask her but it seemed rude somehow. She had been taught not to ask personal questions. If she'd come for adventure why was she working in this horrible place? It was more like a nightmare. Elsie wished she could understand her better and not have to keep asking her to repeat herself. She was the Sister, the only Sister in the Home. Surely it was her job to take these young girls in hand and teach them how to treat people. Of course it was really Matron's job but she was just working her passage to retirement, anything for a quiet life. That's what everyone said anyway. Sandra wasn't as bad as Angela.

In fact she could be quite kind, but was scatty and thoughtless, Angela's cohort. Nothing much passed through her pretty head but where the next boyfriend was coming from. Elsie's mother, brought up in the Victorian era and extremely 'strait-laced', would have called her a tart, she was quite sure.

Elsie's thoughts soon turned back to her body and her inability to move about. That was tiresome enough, but most of all it was the pain. She could scream with the relentless nagging pain. It stopped her doing anything and if she couldn't do anything she had all the time in the world to be absorbed by the pain. She could have Disprin of course but not too many, as they had side-effects and they made her feel sick sometimes and they did no more than take the edge off the pain.

Elsie didn't understand why the disease had come upon her so quickly. One day she was relatively fit, running her own little shop, mistress of her own affairs; three months later, she was almost ready for the wheelchair. She had been lucky with a remission, when for six wonderful months she had been almost back to normal, in the shop every day. Elsie missed her shop dreadfully. The haberdashery shop, Buttons and Bows, had belonged to her maiden aunt, Sybil. Elsie had enjoyed serving the customers and learning about the business, first during the school holidays and later when she left school. She had been overjoyed when her aunt had left her the shop in her Will. She had loved the pretty buttons, lovely ribbons, bright, soft wools, the nice people who came into her shop.

"It's a joy to come in your shop Miss Hammond," everyone said. Elsie did not encourage familiarity but then the people who sewed were always nice; genteel, properly brought-up ladies, who would never think of addressing her as anything other than Miss Hammond, or that was what she'd found. Elsie prided herself in having everything sewing ladies would want.

"Have you any purple velvet ribbon, Miss Hammond?"

" Of course, Mrs Bonville, how much would you like?" Elsie would reply.

"May I have a pair of number 9 knitting needles and 6 pearl buttons, please Miss Hammond?" asked Miss Forbes, who was a champion knitter. Then there was the time when

Mrs Durrant, wife of the Mayor, wanted a pair of light navy, real leather gloves. Not just any navy. They had to be a specific shade, the same as her shoes. She even brought one shoe in to see if Elsie could match the colour. Elsie had rung the head office of her supplier and she had got the very shade of gloves. Mrs Durrant was very pleased and told all her friends which was good for business of course.

There was always a fresh, clean smell in the shop – not like where she was now. She didn't smell, because she made sure they used the talcum powder Joyce always brought her, but an awful smell of urine often invaded her room. Ugh. She could smell it now. Poor Mary was shuffling by and Elsie could tell she'd wet her pants again, by the wet stain on her dress. It was worse than that sometimes. She knew it wasn't Mary's fault. The girls should make more of an effort to take the poor dears to the toilet, before they were desperate and had accidents.

To Elsie, her disease was a mystery. Why did it appear to get better, and then come back with a vengeance, invariably worse than before? Of course there was no chance of her getting better now. She longed to be able to move, to change position, when she wanted to, not when someone else came to turn her. IF they did. Sometimes she had to wait for hours before anyone came to see if she needed anything. Some days, to fill the endlessly boring hours, Elsie would concentrate as hard as she possibly could, to move her legs, but it was no good. They were fixed in a bent position. Her arms too were clamped to her sides, her hands barely able to reach her mouth. At least she could still feed herself but it was impossible for her to scratch her nose or rub her eyes. A day did not pass when Elsie did not wonder why she was still here, in this Hell on earth. She was thin too, scraggy as a chicken. Muscle wastage the doctor said. If you don't use them you lose them. It was true of brains too. She would keep reading, keep asking questions, try to keep up to date. For now, her mind was intact and that was a blessing. Nobody was ever the shape they wanted to be when it mattered. Elsie had been dumpy when she was young. Then she'd wanted to be slim, now she could do with some extra flesh to cushion her painful bones.

OOoo! No! As well as the pain, there was now a fly to contend with. Elsie was at her wits end. The fly was the last straw. First on her chin, then on her nose and someone had removed the fly swat she always kept within reach. In her exasperation Elsie shook her head, or tried to. It was a mistake as the pain went shooting up her neck and sending it into spasm. Elsie felt she would go mad with the pain and the fly. She blamed Angela for moving the fly swat. It was bound to be her, just to be nasty. Someone was coming down the passage so she grasped the bell, which was always by her hand and pushed the button several times. But Elsie was out of luck that afternoon as Angela was still on duty and she heard her say in her hard coarse voice, as she passed the door, 'Let the old fool wait.'

'Oh Angela, we should go to her. What if she needs something urgently?' Sandra gave a nervous giggle but the two girls passed on.

Poor Elsie wanted to scream with frustration and pain. She knew she should try to stay calm as everything felt worse when she was upset but how could she, with the terrible pain. On and on it went. Anger welled up inside and she felt she was going to cry.

No, no, she mustn't cry, because then her nose would run and she couldn't blow it. She mustn't get angry, she must forget the fly, she must concentrate on something else. It was strange how people saw someone crippled up, hear that they had arthritis and know they couldn't do anything, but they never understood the pain. Why didn't they realise that they must be in pain? Elsie supposed that unless they had experienced it themselves they couldn't understand. She never suffered so badly when she was in the shop as she had something to do, something to keep her mind off it. Everything ached by the end of the day of course, but never the nagging, biting pain she experienced now.

Concentrate on the shop, stop thinking about the pain she admonished herself. Everyone had said how brave she was, struggling on when she was working. Well, what else could she have done? There was nobody else to do the shop. Besides, Elsie would not have trusted anyone else to look after it properly, cherish the customers and help them choose what they needed. Her niece, Joyce, understood. She stood in when it was necessary and she was there now. Elsie intended to leave Buttons and Bows to Joyce but she had tried to manage on her own until it became impossible. It was a shame Joyce had never married but it did mean she could concentrate all her efforts on the shop and she came frequently to report on the business to her Aunt.

In spite of her efforts to concentrate on other things, Elsie's pain kept growing. It came in waves, rolling, swelling, filling her whole horizon, blotting out everything else. Sometimes it was like a knife twisting inside, sometimes a hammer thudding away or a fire scorching, burning, but the needle, suddenly, fiercely, stabbing, that was the worst. STOP thinking about the pain Elsie, she told herself, you know it doesn't help. She tried to be calm, reasonable, not get upset, and not complain. Elsie thought she hardly ever complained. She didn't believe she was a complaining type of person but the sad thing was, the staff thought otherwise. Nobody could walk into her room without Elsie had a complaint of some sort. That most of them were justified, given her condition, made little difference to girls like Angela and Sandra.

In desperation, Elsie rang the bell again. This time it was the new girl, Kristine who answered the bell.

'Will you help me? Please can you get rid of this horrible fly.'

Kristine introduced herself, found the fly swat and dispatched the fly with one quick swat. She gave Elsie a drink of water and asked her if there was anything else she wanted. This was such a change from the usual treatment Elsie received that she forgot to complain about her pain and launched into a conversation with Kristine. How long was she going to stay? Did she live in the Nurses' Home? What did she do in her time off?

'I hope you don't mind me asking all these questions but you have been so kind.'

Kristine smiled and said she didn't mind at all. 'I shall be here until I start my nursing training in January. I live in the Nurses' Home and I read a lot and go for walks and to the cinema. I'm very happy here,' she lied.

'Oh, what books do you like? I have several here you may borrow. They are mostly biography if you like those,' said Elsie.

'I have quite a lot to read at the moment thank you, but I should be happy to borrow something when I run out,' said Kristine. There was no point in telling her woes to this old lady who was obviously in pain and had enough trouble of her own. Before she left the room, Kristine put the fly swat where Elsie could reach it and told her to ring if she wanted anything else.

Elsie felt better already from these small acts of kindness. She just hoped Kristine did not get infected with the bad habits of the other two. Any new ones never lasted long. Others had started but within a month or two they'd left. It may be that they didn't like the work but Elsie suspected some of them didn't last because of Angela and Sandra. It was true that Sandra on her own was quite kind and on rare occasions, thoughtful even, but she and Angela nearly always worked as a pair and together they intimidated any new girls. Elsie would pray that Kristine stayed and kept her kind and pleasant nature. Joyce was coming to see her tomorrow and she might bring freesias, her favourite flowers. They had such a delicious scent they went some way towards masking the unpleasant odours always wafting around. She would also be able to tell her about the horrid treatment she received. Joyce always seemed interested.

Edith Nolan

Edith was thoroughly confused. What was the grey thing hanging up beside her? Was it her dress? But she didn't have a grey dress, or did she? She couldn't remember. Was it hers or someone else's? They did dress her in other people's clothes sometimes but she didn't know where they got them. Were other people wearing hers? She didn't even know where she was or what time it was. It was light, but not very so it must be morning, or was it going to be night? She wished she could move her right arm or turn over. She could see a glass of water on a table by her bed but there was no way she could reach it. Oh, how she longed to turn over. Her right leg was so heavy, she couldn't move that either. She felt so utterly useless. Everything was such a muddle. The grey thing couldn't be a dress, it was hanging all around. Now it was moving, was it alive?

'Wakey, wakey, rise and shine.' The curtain was pulled back and Edith was shocked into remembering that she was in that horrible place with the awful, nasty Angela. She felt the bed wet underneath her and cringed away from the expected slap. Angela always slapped her bottom if the bed was wet. Edith slipped back to the safety of her childhood. Her lovely soft, cuddly Mummy and big strong Daddy. He sometimes shouted but he never hit her or her sister. Her mother never hit her when she wet the bed. She didn't mean to, it was an accident. Mummy understood that. She was always kind, just quiet and gentle. She wished her parents were there.

'Good Morning, Mrs Nolan, how are you today?' Kristine

stood beside the bed and took Edith's good hand. 'I'm the new girl and my name is Kristine. I've come to wash and change you, ready for breakfast.'

'Mmmm, mmm, mmm,' was all Edith could say. It was the *only* thing she could say but she understood most of what was said to her. Not to see Angela was an enormous relief, not to have her shouting at her and slapping her and she was delighted to be called Mrs Nolan, instead of "old Ma Nolan", or worse, by Angela. She was still Jack's wife, – well his widow, really, but Mrs Nolan made her feel more comfortable, more like she used to be.

'Mummm, mmm,' Edith didn't know why she couldn't speak. They'd told her she'd had a stroke so perhaps she had. One day she was in her own home and the next she was in this awful place. She vaguely remembered being in the hospital too but she wasn't sure. Edith had no idea what had happened to her house. Had it been sold? Where did the money go? Nobody told her anything. Matron just said, "All that has been taken care of. Don't worry your head about that. You just concentrate on getting better."

Edith knew she was never going to get better, well certainly not if she stayed in this place. Why didn't they tell her things? Just because she couldn't speak, didn't mean she couldn't understand. She still knew things, wanted to know them. It was far more of a worry not knowing.

Kristine put a bowl of hot water on the locker and pulled the curtains back around the bed. Edith's bed was on the veranda with three others and the curtains provided the only privacy. Kristine set about washing Edith gently and carefully. All the time she spoke to her quietly in a soothing, calming voice. She explained what she was doing and what she was going to do next. She talked too, about the lovely day, the pretty flowers in the garden, anything she could think of to reassure Edith. Edith felt it was the best wash she'd ever had.

Sister was gentle too but she didn't speak very good English so sometimes Edith couldn't understand her and she couldn't ask. Kristine rolled Edith on to her side to change the wet sheet then she washed her back and her bottom, patting it dry and then massaging her buttocks with methylated spirits. She told Edith that it would stop her getting bedsores. She found a new tin of talc, 'Wild Violets' in the cupboard by her bed and sprinkled it under her breasts and in her groin. Kristine was not to know that the powder had been a Christmas present and this was the first time anyone had thought to use it. Edith felt clean and comfortable and she smelt lovely.

'I'll get you dressed after breakfast and you can sit out in a chair for a change,' Kristine told her. It would be a change. Edith went off into a dream. Perhaps Jack would sit out there with her. Out in their garden. Jack would read the papers and they would chat about the news. But she couldn't talk. The thought brought her back to the home. There was no Jack. Dear Jack had died suddenly of a heart attack at 81 some years ago, and her sister had died at 68. Poor Edith didn't remember how long ago these things happened but it meant there was nobody to visit. They didn't often get her up because it was too much bother. She was heavy and couldn't help herself. Besides, it was easier to change a wet bed than her clothes.

'Mummm, mummmm, mmmm.' Edith was trying to thank Kristine for being so kind but the same old noise came out. It was so frustrating.

'What would you like for breakfast, Mrs Nolan. You can have scrambled eggs or Weetabix and would you like some toast?'

Jack would have eggs and bacon, he loves them and toast would be lovely, but before Edith could make a sound, another voice chipped in from the end of the veranda.

'Don't bother asking her,' said Angela, 'she can't answer and we always give her what makes the least mess.'

Kristine ignored Angela and asked Edith to squeeze

her hand once if she wanted scrambled eggs and twice if she wanted Weetabix. Nobody had ever asked her what she wanted before and Edith wasn't sure if she could squeeze hard enough for Kristine to understand. She must have managed one squeeze because Kristine said she would bring her some scrambled egg. Edith was over-joyed. At last, someone could understand her. She prayed Angela would not spoil things and prayed that Kristine would take no notice of her.

'You're wasting your time, she doesn't understand a bloody thing,' said Angela from behind the curtain.

'I think she does,' said Kristine. 'I knew someone else who'd had a stroke and he could understand but he couldn't talk.'

'Well you're wasting your time with that one, she's just dim. You can clean her up if she makes a mess.'

Urgh! How Edith longed to scream at Angela. She was saying horrid things about her, calling her dim, and she couldn't join in. Edith was the first to admit that she wasn't very bright but she wasn't dim. She had left school at 12, but then so did most people back in the 1880s. She only knew one person, woman anyway, who went to university then. Just that Molly Harvey, no, Harper she was called, but you didn't have to be clever to do useful things.

Edith had had a job in a dress shop for many years, and the boss had even offered her part time when she married Jack so she must have been all right. Jack had thought it would do her good when they'd discovered they couldn't have children. He'd been very disappointed and so had she. It didn't seem right to her, not having children. Everyone had kids; all the girls who'd been at school with her, they'd all had kids popping out all the time. If her and Jack had had children, she'd have someone to visit her now. She might not even have to be in this awful place. A daughter might have looked after her at home. Edith didn't understand why they hadn't had children but she supposed God had decided against it. Maybe it ran in families, not being able to have children. Jack's brother didn't have any either and Edith's sister didn't but then she wasn't married so she wouldn't have had any.

Edith consoled herself that she was luckier than her sister, because she had Jack. Poor Jeanie hadn't had anyone and she died all alone at 68. Now that Edith too, was alone, she may as well be dead for all the use she was to anyone. Still she reasoned, God might have a use for her, who could tell? Perhaps he was keeping her there to spite that Angela? Edith quickly dismissed the thought. She shouldn't say that about God as he didn't deal in spite. He might be trying to teach her a lesson. Trying to show Angela that she might be like the patients in the Home one day herself. Trying to encourage her to be kind. Edith didn't think it would work. Angela was so cruel she frightened her and she couldn't tell anyone.

Kristine's Letter

Dear Mum and Dad and everyone,

How's things? I'm fine here. I didn't tell you on the phone but the railcar was a good way of coming up from Wellington. It was quite quick and I got a taxi here, which didn't cost too much. Perhaps I'll fly when I come home – that would be even quicker and I wouldn't have to risk a rough trip on the ferry or stay a night in Wellington. It was nice to see Aunty Mary and Uncle Sam but the kids are a bit rowdy and don't seem to do as they're told! I haven't seen the mountain yet. Can't believe it's really there. If it's so big and so close I can't understand why I can't see it. They say it's covered in cloud. I expect Edmund Hillary has been up it. Probably ran up for exercise! The job's very interesting. Some of the old people are very nice, that's the ones that can talk. Some can't say anything, or just mumble. Those are the ones who've had a stroke. One or two are very clever, or were. One chap's written a couple of books on mathematics. Matron's OK. She's about as tall as me but very plump. She wears a blue uniform with a very stiff starched collar and a little hat with a ribbon under it. She doesn't bother us much. Sister Johansen's the best. She comes from Norway and has a funny accent, which she makes worse by not opening her mouth properly when she talks. I think she might have loose false teeth and doesn't want them to drop down. She's very kind though and helps you and tells you things you need to know. Pity she doesn't live in. It'd be interesting to find out more about her country.

The other two girls who live in are a bit different – a bit rough, rather tarty, you know what I mean. They only want to go out with boys and one even smokes! I think they drink a lot too. Matron sometimes smells of drink too, but it's probably sherry, not beer. When they go down town, Angela and Sandra, they sometimes get into cars with strange boys, ones they haven't met before. Can you believe it? I don't know where they go or what they do and I don't want to. Don't worry, I won't do that. I just walk on and do my own thing.

The food's quite good and we can make our own tea and coffee, and toast in a tiny kitchen at the end of the passage.

I could walk to town but it is quite a long way so I go on the bus on my days off. I'm going to the pictures this week to see the Coronation. It's on for at least another week. Have you all seen it? I read in the paper that the people in England could watch it on television while it was happening. It will be great when television gets properly to NZ. The hospital where I'm going in January is two or three miles away; you pass it on the bus. It looks really big but the Nurses' Home has lovely flowerbeds and someone told me there is even a swimming pool.
I'm sure I shall like it there. I could go to the beach when the weather's better but the sand is all black. Iron sand it's called, not golden like ours and it gets boiling hot. You have to wear flip-flops or your feet would burn.

I miss you all. Why don't you girls write? I had a card from Philip last week. If he can write while he's in the Army and working every day then you should be able to, doing nothing. Only joking! Practise your essay writing, pretend it's homework, ha ha. Please write soon.

Love,
Kristine.

Angela

Ugh. Angela was feeling sick to her stomach. She knew it was nerves and it would be OK once she'd done it. The first one was always going to be the worst. She hadn't expected it to take her nearly a month to pluck up the courage to carry out her plan. She knew it was the right thing to do. Many of these people would be glad to be put out of their misery. What sort of life did they lead? It wasn't really life at all, it was existence. What she was going to do was mercy killing. Yes. She was providing a service and tonight was the beginning. First, she was going to knock off one of the old girls. It had to be a woman. There were only a few men and they were stronger, would put up a fight and make a lot more racket. Not that they didn't deserve to die, they were just as gaga as the women, but they'd have to wait. Angela had decided to start with 'old Ma Nolan' as she called her. Her 'mumm, mummm, mummm' was getting on Angela's nerves; she had no relatives and was no use at all. To make matters worse, the new girl, Kristine, was trying to encourage her to talk or say what she wanted with stupid hand signals, squeezing one for yes and two for no and other such rubbish. She'd told her that Edith could understand but Angela knew that was rubbish. Of course she couldn't so it was time she went. Angela also had a sneaking suspicion that if, by some fancy chance, Edith was able to communicate, she might tell Matron that Angela didn't like her and that she smacked her. It was true, but then she didn't like any of the patients. Nobody came to visit Edith Nolan except another old biddy who used to be her neighbour and looked to be in need of a home herself. No, if Edith had any relatives they never came near.

Angela went to the office to look at her notes to check on her next-of-kin. She pulled out the drawer marked M – Q of the filing cabinet and found Nolan. She quickly flipped through the sketchy information. It was OK. The only one to notify if Edith popped off was the old biddy neighbour. She decided to go ahead with her plan that night. Angela had barely returned the file to the drawer and was about to shut it, when Sandra came into the office.

'Whose notes have you been reading then? Not like you to take an interest in someone's history,' she teased.

'Quite a few if you must know,' Angela lied. Better to pretend she'd looked at several rather than one.

'Some of them have been here for years. That Elsie Hammond has been here for two years. TWO YEARS, ringing the bell every day, sometimes ten times a day. Can you imagine we've put up with it so long? Edith Nolan is 83 and she's been here nearly three years, not able to speak, just that boring mumble. Can you imagine living three years in that state?'

'Better watch out, it might happen to you, when you get old,' quipped Sandra.

'Not bloody likely, I'd gas myself before that happened. Come on, lets get the work done and we can have a cup of tea and a fag.' Angela was anxious to change the subject. She didn't want to arouse suspicion by doing anything out of the ordinary.

There was another reason for choosing Edith as her first victim. Her bed was on the veranda, the last bed of four and the next bed to her was empty. From that position, Angela would be able to see and hear if anyone was coming. Her plan was to do the deed near the end of her shift but before it was light. Her first thought was to tell Sandra she was going to change Edith; she was always wet by about 4am. She would 'do her in', then when they next went out there together they would find her dead. But what if Sandra decided to come and help her change Edie? No. A better idea would be to get Sandra to help change Edie first then she'd be able to prove that she was alive when they last saw her. She'd then ask Sandra to make them a cup of tea. That would take her about ten minutes by the time she waited for the kettle to boil. There would be plenty of time for Angela to go back and finish Edie off. She wasn't anticipating any difficulty. A quick pillow over her face and it would be all over. It should be easy. Angela was really quite excited about it and in her own mind she was certain that Edie would be a lot better off.

Kristine

Kristine woke early. It was Monday and she was on duty at 7am. At least she would be occupied for most of the day and wouldn't have to talk to the others. As far as she could tell, they didn't have a single thing in common and they smoked all the time. Kristine pulled back the curtains, and gasped. There in front of her was the mountain. The one everyone talked about, Mt. Egmont, the one she'd never seen, until today. It was so beautiful it took her breath away. How had she not seen it before, not even a glimpse, in the seven weeks she had been there? Seven weeks! It was hard to believe she had been at Mountain View that long and yet this was the first time she had seen the famous mountain. It was almost a perfect shape and the sun glinted off the snow-covered peak. She could rejoice that there was something beautiful to cheer her up. She still failed to see how something so big could be hidden for so long. Apart from the garden and a few houses there was nothing else to see out the window.

Dragging herself reluctantly away from the amazing sight, Kristine put her dressing gown on and went to the bathroom but she couldn't get the mountain out of her mind. Perhaps she could climb it? She'd heard it said you couldn't go up on your own and anyway, how would she get up there? Then she panicked. She mustn't mention wanting to go up the mountain to the others. The girls would get some boys, any boys that came along, to take them, and then what? Most of the boys they went about with had drink in the car, the road would be winding and narrow and they could go over the bank. Kristine's imagination was running wild.

She was imagining the papers, "Girls in car with drunken youths crash down the mountain." Everyone would say they'd all been drinking. They'd all smell of it. Kristine just knew her parents would die of shame.

She'd heard that people had died on the mountain. Going up without telling anyone, then losing their way when the mist and cloud came down suddenly, as it obviously did. Apparently there were guides who would take you up there when it was safe and they also did a dawn climb. That would be fun but hard work she imagined. She had been there for seven weeks and it had been covered in cloud all that time. It was pointless thinking about it as she had no way of getting up there and besides, there would be plenty of time when she was doing her training. Other girls would be bound to want to climb it and they may even have guides who took nurses up there. Just looking at it every day would help her to survive her time in Mountain View. Another six months and she would be finished.

She'd never believed it would be so awful, such dreadful girls. She resolved not to go out with them again, not after the last time. It's almost as if they only went to town to be picked up by just anybody. She would join the library, get out loads of books. Kristine was very fond of reading, nothing specific, murder mysteries, biographies, anything at all and Miss Hammond had said she might borrow some of her books too so she would have plenty. She was unlikely to be bothered by Angela or Sandra wanting to borrow a book. She'd not seen either of them reading anything since she'd been there, not even the newspaper.

She would rather go out of course, but where to? Kristine had intended to go to the pictures the previous week but had got cold feet about going on her own. She knew this was pathetic and her brother would have certainly told her so. She made up her mind there and then to go to see "The Coronation" on Thursday of that week. It was her day off and the film was unlikely to be on for much longer. Matron had seen it weeks ago. With no television yet in New Zealand, the cinema was the only place anyone could see this historical event. Kristine would go to the matinee then she'd be able to get a bus back or walk if it was fine although it was a long way. She wasn't much good at calculating distances but thought it must be about three miles to the town from Mountain View with not a lot to see, just rows of houses. It was no good in the evening as the last bus was 9.30pm. Kristine thought she might get a bicycle, it would be good exercise. Perhaps one day she might be asked to a party or to visit someone. Kristine would do her best to be positive and live in hope.

Angela

Angela was feeling very pleased with herself. Putting Edith Nolan out of her misery had been much easier and gave her more satisfaction than she had ever imagined. Angela could not believe how easy it had been. To think she had agonised for weeks about doing the first one. She could have done it ages ago. Nobody suspected a thing. Edith had hardly struggled at all, just a small feeble effort. Angela had held the pillow hard down on her face for a couple of minutes and she was gone. She'd arranged Edith's head back on the pillow and straightened the covers. She hadn't stopped to check the pulse in case Sandra had seen her coming out of there which might have raised awkward questions. Next time, and Angela was already thinking of the next one, she would wait until Sandra went for a wee so that she would have more time. She also knew that others may not be so easy and it was important that she did not do them too close together. Suddenly, it occurred to Angela that she should do the next one when either Matron or Sister Johansen was on duty, or even Kristine. Then she'd have much more time. They never followed her around like Sandra did. She always wanted to be with someone, especially at night as she said she was afraid of the dark. Angela treated this with derision. Sandra was a baby. What was there to be scared of? It was just the same as the daytime, without the light.

It was Sandra of course, who found Edie Nolan dead. Angela sent her out to the veranda with the early morning tea, while she did the rest of the rooms. Minutes later Sandra rushed back in a great panic,

'Quick, quick get the Doctor', she said, her face pale, her eyes staring. 'I think Mrs Nolan's dead.'

'Keep your voice down, you don't want to kill the others with shock,' Angela joked. 'How do you know she's dead and if she is, what use is the Doctor?'

'I tried to take her pulse and there wasn't one and she's all white and her top teeth have fallen down –and---and, there's quite a smell 'cause she must have wet herself, and more' — Angela interrupted this excited gabble with,

'Come with me and we'll take a look.'

'I'm not going back out there. You go and I'll ring the Doctor.' Sandra couldn't face going out to see Edie again. One half of her was pleased she had gone but she was also quite sad as she'd been fond of the old girl and she'd miss her hopeless mumblings.

Angela went to check and pull the curtain round the bed, which Sandra had forgotten to do in her haste to get away. It wouldn't do for the other patients to see a dead body in the bed, not that most of them would notice.

Phew, the whole veranda stank now but they couldn't do anything until the Doctor had certified her dead. There were no relatives to inform and it did give them both more work as they would have to stay on and help sister 'lay out' the body. While they were waiting, they could start packing up her things. Not that there were many, just a few faded photographs and some badly worn clothes. Sandra glanced through the photographs.

'Oh look, Angela. You can see she was pretty before she had her stroke although she is quite old then. The bloke with her must be her husband – yes it says on the back, Edith and Jack Dec. 1946, and do look, Angela this one's much earlier and she was very pretty then. It says Edith and Jeanie but doesn't give a date.'

Angela glanced quickly at the photographs but wasn't in the

mood to pass comment. She just wanted to get finished and get off duty. She wished the Doctor would hurry up. The morning staff would be there any moment. Sandra was rather sad that there wasn't so much as a card or letter amongst her things.

'Just think, she never got any post all the time she was here.'

Angela was unsympathetic. 'That's what you get for living too long, nobody cares.'

Angela had laid out several bodies before so when she felt they could cope, Sister left the two girls to finish off. Angela had no feeling for the person who had died. She performed the task automatically while she contemplated her next victim. If there were no repercussions, she thought she might try another one the next week. Ideally, it would be Elsie Hammond as the woman riled her beyond measure. Moaning, moaning, moaning, that was all she ever did and Angela couldn't stand it much longer. She would be more difficult though as there was nothing wrong with her mental state and given half a chance, she would scream, and might even scratch. Elsie also had a niece who came fairly often. Angela was sure she wouldn't care if she didn't have to come any more and she might even get left a few quid, which would be a bonus. The old girl had a shop so there could be quite a lot of money involved. The niece might even thank Angela if she knew. No, Elsie would need more thought and she'd have to work out the best way of doing it. Someone else would have to be done before her. Sandra broke into her thoughts. 'What are you smiling at? This is not a fun job.'

Angela realised she would have to be more careful or she'd give herself away.

'I'm glad to be going off to have a bath and wash this stinking place off me. Got a couple of nights off now so might go home when I've had a sleep. Can't bloody sleep in the day when the kids are off school but may as well have a free meal or two off Ma.

Bill Harkness

Life was boring. Boring, boring, boring. Bill was thoroughly fed up. There was nothing to do but read and nobody of any sense to talk to.

He knew that was an exaggeration. Old Elsie Hammond was OK. In fact Bill considered her quite bright and he made a point of chatting with her at least once a week. She had told him during one of their discussions that she was a first generation New Zealander. Her parents had come out from England with a shipping company and decided to stay. She had not had much education but her mind was as sharp as a tack. The problem for Bill was that Elsie was always in bed or sitting in her room. It didn't seem right visiting a lady in her bedroom, well not at his age, although he had to acknowledge it would have been his aim in his youth. Agnes was all right too. Bill gazed out the window, bemoaning, not for the first time, that the window wasn't on the other wall where he would be able to see Mount Egmont. All he could see now was grass and a couple of straggly bushes. He offered up thanks to a God he didn't really believe in, for the ability to get out of his room under his own steam, without having to rely on "those bloody girls" as he called them.

Generally, Bill thought the Staff was pretty useless. The Norwegian was all right he supposed. She was quite chatty but had a hopeless accent, which made her so difficult to understand. He'd heard there was a new girl but he hadn't met her yet. Perhaps she would turn out to be a brilliant conversationalist. What a hope! He couldn't be so lucky. The trouble was they were all just bloody kids. They'd seen nothing, done nothing. This new one was supposed to be going on to do her training so she must have a bit more about her than the other two more permanent ones. When Bill had asked Sister Johansen why those other two were kept on she'd said that it was so hard to get staff you had to take anyone who turned up prepared to work in a place like this. At the time, he'd replied that they should pay them more and throw out the bad ones but he guessed it would not be easy finding people to wipe strangers' backsides and mop up dribble, eight hours a day. These young girls couldn't know what they were letting themselves in for.

Bill got to reflecting on how it would be if they were animals reaching the end of their lives. They'd be put down, no question. There were a few people who talked about euthanasia but Bill didn't go along with that. They would have put him down long ago because he looked ugly, with his drooping lower lip just like Agnes – that's what it would lead to. Their facial deformity seemed to go with the Parkinson's but he couldn't understand why. Perhaps it went with the speech being slow and awkward. He just didn't know. Any disfigurement and you'd have to go. Never mind the brain. Agnes would've gone although she had a good scientific brain. Bill himself would be gone, mathematical brain and all. Even Elsie would go because she was unable to do anything for herself. It wouldn't be long before babies would be knocked off at birth if they had mongoloid features or even a harelip. It would become acceptable to get rid of them early to save trouble later. No, he decided, euthanasia would never catch on – at least he hoped not.

Bill felt very sorry for Agnes. She was in despair all the time over what she looked like. She was so withdrawn, ashamed of seeing anyone because she was ugly. Bill tried to build her confidence by assuring her that it didn't matter. Most of the people in Mountain View were ugly and a lot of them not just in the body either. Agnes was interesting to talk to although he did wish he could understand her better. Still he accepted that he was pretty incomprehensible himself most of the time, or so they told him.

The door to Bill's room was ajar as usual. Perhaps it was something to do with being a mathematician that he was incredibly curious but he liked to be able to hear what people said as they walked past. This was how he knew what was going on. He was sure he was more aware than Matron or Sister, of how some of the patients were treated. He'd hear the girls discussing the patients, often in very uncomplimentary terms. Angela and Sandra were the worst. "Let's leave Elsie till last today," Angela would say. "She's done nothing but ring that bloody bell all morning," or "Don't put any pants on Agnes when she wants the commode, it takes too long to get them down and everything else gets wet."

Suddenly the door flew wide open and Angela breezed in flourishing a urinal. She plonked it on the locker, made a few suggestive remarks, accompanied by a sly grin as to what Bill might do with it and left the room.

'Why don't you learn to knock,' he shouted after her, but he knew it was useless. He took out his handkerchief before touching the bottle, just to be on the safe side. Last time he'd asked for a urinal he had been in bed and was nearly caught short. Angela had brought it to him quickly enough but straight from the sterilizer. She pushed it under the bedclothes and rushed out again. It had been boiling hot and had burnt his leg and the side of his penis. He'd ended up with a wet bed from the shock of it. In Bill's opinion, Angela was a sadistic bitch. He'd heard that she ill-treated some of the other patients too, particularly the ones who couldn't fight back or complain. He'd told Matron but she wanted to know if he'd actually seen her and he had to admit that he hadn't. If he caught her at it she'd know all about it.

Bill had also heard that she was free with her favours to anyone who was willing. God if he was young again he'd teach her a thing or two. But then again he decided she wasn't worth it. You didn't want it when it was thrown at you. He thought her friend Sandra would be more fun but he'd always liked a bit of brain with it, made it more of a challenge. There hadn't been many good lookers when he was at University. Gentian Thistlewaite had been glamorous enough, tall and rounded in all the right places with long brown hair done up in a fancy knot thing but her God-awful name and haughty manner had put many a bloke off. Being brought up in England probably made her like she was. Heather Wilson had been another one but she'd been too thin for his taste. You needed something to get hold of. From what he'd heard though, she'd done rather well, going to America to work on the space programme. He'd had one or two conquests but he'd not been ready to settle down and when he thought it might be a good idea he hadn't found the right one. He wasn't sorry though, he'd always preferred to be a free agent. Then if he'd wanted to go to America or outer space, he'd have been free to do so. Not that he thought there'd be much point. It might be interesting to look back at the earth to see just how insignificant it was.

Most of the girls he'd known had brains, though they'd kept their heads in their books with no interest in men. Perhaps that had just been a front to stop the men pestering them. Still it was no good him thinking about that now. It was all in the past.

He decided that the new girl, Kristine, was quite intelligent. She'd brought him hot tea, almost unheard of in Mountain View, and she'd made sure he could reach it. She told him she had four sisters and a brother, which must make quite a houseful.

She'd also got her school certificate and had decided to do her nursing training instead of going to University.

'Would you like to go to University?' he asked her.

She blushed, 'Oh I'm not clever enough for that, and I wouldn't know what to study.'

'You could be a doctor.' This seemed the obvious answer but she seemed embarrassed so he hadn't persisted. She was a real good looker though, so her value to the nursing profession was probably nil as she was bound to run off and get married before she finished the course and have umpteen children, like her mother.

Now he couldn't find his book. One of those bloody girls must have moved it, all under the pretence of tidying up. What did it matter how tidy he was? Nobody except him was going to see his room. He needed the book with all his latest calculations. Not that they were important but they were brain exercises and Bill was determined to keep his brain active and in good shape. He didn't want to go doolally to add to his disabilities. Bill wheeled himself to the door and shouted,

'Nurse! Come in here and find my book. I've got work to do, even if you haven't.'

Angela

Angela put her coffee on the table and flopped into an armchair. She'd done three now, and it was getting easier. Nobody suspected anything. Not that there was any reason why they should. Anyone who came into an Old Peoples' Home was usually 70 or 80 years old and didn't expect to go out again. Three deaths in three weeks in a place like Mountain View were about what you'd expect. Angela was sure the other nurses would thank her if they knew that it was she that was making their workload easier. All those who she'd "helped on their way," had either wet their beds or soiled them, or both. None of them had been able to have a conversation. Nobody cared for them. One old bloke who had come for Maggie's things had only wanted to see if there was anything for him, or so Angela believed. He'd never come to see her when she was alive or if he had, she hadn't seen him. They were all the same. They put their relatives into a home for someone else to have the muck and bother so they could go off and enjoy themselves. Well, for Angela, it was good riddance to as many as possible.

She shivered. It was cold in the sitting room now the sun had gone. She pulled the curtains as it would soon be dark and it would make it warmer. One electric fire was not enough for the size of the room. Still, it wasn't a bad room for three people and would still be big enough for six if the other three bedrooms were full. It was nearly twice the size of the one at her home which six people had to share. Angela continued to mull over her plan. The trouble was, there didn't appear to be an end to it. For every bed she emptied someone else arrived to fill it, often the very same day. Matron didn't seem to want empty beds. But then it didn't matter to her, just swanning around doing nothing anyway. She didn't seem to mind them popping off either, except she or sister had to be there to lay them out.

Reluctantly, Angela decided she must give her plan a break for a couple of weeks. People were expected to die in these places but too many at once might make someone suspicious. She couldn't afford to have anyone asking difficult questions. Even Sandra had looked worried yesterday and said "people seem to be dying like flies around here."

"What do ya mean? Only one this week and what's one in a place like this? They come here to die don't they?" Angela made out like she hadn't noticed how many had gone.

"There's been four in the last three weeks and that's more than usual," she'd said.

Angela nearly put her foot in it by correcting her, "no, only three," because that was all she'd done, but she remembered just in time that one old fellow had kicked the bucket all by himself. That was one less for her to do. The next one had to be Agnes. She'd like to do Elsie but she would be much more difficult, and what's more, the niece might be a problem as she visited regularly. No, Agnes would be next. She was getting worse, much worse. Three times Angela had had to change her yesterday and it had been twice already that day. Kristine was making it more difficult by insisting that they all had to wear knickers. "Not decent!" she said. Kristine was really getting up Angela's nose. It was a load of rubbish. What did the patients care about whether they wore knickers or not? Most of them wouldn't even know what they had on. Angela went without them herself sometimes when it was hot or she didn't have any clean ones.

Bill was the only one who might question Agnes' death

although Angela couldn't see why he should. Old people died all the time, especially in there. The only difficulty she could see was that Agnes wasn't old, just 58 or thereabouts. Well, she could have a heart attack, people often did in their fifties and sixties. Or a massive stroke? She might have cancer they didn't know about. Whoever was to be her next victim, they'd have to wait. She couldn't risk doing any more for a few weeks, particularly as there were one or two who were sick and they might die anyway. She would have to get it just right. Maybe she should do one or two before Agnes and for her, it would have to be on Kristine's day off.

Agnes

Agnes was in a state. She was so frightened it was making all her symptoms worse and this was compounding the problem. The more she shook, the more she dribbled, the more accidents she had, the more horrible Angela was to her.

What could she do? She decided to ask Bill his opinion when he came along to see her as he did most days after she had told him Angela frightened her. She just hoped he would understand her.

'Sthee never leths me sit in the sthitting room these days. Sthays I mucked up the cthairs cos I was always wet.' If they put her on the commode more regularily or when she asked, she wouldn't make a mess. Not that Agnes wanted to sit in the sitting room very often as it was a dreary room; dull green walls, brown linoleum on the floor with a few nondescript rugs. The five pictures probably came from a jumble sale as they too were dull and did nothing to lift the spirits. But it would be a change.

'You should stand up to her Agnes. Shout at her, tell her not to push you around or you will report her,' advised Bill. Poor Agnes couldn't shout at anyone. The sound came out as a screech. She wouldn't even be heard outside her room.

'Sshister leshs me sit oustshide on fine days. Shister puts me by the flowers and there's no nashty shmells out there,' said Agnes.

'I'd stick to going in the garden with Sister or Matron. I shouldn't risk it with that Angela, she's likely to forget about you or leave you out there deliberately and you could be there all night,' warned Bill.

Agnes shuddered. What an awful thought. It was a pity, as even when she was outside on her own she didn't feel lonely or miserable like she did when inside. It was healthy to get the Vitamin D too. Agnes had told Bill about Angela putting her hand on her neck, putting pressure on with her thumb. She had been getting her dressed and had gone behind her to straighten the collar. She'd folded it down and under the pretence of creasing the fold to make it sit right she had pushed her fingers hard into Agnes' neck, her thumb partially blocking off the blood vessel.

'I'm sho frightened, Bill. When she put her sthumb in my neck I felt quite faint and thsick. Shees trying to sckill me.'

'Oh, I'm sure she's not. She was probably being her usual rough self. She's like that, she should be more careful.' Bill said. Agnes knew it was more serious than that but unfortunately she couldn't explain herself well enough for him to picture what really happened. Angela frightened people. That incident had terrified her. She feared for her life and everyday that Angela was on duty had become a nightmare for Agnes.

Bill Harkness

Bill had only three more calculations to finish on the section of the article he was working on but he couldn't concentrate. Time Travel was a difficult concept and needed undivided attention.

Poor old Agnes. She was working herself up into a tizz. She was firmly convinced that Angela was going to knock her off, or at least try to. Bill didn't believe she had the guts. She was all bluster and hot air but he knew she was cruel enough. Nasty for the fun of it. There was a knock on the door. Now what? It had to be Matron or Sister – the others didn't bother to knock. No, it was Kristine's head that appeared round the door to ask him if he wanted anything.

'Well I wouldn't mind a cup of tea since you're asking and when you come back I've something to tell you.' Kristine soon returned with hot tea and a biscuit and put it on his locker.

'You said you wanted to tell me something, Mr Harkness?'

'You can call me Bill, everyone else does. Now you're not going to believe this but Agnes Thorwood believes Angela is trying to 'knock her off".'

Kristine gasped, her eyes wide and staring, 'Bill! You can't say that. It's not true. Oh, that's horrible! Of course she's not. You mustn't spread stories like that.'

'I didn't say it. Agnes did. That's what she believes and she's very frightened. I thought somebody should know, that's all.' The poor girl looked so shocked, Bill wished he hadn't mentioned it. Too late now but somebody should know.

Kristine couldn't believe her fellow creatures were not as

nice as she was. Bill was afraid she had some rude awakenings in store. Seriously, he did not think Angela would try anything although he did know there were people about that would. Deaths were not unexpected in a place like this as it was the only way any of them were going to leave. Thinking about it, he came to the realisation that there had been quite a number of deaths in recent weeks. But they were all old and Agnes was only 58. She had a long way to go yet although she probably wished she hadn't.

Perhaps he had better warn Elsie too. She was quite a pain to the girls, always ringing the bell because she could do so little for herself. If someone was knocking the patients off, Elsie could well be on the list for an early exit. No, he decided, it was all too far fetched. How would she do it? Angela was only an aide, with no access to injections, or tablets even. Matron had them all locked up, the ones that would be any use. She would surely notice if some were missing and he was pretty certain they all had to be accounted for. She couldn't just hit the patients on the head as that would be too obvious. The same went for strangling and he'd just like to see her try it on him. Come to think of it, Agnes did say Angela had pressed the vein in her neck so hard she felt faint. Perhaps that was how she could do it, make them pass out and then smother them? No. Altogether too far fetched. It was a waste of time speculating about a 'pie in the sky' notion.

A person could soon get paranoid in Mountain View.

Kristine

Kristine couldn't believe it. Bill must have got it wrong. Angela wouldn't dare do such a thing. She wouldn't WANT to, for Heaven's sake. Nobody would, well not unless they were mad. Angela might be unkind, cruel even, but she wasn't mad. It was obvious she didn't really like old people and Kristine couldn't work out why she was there, but it wasn't to kill people, she was certain of that. It was too awful to think about.

It was a pleasure to take her break, sitting outside in the sun for a change. Kristine glanced at her watch. Great, she had another ten minutes. Time for another coffee. She went in and made a fresh cup, taking a biscuit from the tin on the way. She had to think. Bill couldn't be right, he must be imagining things. Perhaps he was making it up? Kristine knew old people did that sometimes, to get attention. Still, maybe she should tell someone else, just in case, so they could watch out? But tell who? Watch out for what? No. It was too ridiculous. She had no proof. Nobody would believe her.

It was true that quite a few people had died since she'd been there. Matron had explained that there were always deaths in old peoples' homes and she must try and get used to it. Nobody came to these places unless they were old and frail and they would not be going out again. It was obvious that they would eventually die there. All those who had died had been old though and Agnes was not old. Kristine thought she was lovely. Nobody could possibly hate her. Bill had to be imagining it. Angela was just rough, rough with the patients and just as rough in her personal life. It was probably the way she had been brought up.

But then Elsie had also told her to keep an eye on Angela. That made two of them who were worried about it. It wasn't surprising that neither Bill nor Elsie liked Angela. She was quite beastly to both of them but to suggest that she'd "knock them off" as Bill put it, was too harsh. Even she couldn't be that wicked. What could she do anyway? The girls didn't give injections and even the tablets were checked. If she tried to do anything else someone would notice. It couldn't be done and Kristine was convinced she wouldn't try. Bill was just being dramatic and they would have forgotten all about it by the time she came back on Friday from her days off.

Angela

Angela was feverishly trying to force all her belongings into her one suitcase, cursing and swearing to herself as she did so. She didn't have much but she'd collected a few Elvis records and other rock 'n roll ones and she wasn't going to leave them behind. She'd have to wear her jacket even though it wasn't cold enough.

Over and over she repeated, 'God! That was awful. Awful. I'm not doing any more, I'm getting out of this bloody place, now, this minute.' She knelt on the case, forcing it shut and gathering up the rest of her things; hair drier, her hair brush, toilet bag and a couple of magazines. She stuffed them into an old canvas bag she'd forgotten she had.

Angela couldn't stop seeing Agnes' face; choking, purple, wild eyes. It was a nightmare. She was choking, all that saliva bubbling out, her terrified eyes staring accusingly at her. Why couldn't she have gone quietly like all the others?

The doctors wouldn't know – they couldn't. Nobody would be able to tell what made her choke. She'd always had too much saliva. Uughh, Angela wanted to throw up. She forced herself not to think about it or she was never going to get out of there. All over the pillow it was, when she'd pushed it down. She put it under her face so they wouldn't know, they'd just think she couldn't get rid of it. It was bound to happen some time.

Angela had to get away, to stop seeing her face. "Go away Agnes. *Go away*" She screamed inside her head. "You know you didn't want to live. Well, now you've gone. Be happy, I did it for you. Don't you see, you didn't have a life, so what's the difference?"

She'd get the bus. There was one at twelve o'clock. Bloody Matron was furious she was leaving.

'You can't just leave, you are supposed to give two weeks notice. You will leave us seriously short of staff. Why is it so urgent that you go today?'

'I've had enough. I'm tired of cleaning up after people; dirty bottoms, dirty beds. It's making me sick and people are dying all the time. I've got to get away and get a different kind of job.'

'You do realize that you will not get paid for the two weeks in lieu of notice,' Matron said trying to encourage her to stay to work out her notice. But Angela refused.

'I don't care about the money. I'm going today and that's it. I hope you find someone else to do the job.' Angela muttered goodbye and left the office, stifling the urge to slam the door. Matron should be pleased because she had one less patient to look after. One who took up a lot of time. She should thank her but she wouldn't of course. Angela would be up for murder. She couldn't understand why. All the smart people called it Youthinasia or something like that and they didn't get done for murder in other places. It's not murder she insisted to herself, it was putting useless people out of their misery, helping them on their way. Religious people should be happy. Angela was sending them to a better life according to them.

Sandra started crying, 'Why are you leaving, all of a sudden?'

'I'm fed up, that's why. Tired of all the hard work and getting no thanks. Not enough money for all the disgusting things we have to do.'

'What am I going to do?" Sandra wailed. 'Here all on my own with goody, goody two shoes. Nobody to go out with.'

Angela told her she was pathetic. 'Stop weeping and

wailing, thinking only of yourself. I've enough problems of my own, no money, and now no job. You're grown up now Sandra, although you wouldn't think it sometimes. You're such a baby. You'll just have to look after yourself. You can always leave if you want to.'

Kristine was just as bad. She'd been crying too because her darling Agnes had died, and such a horrible death.

'To choke must be so awful,' she'd sobbed.

'Oh for God's sake shut up,' Angela snapped. 'Grow up. People die all the time, specially in places like this and what's the difference between choking and having a heart attack? You're still dead aren't you?' She wished Kristine had not mentioned choking. There was that horrible blue mottled face again, staring, accusing, swimming before her eyes. Angela nearly threw up.

She was going. She was out of there. *Now.*

Matron

'Why me? Why now.' Matron was furious, exasperated, slightly nervous. Here she was with just one year to go. She didn't need it. Agnes had been sick. She was unhappy, anyone could tell that. She had no quality of life. She had little control of her bladder, dribbled all the time. It was bound to happen at some time. It was true that she wasn't old; younger than Matron in fact and the doctor had not seen her for nearly a month. But a post mortem! This was only the third time in her career that a patient of hers had been ordered a post mortem. It was an old peoples' home, someone died every other week.

'All sudden, unexpected deaths require a post mortem. You know that Matron.' Dr Bradford explained that, coupled with the fact that Agnes' death had been unexpected, she was relatively young and two of the patients had voiced their concerns, he was duty bound to investigate.

'Concerns? What about?' Matron was bemused. This was the first she'd heard of any 'concerns.'

'One of your staff, the good looking one, was very shocked and she said that Agnes had told her she was frightened. She said Agnes had told several other patients she'd been threatened by one of the staff some days ago.'

'Oh, come on. Who is going to threaten a harmless creature like Agnes. It would have been Kristine who told you all this. She's always shocked when someone dies, seems to think they can go on forever. If Agnes had been frightened she'd have told me. She'd probably had one or two choking fits and got scared. She just died for Heaven's sake. All right, she choked. People do.'

'I do agree that's probably what happened but in view of questions being asked, I have to order a post mortem. Apparently, a relative has made enquiries too it seems, so I must take the form in now. I'll be in touch if I need to know any more.' With that Dr. Bradford departed.

Matron was furious. What relative? Agnes didn't have any relatives. It must have been Joyce, Elsie's niece. Bill and Elsie would have put her up to it. She would give them a piece of her mind and tell them not to go frightening everyone. She was convinced they wouldn't find anything. There were no drugs missing, no strangle marks, nothing. Dr. Bradford was making a mountain out of a molehill.

Now they were short of staff. Today of all days. Angela might have given her more notice. She'd demanded to see her saying it was vitally important then announced she was leaving. Said she was fed up and would be going this afternoon. She wasn't the only one who was fed up. Matron Gardiner wished she, too, could just up and walk out.

PART TWO

England, 1997

Kristine

Chapter One

'You can't put it off much longer.'

'I know, I know, but these places are so awful.'

'How can you say that? You haven't seen them.'

'I've experienced them. I know what goes on inside.'

'For Heaven's sake, Kristine, that was over forty years ago, and in another country.'

'Why should it be any different, Derek? An old peoples' home is likely to be just as bad here if you can believe the horror stories in the papers, now, not forty years ago, but this week.' She'd never told anyone the full horror of Mountain View, not even Derek. Lately, with the current bad publicity, the memories had been flooding back.

'That's true but it was a long time ago, things change. Only the very bad ones get into the papers. There are hundreds of Nursing Homes. There are bound to be good ones somewhere, why not here, and we have to resolve the problem of mother.'

'So she's a problem to you now, is she?' snapped Kristine, who'd often found Derek's mother a problem.

'Of course she's a problem, in the nicest possible way. We've already agreed she'll have to go somewhere.' Derek's way of dealing with this was the way he dealt with all problems. Find a solution, execute it, problem solved, deal with the next thing. He was sharp and decisive, unusual in an accountant, or so Kristine thought. Until she met Derek she had always thought them dry old sticks and would never have imagined herself marrying one.

'It's all very well but it's your own mother we're putting away.' Kristine was struggling to hold back her tears.

'Look love, I'm not trying to be difficult but we did agree that we're not able to look after her here.' Derek moved over to Kristine, putting his arm around her and giving her a comforting squeeze. 'And we're not "putting her away" as you call it. We're just trying to make sure she has the care she needs and deserves.'

In a voice barely audible against his shoulder, Kristine murmured, 'Perhaps we could look after her here, after all – I feel so mean, being a nurse and – we've got the room and I could give up work and there must be some benefits we could claim and she is 84 this year – she can't go on for ever.' Her memories of old peoples' homes were haunting her. How could Derek be expected to understand?

'You're not starting on that again,' exclaimed Derek, moving away in frustration. 'We've been through it all a hundred times.' Catching sight of his reflection in the glass door reminded him, not for the first time, that the years were catching up with him, 63 at the next birthday; grey at the temples, a few more lines. Kristine still looked younger although there was only a year's difference. Her weight had barely increased over the years, perhaps a little wider on the hips if he was being objective. Her glossy dark hair was only sparsely streaked with grey and hardly a wrinkle, just a few laughter lines around her eyes. It would be them next, wanting an old peoples' home. Well, it wouldn't be his problem. Rebecca and Ralph would soon organize them into a home once they started to become difficult.

'But I should be able to look after her. What will people say?'

'So that's it! You're worried about what others think. To hell with what anyone else thinks – it's our life. You must admit, you get too emotional about it. I didn't think nurses were supposed to let personal feelings encroach on their professional judgment?'

'That's not fair. This is your mother we're talking about; she's family so I'm bound to think differently about her. Anyway, it's your mother's life you're organising, not ours.'

'It's ours too. Having my mother living here would change our lives completely — you'd better believe it. I love her and want to do the best for her but I for one, am not prepared to put up with the upheaval. Before long we would grow to resent her, however nice she was and you know as well as I do how difficult she can be. That wouldn't be good for her, or for us.'

Kristine knew only too well how difficult Derek's mother could be. Having her live with them was the last thing she wanted but she had a horror of old peoples' homes. Didn't she boast when she was in Mountain View that she would never dump her relation in an Old People's Home? Now she was contemplating doing just that.

Derek walked over to the window and stood gazing into the garden. It was only the middle of March but he could see already the faint green haze of new leaves. Kristine sat on the sofa, sick and hunched over with guilt and indecision.

Finally Derek turned and said, 'Let's approach this sensibly. Why don't you make an appointment to go and see some of these homes? See what they're like these days. See what facilities they provide, what the staff is like – and how much they cost?' He wasn't mean and would happily spend the money on his mother, but he wasn't inclined to waste it either.

'Will you come with me? She is your mother.' No way was a Home for her mother-in-law going to be Kristine's decision.

'Yes, if you want, but I don't know what to look for. Why don't you suss out two or three of the best ones then I'll come with you for the final choice.'

'What about your mother? You know her. She won't be pushed about and she will insist on having a say, if not the whole say. What if she won't go?' Kristine could just hear her, "How ridiculous, what would I want in one of those places?"

'She'll have to, eventually. Oh I know she can look after herself at the moment but she is getting forgetful and the day will come when she's unable to make a rational choice.'

'You know her favourite saying, "Please don't treat me like an idiot"' parodied Kristine. 'She'll have to be properly assessed and they'll want to know what she can do for herself and how reliable she is. I don't think she's ready for a home quite yet. Perhaps we should get the assessment done first?'

'We might have to wait months for that. We should find out what's on offer then the home we choose will hurry up the assessment. It's in their interests.'

'You make it sound so clinical and financial – she's a human being. They won't take her if she can still look after herself, no matter how old she is. The big drive these days is care in the community, but I suppose they could put her on their waiting list. They won't keep a room but at least they'll have seen her and she will have seen them.'

'I'm just being realistic and I think we'll soon find out just how financial it all is,' replied Derek gloomily as he went out to finish polishing the car. He'd come in for a cup of tea, not to be harangued about his mother. Still, he supposed it had to be discussed. Even if Evelyn was his mother, Kristine took the brunt of the visiting. She resolved to go and look at some Homes over the next few weeks.

Chapter Two

'Hello Evelyn, it's me,' Kristine called, letting herself in through the front door. She often wondered if she should encourage Evelyn to keep the door locked but knew she wouldn't be thanked for suggesting it.

'Come in dear, how nice to see you. I haven't seen anyone for over a week.'

Evelyn was sitting in her favourite chair, The Times on her lap and a dictionary to hand. She had taken her usual care with her appearance; green blouse that matched her tweed skirt, pearl necklace, always the pearls, and matching earrings. Kristine didn't think she even took the pearls off at night. She had been a good-looking woman in her younger days and apart from being about a stone over-weight, she still managed to look elegant most of the time. Her white hair had been carefully folded into a tidy chignon at the nape of her neck. Her skin was good, like many English women who'd never spent a great deal of time in the sun. Kristine's compatriots of a similar age usually sported dark, leathery skin from a lifetime of outdoor living. Although Evelyn had spent many hours in the garden, she'd always worn a hat and gardening gloves. She had a gardener to look after things now.

'I saw you yesterday, don't you remember?'

'Not yesterday surely, it was ages ago!'

'No. I brought you some chicken soup for lunch.'

'Was that only yesterday? I could have sworn it was a week ago.'

Yes, thought Kristine. You'd be prepared to argue black was white rather than say you forgot. Gosh, I hope I don't get like that. I'll get Derek to shoot me first. Maybe I'm nicer to start with. But then, maybe I'm not. You never can tell how people are going to end up.

'Never mind, I'm here now. You remember I said yesterday we need to have a talk about your future and how we can best look after you.' Kristine had spent an hour on social chit-chat the day before so felt she could launch into serious business this visit.

'I'm just fine here, thank you. I've been here for forty years, as you well know. I'm sure Derek will sort this out. He looks after my affairs now dear Brian has gone. Why don't you put the kettle on and we'll have a cup of tea. There's cake in the tin. Mrs Humphrey baked it yesterday.'

Kristine made a mental note that she was not the only one who had visited yesterday. Evelyn had never learnt to cook, other than basic meals and she used a local woman to do any lunch parties she gave and to do some baking once a fortnight. She'd given up dinner parties several years ago as none of her friends, mostly widows, wanted to venture out in the evenings.

'Of course, it is his domain and he will be making any new arrangements. He thought you and I might like to discuss the more personal aspects, woman to woman, see what's best, you know what I mean,' Kristine replied as she disappeared into the huge kitchen. She tried not to notice the clutter or the fact that it was not as clean as it should be.

'I can't hear you, dear. We'll talk about it when you come back.' Not that Evelyn wanted to talk about moving. She was perfectly all right where she was and that was that.

Back in the living room with the tea, Kristine looked around at the faded curtains, dull wallpaper and badly worn carpet. There were a few cobwebs draping the corners too. Evelyn wouldn't have anything changed, and she only wore her glasses for reading so didn't see the dust. Derek's father, Brian, had liked it as it was, or so Evelyn said. Kristine didn't think he had much choice but then he liked a quiet life. The room had been lovely when newly decorated just before Brian died, but the last ten years had taken their toll. Evelyn wouldn't accept that everything had now become very shabby. Molly Davies was very kind to Evelyn but she wasn't the most conscientious cleaner. She came twice a week to 'do' for Evelyn, but she couldn't refurbish what needed replacing. Having an open fire in the room for many years had not helped the decoration but Derek had replaced it with a gas fire four years ago so Evelyn didn't have to carry wood and deal with ashes. At least one room in the house was easy to heat. Some of the window frames needed replacing and before long the roof would need attention. It was also totally unsuitable for an elderly person: large rooms, difficult to heat and a rather steep staircase. Derek was always on about how much it would cost to put right. Although it was the family home, he was keen to sell while they could still get a good price, but that was certainly not an argument she could use with his mother.

'I don't know what there is to discuss. I'm quite happy here. Mrs Humphrey certainly makes good cakes.'

Kristine was not going to be deflected from the subject.

'I'm afraid it's not possible for you to stay here much longer, Evelyn, especially when the winter comes. The house is too big, not to mention the garden. You really need someone to look after you – see that you eat properly, help you with a bath, things like that. You know you've had a couple of falls lately. We've tried Home Helps, haven't we, but you didn't find them very satisfactory, did you? Often off sick, or their children sick, agency short of staff, lack of transport and other excuses.'

'You could look after me. You come in nearly every day.'

Not for the first time, Kristine noticed, Evelyn was able to remember things when it suited her.

'I can't be here all the time. I do have a job and we do go away and then there are the children.'

'You can't call them children, they're grown up and should be helping you. You don't have to help them.'

'No, I don't mean that, but now Rebecca is married she's likely to have a family of her own soon and I'd like to be free to help her out. And when Ralph comes home I'd want to be free...' Her voice trailed off rather lamely. Why hadn't she made Derek do this? Sadly, Kristine had never had to have this conversation with her own parents. Her mother had died of cancer at 54 and her father of a heart attack just two years ago, aged 83. Her sister Colleen had lived near him and kept an eye out but he'd been hale and hearty until the last, and fiercely independent. Kristine was timid, like her mother, more sensitive to atmosphere and criticism. She reflected that Derek thought she was too sensitive and often expressed surprise that nursing hadn't toughened her up.

Evelyn brightened up, 'If I must move I could come and live with you. Is that what you're saying?'

God forbid, thought Kristine. Why had she ever thought that was an option? If that were to happen she'd be strangling her mother-in-law within the week.

'No, that wouldn't be very sensible as we're both out all day so you'd be no better off. We thought we should look at residential homes where you could have continuous care. You'd have your own room of course and these days you can take your own furniture too. Many of them let you have breakfast when you want. They go on outings. Have musical events. You can get your hair done on the premises. Some even paint your nails for you.'

'If I want my nails painted I'll do them myself. The whole idea sounds perfectly ghastly.'

'I'm just trying to give you an idea of how pleasant it would be. You'd always have company. Never be left alone.' Kristine felt she was digging herself into a hole but wasn't quite sure how she could extricate herself. She didn't feel her voice carried sufficient conviction either, coloured as it was with her negative experiences of nursing and residential homes. She refilled Evelyn's cup and considered trying to change the subject but knew she had to press on with it.

'I should hate that. Never being on my own. Not being able to get away from people. The forced communal spirit is what's so horrible about those places. Most of them are ga ga anyway.'

'I'm sure you could stay in your room if you wanted to, even have meals there but there would always be someone to talk to if you wanted company. Residential homes are not like nursing homes. Many of the residents go off into town or out with their relatives. You could still see your friends and play Bridge.' Kristine realized too late she should have refused to discuss the matter with Evelyn. Derek was the only one with any influence on his mother and he would have to talk to her.

'You sound determined on it. Am I not to have a say? I suppose you've booked me in already.'

'Of course we haven't, Evelyn. We wouldn't dream of it. That's why I wanted to have this discussion.'

'I could have a companion. There are plenty of "little women" who want a home and would be happy to do for me, in return for their keep. We'd hardly have to pay them at all.'

Kristine tried desperately to hide her frustration. There she was, way back in her fantasy world of the '50s when she'd been spoilt to death with domestic servants. She supposed there must have been a time when Evelyn looked after herself but Kristine had no knowledge of it.

'I'm sorry Evelyn, but things aren't like that any more. There are no "little women" as you call them, these days. They all want their own bathroom and sitting room, paid holidays, two days off a week and no night work. It would cost a fortune and we just can't afford it.'

'You can afford to go gallivanting about on holidays all round the world. I've never been on holiday – well not for years and years.'

No, and that's your own fault, thought Kristine. Evelyn had a phobia about planes, trains, tunnels, anything that involved being closed in. Not that she'd ever been in a plane so had no idea what it was like. She also had diabetes and the beginnings of osteoarthritis in her knees. The idea of 'going abroad' didn't appeal to her and she didn't trust foreign doctors.

Kristine didn't rise to the bait. Evelyn knew perfectly well that they went to the other side of the world to see her family and on her more pleasant days she agreed it was essential. Kristine tried another tactic.

'Dr. Nicholls said it would be wise to have access to medical supervision. You know you sometimes forget to take your medication and that can be dangerous for a diabetic.'

Evelyn cheered up at the mention of Dr. Nicholls. A cynic would say she enjoyed ill health. 'I could have a nurse living in. She could keep a close eye on me and cook a few meals. She'd probably run the vacuum round and dust occasionally, although I can do that. After all, I wouldn't need nursing care all the time. You'd be ideal. I could even pay you a little. As you're family it would be insulting to give you proper wages but I'm sure you'd like some pin money.'

Kristine had had enough. She finished her tea, gathered up the cups and took them into the kitchen. She washed up and decided to leave before she said anything she would regret.

'I think we've been over all this before. The best thing I can do is go and look at some homes, then we can talk about it again. I'm sure you'd like to discuss it with Derek.'

'He won't want to put me in a home and I'm sure he'll agree with me that my idea is the best. In our family, we always did our duty by our loved ones. Look after your own, I always say. I looked after my niece when she was ill, nursed her until she died and I hadn't had any training. I went to my mother every day too.'

'Derek will come and see you about it. I must go now.' Kristine picked up her bag, gave her mother-in-law a peck on the cheek and calling, 'I'll see you soon,' she made a hurried exit.

Once in the car she turned the music up loud and shouted Damn! Damn! Damn! Why do I let her get to me? Kristine was sure Evelyn knew she was more vulnerable to attack than Derek and if she could make Kristine feel guilty then she would get what she wanted in the end. Derek was right. They could not have Evelyn living with them or Kristine would go mad, or hit her, or both. Evelyn would be like the old mother in a film she'd seen years ago, banging her stick on the floor for attention. Day and night, week after week, month in, year out. Kristine couldn't bear to think about it. She was shocked to think she had changed so much. Where was the love and compassion she had lavished on those old people in Mountain View so long ago? What if it was her own mother? Her mother had always said she wouldn't live with any of her children, as it wasn't fair, caused too much disharmony in families. Sadly, they never had the chance to see. Her sisters, Helen and Margaret, Marlene and Colleen, would all have looked after her willingly, and Kristine believed she would have too if she'd lived in the same country. Had she become no better than Sandra or Angela?

Kristine argued backwards and forwards with herself. No, no way am I like them, I'm sure I'm not. *Well you were so sure back then that the relatives of those people in Mountain View were uncaring. What do you think of them now?* It's just that I had nobody else to consider back then. I've got other responsibilities, Derek, the children. I'm much older too. *Perhaps Elsie Hammond's niece had too? You were rather critical of her at the time. She must have*

been at least as old as you are now and she was running Elsie's shop.
I know, I know. Don't remind me. Haven't the energy, not so
fit. Still, other people do it. Why can't I? Am I that much more
selfish?

She didn't think so. All she wanted for herself was more
time. Time to do a few of the things she'd like to do, things
for herself, painting, art appreciation, writing a book, doing
whatever took her fancy, instead of having every minute filled
with what she had to do. Still, she was a nurse. Whatever Derek
said, people would think she should look after her mother-in-
law, at least for a while. But then how would she stop? It might
get too much for her. She would certainly feel resentful about
not being free to do what she wanted, when she wanted. In her
eyes, that boiled down to being selfish. Evelyn was elderly and
needed to be looked after. It was Kristine's duty to try, but she
just knew there would be a big row, ending in a major falling
out, if they went down that road.

No. This was the best way. Kristine started the engine and
drove home, calmer now and resolved to find a nice home for
Evelyn. Fairly close by – not too close – and she would visit
often, take her little treats, take her out. Yes, that was the best
solution. The problem now was to find a good home.

Chapter Three

Kristine sank into the chair and closed her eyes. The Spring sunshine bathed the room and the music of Swan Lake wafted gently around her, soothing her jangled nerves. Kristine loved Tchaikovsky although she'd never quite forgiven Barbara for telling her that her preference meant she was musically unsophisticated. Maybe she was, but she hadn't taken any interest in classical music until well into her thirties and the first proper concert she'd ever been to had featured Tchaikovsky's first piano concerto, which she'd loved. The music calmed her and the late afternoon sun warmed her legs, making her feel drowsy. It had taken her months to get around to looking at the local homes for Derek's mother, partly because she was working most days but mainly because she couldn't face the trauma of it all. Christmas had come and gone since she first broached the subject with Evelyn. No doubt she thought they'd forgotten about it. Kristine would never find a home for Evelyn if all the homes in the vicinity were like the two she'd seen in Marwick today.

'Well, how did you get on?' She was so despondent she hadn't heard Derek come in. Kristine didn't answer immediately. She went into the kitchen and filled the kettle and took a matching cup and saucer from the cupboard. She'd be quite happy with a mug but she was so used to Evelyn's disapproving looks, using a cup and saucer had become a habit.

'Would you like some tea? I haven't had any yet, it's been a depressing afternoon.'

'In that case, I'll have a gin and tonic and skip the tea and you can tell me all the horrors of nursing homes.'

'A very depressing experience, I'm afraid. In Peace Haven there was anything but peace. Three of the staff were gossiping about their own affairs and one sighed quite openly when someone rang the bell for attention. Your mother would hate it: music blaring from someone's radio, racing commentary barking from another and the television at top volume with most of the residents dozing in their chairs or looking blankly into space.'

'They were probably quite happy, living in their own little world, not having to worry about anything, warm and comfortable, plenty to eat.'

'Oh. That's another thing. They were getting the lunch ready and the food smelt pretty awful, liver and onions it was. Ugh!'

'Some people like liver and onions. Probably reminded them of the old days, rationing, stews and such like.' Derek was quite fond of liver and onions but seldom had it as it was not Kristine's favourite thing. 'Did you manage to speak to any of the residents or were they all past it?'

'Well some were sitting there staring into space but some of them were quite 'with it' and I had a long conversation with one old chap. He must have thought I was a member of staff because he asked me when lunch was, as he was starving. Once I explained that I was a visitor he let rip with his less than complimentary opinion of the place. He thought that day's food smelt like boiled cabbage and he just hoped it wasn't. He couldn't imagine anyone liking boiled cabbage. He said the money all went on plush carpets and antique furniture in the entrance hall to attract the "punters" as he put it, but they cut corners on the food. His niece usually brought him tasty treats but she'd gone to Devon on holiday and wouldn't be back for three more days. She'd brought him a big box of chocolates before she went but he'd eaten them all at once so now he'd probably starve.'

'I'm sure he was exaggerating,' Derek was sceptical that it was all that bad. He had no recollection of ever stepping foot in such a place and had no idea what they were like. Kristine pressed on, trying to make him understand.

'He also complained about the music. He said he didn't mind a bit of background music but they played loud pop junk all the time and it got on his nerves. He claimed the staff liked it and it was for their benefit, not the residents. The same with the television, that was on all day whether anyone was watching it or not. I think he would have gone on complaining if the gong hadn't gone for lunch. He excused himself, saying he had to rush and get there ahead of the mob to get a seat at a table where nobody needed feeding. People dribbling their food rather put him off his dinner, even though he knew they couldn't help it. The whole thing sounded terrible and doesn't seem much different from what I experienced forty odd years ago. The staff didn't seem that interested in the residents. It was just a job.'

'Does sound pretty ghastly,' Derek conceded. 'So what about the other one? Eventide, wasn't it? You'd think they could come up with more imaginative names.'

'It was far better as far as the noise was concerned, just the opposite in fact. It was so quiet, there was a rather empty feel about it – and there were no pictures. It was really strange, there were no pictures anywhere. None in the hall, or the public rooms. Miss Harrison, that was the Care Home Manager, they're not allowed to call them Matron anymore, and I suppose most of them are not anyway. Trained I mean, not even nurses unless it is a nursing home. Where was I? Oh yes, Miss Harrison showed me a room belonging to one of the residents. It was quite nice, big too, with a bay window, but I don't think they're all that large. She showed me one of the better ones. She was quite fierce about the money too. "You'll have to pay every month, by standing order and any default, I'm afraid you'll lose the room". And all that before I'd even said I wanted a room.'

'I told you they're mercenary. I suppose most of them are on a tight budget and they want to make as much profit as they can. What about the food? Did it smell any better?'

'Miss Harrison said they all had small appetites and didn't eat much and elderly people didn't need a lot of food, it was bad for them. That might be true but they don't have much else to look forward to. I can't say the residents looked very happy, the few that I saw. They looked rather cowed somehow and none of them were doing anything. Not reading, knitting or even chatting to each other. I can't explain it but it made me feel quite depressed. There wasn't a nice atmosphere.'

'It doesn't look very promising I agree, but there must be others. You probably need to go a bit further afield to get a better selection. Bilston should be more promising. Don't you know anyone to ask? Anyone who has been in the same position?'

'I suppose I do. Yes, I could ask Beverley. Why didn't I think of her? Both her mother and mother-in-law were in a home, and that was in Bilston. One was in a wheelchair so she was probably in a nursing home.'

'What's the difference? If they're better perhaps we should look at them.'

'The difference is that they're much more expensive. They have to have trained people in charge and they're for people who need a lot of nursing care. Your mother can still do things for herself, she only needs supervision and company.'

Derek laughed. 'What's so funny?' asked Kristine sharply. She wasn't finding any of this a laughing matter.

'I was just conjuring up the image of "she who must be obeyed" being supervised. She'd be so insulted if she could hear us.'

'I could always ask Mary too. She's a Councillor and must know the reputation of some of these places. I'll ring them both this evening. Are you going to see your mother tomorrow? You're going to a meeting in Little Marston aren't you? It'll be on the way. It's your turn and don't forget to bring up the question of a home. It's months ago since I told her you were going to chat to her about it. You keep putting it off. She'll think it's just me and we won't get anywhere. She probably thinks we've forgotten about it anyway.'

'Don't worry, I'll go in there all positive and say I'm so glad she thinks it is a good idea. How many are we going to let her look at?'

'Let's wait until I've found a few good ones, if I ever do, then we'll decide.'

That evening Kristine tried Mary first as she was the Councillor in charge of Social Services. She would at least know which homes had reasonable reputations. Mary's best advice was to check the internet for the latest inspection reports of the various homes and she gave her a list of those in the vicinity.

'Most of them are not too bad, if you measure them against what you get in other parts of the country.'

'Is there nothing in between? You know, sheltered accommodation where they can do their own thing and someone just keeps an eye on them?'

'There are such places, but not round here. There are a few near Bath – places are as scarce as hen's teeth--oh there are some in Birmingham too. Unless your mother-in-law has relatives near those places she'd be worse off. She wouldn't know anyone and would be very lonely. Besides, as she doesn't live there, it's unlikely she'd get a place.'

'I'm afraid she doesn't and all her friends are here. Can you recommend anywhere in particular? Derek's mother is so fussy and she's refusing to go anywhere at the moment but we need to find out what's available.'

'If it's residential you want then Oakhurst is as good as any, oh and Lakeside is OK too, from what I've heard. Both are no more than half an hour from here.'

'We'll see what we can find. Many thanks for your help, Mary. I'll let you know how we get on.'

Kristine then rang Beverley to pick her brains about her experiences of residential and nursing homes. She wasn't altogether reassuring. Her mother had been in Merrivale, a Residential Home about a mile out of Bilston. Beverley said her mother had been fairly happy there and had made one or two friends but she hadn't needed much care and had died quite suddenly of a heart attack. She had, though, reported to her daughter on several occasions that people often got left for long periods on their own. They were not badly treated so much as rather neglected. Her mother had often commented that she was glad she wasn't incapacitated because "they don't look after you very well." Beverley's mother-in-law had been in a joint registered place called Westwood, which had now closed. It had been reasonably satisfactory, but again there were occasional stories of neglect. In Beverley's opinion this was usually due to shortage of staff and poor training.

'If the staff are local it's not so bad but a few foreigners are creeping in these days, you know, Poles, Rumanians, Ghanaians. Their language skills are limited but on the other hand they are usually kind. Take a good look at the Matron or Manager. She, and it's usually a "she", will set the tone of the place. That's my advice. I don't envy you having to find somewhere but I have heard there are a few better ones now. Good luck.'

Kristine then went to the computer and looked up both

the homes Mary had suggested, carefully reading the latest Inspection Reports. Both seemed good, although both had suffered from staff shortages at various times. Oakhurst was relatively new so didn't have the maintenance problems reported in Lakeside. They had to do major work on the building to comply with the latest regulations. At least they were both worth looking at.

Chapter Four

'Hello Mother, how are you today. You're looking lovely as usual.'

Evelyn was wearing a blue pleated skirt today with the powder blue cashmere sweater Derek had given her last Christmas. As always, her pearls completed the picture.

'Hello, darling boy! It is lovely to see you. I'm just fine.' At the sight of her only son Evelyn became more cheerful. Derek wasn't quite as compliant to her wishes as Brian had been but she did know how to invoke his sympathy. He was much more amenable than her daughter-in-law. Derek was so like his father to look at, that whenever she saw him, Evelyn always felt more keenly the loss of her dear Brian.

This is going to be a piece of cake, thought Derek. In his view, Kristine became over emotional when dealing with his mother. He found her quite easy to handle if he flattered her, buttered her up a bit.

'I thought I'd come and talk to you about this home you're going to move to. Find out the sort of place you'd prefer, locality, all that sort of thing.'

Evelyn threw her head back and laughed. 'You are a comedian, aren't you Derek! Kristine came ages ago with some funny notion that I should go into a home but I think it was just something to say. She wasn't serious and hasn't mentioned it recently. I know you wouldn't put me away.'

Derek sat down facing her and took her hand.

'It's not a joke, Mother and it's not "putting you away", as you call it. We really feel that it's time you were looked after on a more regular basis.'

'But I've already told Kristine that I could have someone coming in. She said it would be too expensive but you both come quite often and I'm sure if she put herself out more, she could pop in every day. That wouldn't cost anything. I know you provide well enough for her; she doesn't need to go out to work. Her work could be looking after me. Besides, I couldn't possibly leave here. Tiger would never survive without me. That's settled, then. No more talking about homes. It's dreadfully cold for the end of April, isn't it? I've had the heating on most of the day. I shall be glad when the summer comes. You feel the cold if you can't get about and Tiger likes to be warm, don't you dear?' She reached over and stroked the fat, indolent cat lying on its own cushion, basking in the heat from the gas fire on full volume.

'I must say, it is nice to see you. I never see anyone from one day to the next.'

'You know that's not true, Mother, Kristine was here two days ago and Mrs Johnson told me she called last week. The District Nurse comes twice a week about your medication, the children come, the Vicar comes. Molly Davies comes to help two mornings a week. How can you say nobody comes?'

'I think it's much longer ago than two days since Kristine came and Mrs Davies only comes two hours twice a week. You can't call that two mornings. But I'm not going to argue with you. It still leaves a great many hours when I am entirely alone. It never used to happen to people. Their families all came regularly, even had their elderly parents to live with them. It would be rather enriching for you and Kristine to have me living with you now that the children are grown up.'

Why did I ever think this was going to be simple, thought Derek? 'It's because you are lonely that we are suggesting you go into a home, Mother. Then you would have permanent company whenever you wanted it and you would be properly looked after.'

Evelyn was at her most imperious, 'No member of our family has ever gone to one of those places and I cannot believe a son of mine is suggesting such a thing. Your father would be ashamed of you. I looked after my own mother, your grandmother, and I looked after your poor cousin Caroline when she died so young. It was known as family responsibility.'

Derek got up and started pacing about the stifling room. 'Nobody went to those places when you were young because there were no such places. Families had their relatives at home and had to make the best of it and I'm sure you'll forgive me for saying so, you only visited Granny every day, you didn't have to nurse her. Besides, you know our house is totally unsuitable, with almost every room on a different level and we have no lift. It is quite impossible, Mother and you know it. Besides, you would be just as lonely. We are out at work every day and it's no good asking Kristine to give up her work. She enjoys it, keeping up with the latest surgical techniques, doing something she's good at. It's very important to her.'

Evelyn's face crumpled, 'and I'm not, I suppose. It's obvious I'm a burden to you both. I may as well be dead. After all I've done for you', she trailed off into a sob. 'Tiger is the only one who cares about me. Whatever will become of Tiger?'

Derek was useless when confronted with his mother's tears, or any other woman's for that matter.

'Don't go on so, Mother. You know we all love you very much and want to do the best for you.' Like a coward, he backed away from the subject rather than have a scene. He gave her a hug, 'Let's leave it for now but it's something we have to come back to. We shall look around to find the best possible place and then we shall take you to see it. You'll probably love it.'

'I shall hate it and it will be a death sentence to me. I shall die within weeks of going there, whatever it's like. I know I shall and so will poor Tiger.'

'Tiger will be perfectly all right and so will you. I'll love you and leave you now but will be back in a day or two.' He gave her a kiss, patted her arm and escaped out the door. Outside in the fresh air he took a deep breath and decided to take a walk in the park before going home. He had to clear his head. Was he doing the right thing by his mother? Now he knew exactly how Kristine was feeling and in a way it was harder for her. She was the woman, the one expected to have compassion, yet his mother wasn't even her own relative.

He'd been scornful when she worried about what others would think but it was something to consider. Perhaps they should have her at home? No. All the arguments he'd used were valid. They did have floors on several levels. His mother might fall if she was unused to the house. It wouldn't just be in the daytime. What if she wanted something in the night? What if they wanted to go away for a weekend, have a holiday? They would have to try and find someone to come in. They could look after the dog at the same time he supposed. It would save kennels. No. It would be a twenty-four hour, seven day a week sentence, particularly for Kristine, and his Mother was difficult. She'd been used to having her own way most of her life, certainly since she'd been married. Derek's father had been an easy-going, gentle man and went along with anything for a quiet life.

Evelyn had never really liked Kristine, mainly because she had no say in whom Derek married. It had been a whirlwind romance abroad, the engagement announced and the wedding at Kristine's home in New Zealand, all within three months. Derek's parents could have gone to the wedding but they declined, saying it was too far to go. Secretly, Derek thought his father would have loved to be there but his mother was scared, probably thinking the New Zealanders were a bunch of savages. Kristine wasn't considered good enough for her darling son. Heavens, she wasn't even English.

But then no mother thinks any girl is good enough for their son and fathers are supposed to feel the same about their daughters. Derek could honestly say he thought Rebecca had chosen a splendid chap. Tom approved of hunting, drank whisky and red wine, loved cricket and rugby. What more could a father ask of a son-in-law?

Evelyn had been quite sure Kristine would eat her peas off her knife and be an embarrassment generally. The fact that she'd produced two handsome and healthy children had redeemed her somewhat, but it obviously irked Evelyn that she had never had any control over Kristine. No, life might be hell for Evelyn if she went into a home but life would be hell for all three of them if Evelyn lived at Elmbrook Manor.

Still, Derek was beginning to think that perhaps they should try it for a few weeks? Maybe they could have a three month trial, give them time to find a nice home? Then his mother would know they had made the effort and so would everyone else. Derek wouldn't admit it, even to himself, but his mother had effectively got her own way by dint of a few tears. He'd think about it, see what Kristine came up with in the way of suitable homes. It wasn't that urgent.

Chapter Five

'Good afternoon. I'm Mrs Arnold. I made an appointment to see your home.'

'Yes of course. I'm Eileen Rogers, the Care Manager for Lakeside. Do come in and take a seat. Would you like tea?'

Miss Rogers was tall and angular with a no nonsense demeanour. It was not difficult to see that she was the one in charge.

'Yes, thank you.' This was an improvement on the others, thought Kristine. 'My husband's mother is living on her own at the moment but she is becoming increasingly forgetful and has had the occasional fall. I worry about her and the gas, remembering to turn it off at night, you know, things like that. She still plays Bridge once or twice a week though. She has diabetes, which is under control. I visit her twice a week and of course my husband visits her regularly. We are looking for somewhere pleasant for her to go. Somewhere where she can have some company and general supervision of her needs.'

'You realize we are not a nursing home, Mrs Arnold? Does your mother need nursing care?'

'Mother-in-law, no, she has one or two medical problems like diabetes as I said, she is rather forgetful but no, she doesn't need nursing care.'

'That's all right then. Does she look after herself at the moment?'

'Yes, she does. A local lady goes in and does some cooking for her once a fortnight and she has a meal with us once a week or so. But she can make scrambled egg or heat up things in the microwave. The District Nurse calls once or twice a week to check on her diabetes. She doesn't do much housework as she has someone coming in two mornings a week to do the vacuuming and any heavy things. She potters around with the duster and manages to wash her own clothes in the machine but that's about all. Her sheets go to the laundry. I take her out and she still sees her friends.'

'Does your mother bath herself?'

'Mother-in-law, she's my mother-in-law, not my mother.' Kristine was getting irritated that Miss Rogers, for all her efficient bearing, was unable to remember that Evelyn was not her mother. 'Yes she does bath herself but only when someone else is there.'

'Well I think your mother — excuse me, your mother-in-law, is just the sort of person who would be happy here. Would you like to look around? Oh. We don't have any single rooms vacant at the moment but we do have one bed in a twin room.'

'Oh! That would never do. My mother-in-law would never stand for sharing. I didn't think anyone did these days? How many shared rooms do you have?'

'Only three. Most of the rooms are single but there is quite a waiting list. There are just not enough homes available and all the new regulations are forcing some to close, those who can't afford to do the alterations.'

'So you're saying that if we want my mother-in-law to come here we will have to put her name down and wait until a single room becomes available?'

'Yes, that is exactly what I'm saying. There is tremendous pressure from the hospital too, trying to unblock the beds for those that need to be admitted.'

Kristine walked despondently round behind the Care Manager. Lakeside, the second of those recommended by Mary, was a nice airy home and it didn't smell! It was on several floors but there was a lift. The single rooms that she looked at were bigger than she'd seen anywhere else, even Field View, and most were pleasantly decorated. Some even had splendid views across the lake and surrounding countryside. Three donkeys could be seen in the field behind the main house. The gardens were nicely kept with Spring bulbs just beginning to fade.

'May I ask what the food is like? Do you have a sample menu? Mrs Arnold senior thinks it will be like boarding school.'

'I'm glad to say we've moved on from that. Residents can have a full breakfast or cereals and toast or any combination of that and they may have it in their rooms if they wish. It's set in the dining room from 8am but breakfast is available until 10am. Lunch is at 12.30 and they can have a choice of two mains and two sweets. Evening meal is at 5.30pm and can be something cooked or sandwiches.'

They had arrived at the kitchen while they were talking and Miss Rogers handed Kristine some typewritten menu sheets. There seemed to be a good variety on offer and salads were available. Evelyn loved salads, which was a plus but Kristine doubted whether there'd be a choice of the exotic dressings she was used to.

'The evening meal is rather early, isn't it?' Kristine knew it was a minor criticism but Evelyn seldom ate before 7.30pm and she would make some rude response about 'working class hours.'

'It needs to be early because some people like to go to bed about 8.30pm and they shouldn't go straight after a meal. Besides, if they want a snack later they're quite welcome. Another reason is staff. We only have two carers on at night so we must help those who need assistance with their toilet before the day staff go off at 8pm.'

'Is it difficult to get staff?'

'I'd be less than honest if I said no. The trouble is, the pay scales are not much better than in the supermarket, which requires a lot less commitment and has more social hours. If we paid the staff what they are really worth, nobody could afford to come here and they wouldn't have a job. It's catch 22, I'm afraid.'

'What about entertainment? Do you provide any social activities? What about hairdressing, chiropody, things like that?' Kristine was apologetic about asking so many questions but felt she must mention them as they came to mind. 'I made a list but left it at home.'

'That's quite all right. You may as well get things straight. We do have musical afternoons when residents are encouraged to take part, you know, sing-along with some of the old songs.'

Kristine resolved not to mention this to Evelyn. She could feel her cringe at the thought of community singing. Miss Rogers pushed open the door of an attractive room featuring a piano, a large TV set and video player. There was also a slide projector and a screen in one corner.

Miss Rogers continued, 'You can book this room for a family party or we can use it for a birthday party or to watch any significant programmes such as Wimbledon or a Royal Wedding, things like that, where we can make it into a social occasion. We have a "Friends Group," some of whose members take the more able bodied out for coffee or tea to a garden centre or gift shop. This might be in the summer or another popular time is around Christmas. Now what else did you ask? The hairdresser comes once a week, her charges are quite reasonable. Wish I could get my hair done for £4.50. Then the chiropodist comes monthly and sees all those who need it. That's extra of course and goes on the bill although as your mother-in-law is a diabetic she will have her feet looked at as a matter of course.'

They were back in the office by this time and there was a tray of fresh tea waiting.

Kristine gritted her teeth and said, 'How much are the fees?'

'Would your mother-in-law be self-funding?'

'Oh yes, of course.'

'If she had a single room, the fees are £500 per week and if she had an en-suite then it is another £20 per week. Then there are the extras that I mentioned and she would want some pocket money. Of course her pension would go towards the fees so it is not quite as bad as it sounds. If you'd like to go away and think about it then let me know if you want to put Mrs Arnold's name on my waiting list, that's probably the best.'

Miss Rogers was right. Kristine didn't want to make a commitment without discussing it with Derek, and Evelyn would have to see the home first. Besides, she had promised her three or four to look at. Apart from Oakhurst, which was fully booked with a long waiting list, this was the first she had come across that was remotely suitable. Evelyn might only be able to see two.

Chapter Six

New Zealand 2000
Angela

'It's time you left here, Mum.'

'I'm not moving.'

'You've got to, some time. It's too isolated.'

'I'm not bloody moving and that's that. I've got everything I want here and you bring the rest, so what's to move for?'

'That's just it, I bring the rest. Well I'm tired of traipsing up that rotten road bringing what you want. It wouldn't be so bad if you came down yourself sometimes. You've got the Ute, why don't you? Not as if you're old, sixty-nine last birthday wasn't it? Anyone'd think you were eighty. Last time you were down was Christmas. Two months ago.' Maxine was really riling her mother now.

'So what if I'm sixty-nine. I'll be seventy in July anyway. You're my daughter, daughters are supposed to look after their mothers, in case you've forgotten. I shouldn't have to go out if I don't want to. Besides, that Ute is too heavy on the corners, steering hurts my arms.'

Angela had bought it years ago and it wasn't new then. A 1950s Ford pick-up truck, a big old one like the ones she'd seen in the movies. They often had the gangster jumping on the running board trying to wrestle the steering wheel from the 'goodie' who was driving. It was good and solid; she'd felt invincible on the road. Nobody'd mess with her. Now it was too much. Her shoulders ached after even a short drive and getting anywhere from Whangata was at least ten miles. No. She needed something lighter with power steering. A new car for the new century.

'We could change the Ute for something smaller but up in this God forsaken place you'd have to have a four-wheel drive. I'm warning you now; it won't be once a week in the winter. You'll be lucky if I get up here once a month. And if you want a birthday party for the BIG Seven O, you'll have to come down. This place could be snowed up. Aren't you going to give me a cup of tea, now I've come?'

Maxine was irritated. She'd come all this way and what thanks did she get? Nothing but complaints.

The kettle was always near boiling on the stove so Angela made a pot of tea and put out some bread and butter. Maxine was lucky. There was still some jam from last year. Angela turned her back on her daughter to check for mould in the jar; it was OK. She didn't use much of it and it often went off. She'd just scrape it off when nobody was looking. A bit of mould never hurt anyone as far as she knew. Angela didn't want a birthday party but thought it was decent of Maxine to suggest it. She'd make up her mind when the time came. She could be dead by then.

Angela moved last week's papers and the jumper she was knitting, onto the big squashy sofa against the wall. She sometimes slept there in the winter when it was really cold. The Aga was left on all the time, but the heat didn't quite reach the bedroom.

They sat at the table in silence. For once, Maxine took a long hard look at her mother. She'd barely noticed before that Angela was looking older and greyer, her wrinkled leathery skin prematurely aged by the strong summer sun and the biting winter wind of this isolated spot. A loner, her Mum was. In some ways more like a man than a woman. Always seemed more comfortable with the local farmers, shearers and car enthusiasts. Maxine couldn't remember ever having seen a softer more feminine side to her mother.

Angela was thinking how lucky her daughter was not to have inherited her freckles. God, how she'd hated the freckles. She was shocked to see grey strands amongst Maxine's mousy hair and even a few crow's feet at the corners of her eyes. It brought home to her the advancing years. How she hated the thought of getting old. Maxine was not that far off fifty and her Ken must be fifty already.

'If driving up here is too much for you, why don't you get that useless husband of yours to come up? He's still not working I suppose? Not used to that in our family. Might not've made much of ourselves but we always worked, always had a job and got paid – not been on the benefit. Disgrace that is. How old is he? Not even fifty, is he?'

Maxine jumped to her husband's defence. 'Ken can't help not working. All that shearing done his back in. Not his fault. Shearers work damn hard, you know that, and he's over fifty, well fifty last birthday. He's not a lazy bastard as you're always calling him. He doesn't just sit about all day. He can mow the lawn and he helps me around the house, does odd jobs at Bob's garage. Does what he can. He might come up here for me but you always give him such a hard time, criticise him for not working. Don't see why he should take that, me neither, when we come all this way to see if you're OK, not dead in your bed.'

'Don't you worry about that. I'm not about to die yet and it won't be in my bed if I can help it. Ken should be able to take a bit o' stick. Where's 'is sense of humour, gone the same way as 'is back has it?'

Maxine didn't think that was funny. They often used to have a laugh together but she seldom saw the funny side these days. Having that Ken home all day and her having to do all the work couldn't be very amusing.

'What do you mean by that? Not dying in your bed. That's where most people die.'

She cut another chunk of bread and smothered it with butter and jam. Angela poured them both more tea. She'd got Maxine interested now.

'Aw, I don't know, but if I started to get decrepit, you know, losing my marbles, I rather fancy going in an accident, over the cliff somewhere.'

Maxine was shocked. She stared at her mother, her eyes wide, mouth hanging open.

'You mean, you don't mean suicide, do you? You can't. Anyway you mightn't die, just be mangled up, lying in a hospital, like a cabbage. You mightn't be able to talk, just mumble and dribble.'

'SHUT UP, damn you. Just shut up.'

Angela could see it. The dribble, the saliva, the choking, it was all coming back. Why did Maxine have to mention dribble? It'd gone and now it'd come back, the saliva, the choking. Go away, go away. She thought she'd forgotten, but it was there, underneath the everyday stuff. Waiting, just waiting for her to relax, let her guard down, slipping back, thinking of the past. A simple word and it all came flooding back. She couldn't stand it. She rushed outside into the fresh air where she could see the mountains, see something else, clean and fresh. Get the vision out of her head.

Maxine was trembling. She was standing over her mother, white-faced, crying.

'What've I done, what've I said that's upset you so? I only pointed out that you mightn't die---'

'Stop, stop I tell you. I don't want to hear it. Just remember, whatever else I do, I'll make sure I'm good and dead.'

Angela was still sweating but not from the sun. The snow, last year's snow, still clinging to the distant peaks added a freshness to the air. The vastness of the scene filled her head, calming her. It always did. That was why she stayed there. She must think of something else, talk about Maxine's next visit, say she'd go down to see her next week, then she wouldn't think about what she'd said, wouldn't talk about it again.

Maxine went in and made another pot of tea and asked Angela if she'd like it out in the sun, might cheer her up. She wanted to forget that she'd upset her mother. She didn't want a row.

Angela tried to concentrate. Maxine hadn't been a bad daughter. Not done anything spectacular with her life but neither had she. Job in a shop at sixteen, then the dreaded residential home which she tried to forget, then a succession of dead-end jobs in shops or cleaning. Fond of the fellas, like her Mum, and her Gran before that.

Thinking of her mother irritated Angela. Not much of an example, she wasn't; hard drinking, foul – mouthed, husband who knocked her about. No wonder they didn't amount to much. Well, thought Angela, I didn't. Maxine had done better for herself, going to college, getting that job in a hotel. Undoing of all of them, men had been, she supposed. Maxine was better looking than her mother, with pretty curly hair, blonde once but mousy now. Good skin, none of Angela's freckles or pointed nose. Got her looks from her father. Gary had been good – looking. Only good thing about him. Maxine did get to travel about the country a bit with a hippy Irishman, Kelly. Then there was Rob or was it Dave? No matter, Angela couldn't remember all their names. None of them were any good; just like that hick she'd married.

Pity Maxine and Ken hadn't had any children. Angela quite liked kids and grandkids might have softened her. Maxine had found it hard for a while. Didn't want to accept it but probably best in the end. With a husband permanently out of work, it wasn't much of a life for kids. Angela felt that being married to Gary had been more exciting than it must be for Maxine married to Ken. Well it was in the beginning, before he got violent. Plenty of parties, hunting trips, quite a fun time. Then when Maxine came along Angela couldn't go with him so he went off with other women, wasting all their money. He always spent too much, mostly on booze and cigarettes, then the court case. Eighteen months he got. Lucky really, stealing so much – well, trying to. He couldn't even do that right. She shouldn't have taken him back. He was a bad influence on Maxine, mixing with the wrong crowd. Angela concluded they were both the same, no good at picking decent blokes. Her mother had suffered at the hands of her dad too. She put it down to their genes; no good at choosing. Looking for the wrong thing and ending up with the ones who knocked them about. Maxine said Ken didn't but he was useless anyway in Angela's opinion, too feeble to knock anyone about.

'You all right, Mum? You're in another world.' Maxine had sat watching her mother staring into space, deep in her own thoughts. 'All right if I make my way back now?'

'I'm OK. Don't bother to come up next week. I'll come down Thursday, unless it's raining, then it'll be Friday. Can't manage the hill in the wet – too bloody dangerous – not as quick as I was. Thanks for coming. You probably won't believe it but I like you coming.'

'Bye then, Mum. If you come round 12, I'll give you lunch. Won't be much, beans on toast or some such thing.'

She took off in a cloud of dust. Drove too fast, specially on that hill. It was a nice car though. One of the new Japanese ones. She never could remember the make of it. Jess came out of the house, head on one side, asking for a walk. Angela needed the air, the breeze, the mountains. Maxine had said it was too isolated up there but it was what she wanted. It was the only way she had survived for the last thirty years. No old people up there. Nothing to remind her, nobody could find her. Not that anyone was looking. Not as far as she knew.

It hadn't been a success, living in Christchurch. Too big a place. People, always people. She'd had to talk to them, make friends, answer questions. People always wanted to know where she came from. Then they always knew someone else who came from there. "Do you know so and so? Why not? You must know him if you lived there, he's lived there for years". On and on it went.

It was the same when Angela lived in Masterton, worse really as it was too small a place. Everyone knew everyone else and they all wanted to know your business. She didn't want any questions, then she didn't have to give any answers. Clean slate, that's what she'd wanted and that's what she'd got. Just her and Jess. Jess was good company and dogs didn't ask questions – took you as you were.

Chapter Seven

'Don't know what got into Mum today. Never seen her so worked up. Can't remember what I said, something about dying in her bed. Said she wouldn't.'

Ken was sprawled in the sun lounger, looking worn out.

'I'm pretty exhausted. There was a hell of a lot of grass on that lawn this week.'

Maxine was unimpressed. The lawn wasn't that big. Their house was one of half a dozen on the north side of a back road South of Christchurch. Nobody had more than a quarter of an acre. Everyone grew their own vegetables and most had a few flowers plus a garage so there wasn't much room for lawn. Anyone would think they had a couple of acres to mow. She thanked him for mending the hinge on the gate at long last and he was pleased that she'd noticed.

'That's it, that's what started it. Said she wanted an accident, no way was she going to die in bed. And I said "You might not die, you might be injured."'

'Well what's wrong with that? So she might. Just end up with broken bones or — or, oh I don't know.' Ken was scratching round for some other injuries she might get when it came back to her.

'No, wait. I've remembered. I said she might be a cabbage and just mumble and dribble. That's when she lost her rag. She really lost it, screaming and shouting at me to shut up. Just hope it puts her off having an accident, deliberate, I mean.'

Ken stirred himself and sat up, open-mouthed. 'You don't mean she's thinking of suicide, do ya?' He was staggered. Your mother-in-law didn't commit suicide. Some people might wish they did, but they just didn't. Well he'd never heard of any that did.

'Well, if she did mean that, I hope I've put her off. Oh. She wants to change the Ute. Says it's too heavy, she's finding it hard to manage. That might've been what she meant. She might have had a close shave on one of the bends and realised she could go over the edge.'

'Don't know what we'd change it for. She's gotta have a four-wheel drive living in that God-forsaken place. Might find something small, power steering would be a help. I'll look around.'

Maxine smiled affectionately at him. 'She doesn't deserve you, love. I also said I'd only be going up once a month in the winter, if that. She was pretty rude about you again today. She thought you should go up some of the time. You've got nothing else to do, she said. I did stand up for you.'

'Gee thanks. I bet she called me a lazy bastard too.'

'Yip, got it in one.' Ken knew her well enough. He'd put up with her abuse for over 20 years. He wasn't going to be bothered by it now. Maxine thought it was a bit rich of her mother to criticise Ken. What about her own husband? He was twenty times worse and he hit her. He'd hit Maxine too, when he could catch her. She considered her father a drunken slob. At least her Ken didn't drink too much – well not often, and he never got violent.

'She says she won't move, though. That's how it started, the argument I mean. Me saying she had to leave and her saying she wouldn't. We'll have to leave her for now. One day she might come around to it. If she gets sick, she'll have to move.'

There would be room for her to live with them. Not that they'd like it. The house wasn't what you'd call big but they did have two spare rooms, full of junk mostly. They'd have to clean them out, well one anyway. Angela and Ken wouldn't speak much and Maxine would always be trying to calm things down. If it ever happened, they'd probably get used to each other. Her mother would see how kind Ken was to her. Nobody wanted to get old but that was one thing you didn't have any say over, it just happened, and before you realised it. One minute you're out and about, driving, shopping, going to dances, the cinema; the next thing you know, you're having to ask people to do your shopping. Take me here, take me there. Angela had a point, have an accident and just finish it. No more worrying. But that was the problem, you had to make sure you finished it. Ah well. Hopefully, she and Ken had a few years yet before they had to think of it and her mum would probably die in her sleep. She'd have no say in the matter.

'I might just ask Jack Flint to keep a look out for her when he's going round his sheep, you know, give us a call if he hasn't seen her for a few days.'

'He probably does anyway,' said Ken. 'He'd notice if there was no activity. Jess would bark anyhow. Good thing she's got the dog. Still, I'll mention it if I see him in the pub.'

Chapter Eight

Four months later

'Is Angie coming down for her birthday?' Ken wanted to know so he could clear out one of the spare rooms. Where he was going to put all the rubbish, only the Lord knew. It would have to go in the garage, there was nowhere else. The car never got as far as the garage.

'Don't know. I did mention the big seven-0 back in February but she didn't make any comment then. Haven't reminded her since. She'd better, 'cos neither of us are traipsing up there this weather. We should get her down well before. I'll give her a ring later and tell her we'll get her at the weekend of 16th, that's if she ever answers the phone. She may as well not have one for all she calls us.'

'When's her birthday? Are we inviting anyone else?'

'21st. We could ask Jack from the farm. She wouldn't mind him and Bob Smaills from the garage. No old people. She hates old people for some reason. I don't know why.'

'Didn't you tell me she once worked in an old peoples' home?' Maxine had told him that, but she had never known any details.

'I did but I only found out by accident and she flatly refused to tell me anything about it. It was that time we went up to Palmerston North for Uncle Arthur's funeral. When we were walking down the street, we ran into this old dear. Foreigner of some sort she was, Norwegian or Danish I think. Yes, Norwegian, that's right, and she said "Hello. Don't you remember me? You're Angela Thornley aren't you? You used to work at Mountain View in New Plymouth, back in the fifties?" Mum mumbled a reply, said it was nice to see her but she was in a hurry and had to get on. Quite rude Mum was. The poor old thing obviously wanted to talk about old times. Being foreign, she probably didn't have many friends and we weren't in a hurry to go anywhere. I said as much to Mum but she told me to belt up. She'd talk to whoever she wanted and the last thing she wanted to talk about was old times at that place.'

'Can't have been a fun place to work then. Perhaps that Norwegian bird had been hard on her or something? Your Mum does take against people quite easily though, doesn't she?'

'She's not the easiest to get on with, you should know. Where were we? The birthday, week after next. I'll bake her a cake, icing an' everything. Show her I did learn something at college. I'll have to hide it if she's coming at the weekend. Birthday's not till the Wednesday.'

Ken didn't think his mother-in-law would agree to coming down for nearly a week. Maxine acknowledged he had a point. Her mother was not used to sitting about. She was normally very active; walking the hills, chopping the wood, cleaning the house. She had her faults but she didn't live in a mess. She would also have to bring Jess. She wouldn't go anywhere without her.

'She can bring her knitting. I noticed she's always got some on the go and she can still take Jess for a walk. There are plenty of paddocks and she can go up Devil's Creek if she wants some hills. Lord knows what we'll do with her if it's wet. She'll watch the telly. Be a novelty for her to get a decent picture. The reception's no better, I noticed last time I was up there. Perhaps we needn't get her till Sunday if the weather's OK. Have you heard a report?'

'Fine and clear for the next week. Might be a frost but that's not a problem in our wagon. What are we going to give her for a present? Perhaps we should give her a mobile phone? Make her feel young and trendy. They're quite cheap too. Won't break the bank.' Maxine was impressed. Ken often came up with really bright ideas.

'I think she'd like that and she just might call us more often. We'd have to check that she topped it up but if we showed her how, she'd do it just to show us that she was still capable. Yes, that's a great idea. Can I leave you to buy it? Don't go for the top of the range. We're not made of money.'

'Trust me. I'll get it tomorrow.'

Chapter Nine

Angela didn't know why she'd agreed to go down for almost a whole week. Now she was regretting it. It'd be dead boring. Still, at least the house would be warm and there were some nice walks up Devil's Creek. It would give Jess some new smells and different rabbits to chase. Angela might even get waited on a bit. She'd stopped them coming up to get her because she wanted to drive down and see about swapping the Ute for something smaller. As she was down there so long they could go into Christchurch and look at some of the Jap four-wheelers. Jap stuff was good now, not rubbish like in the early days. There was bound to be something second-hand, suitable for her. It needed to be light to handle but tough enough for the rough terrain where she lived. She spent very little, living in such an out of the way spot so had enough money stashed away to buy something decent.

'Come on Jess, down to civilisation for a week. You'll like it when you get there and give him his due, Ken really likes you, throws sticks, even bought you a ball last time. Bet you don't remember he took you to the beach once. Come on. Hop in.'

At least it was fine and dry. The road was a killer in the wet, with slips and mud, even quite big boulders sometimes. Angela never knew what she would meet around the next bend. She didn't know how Jack did it all the time. Her neighbour was up and down nearly every day. He was younger than Angela but not by much. The difference was, she supposed, he'd been doing it all his life.

'Thank God, Jess, we're down in one piece.' Whew! What a relief. She could feel the tension going out of her shoulders. She never used to be a nervous driver but this hill was really getting to her. It was only three and a half miles, but seemed like twenty. Maxine was always trying to get her to go down on to the flat permanently but Angela was not going to give in. She was prepared to put up with the hill as long as she could. At least the public section was sealed now, complete with all the white and yellow lines and warning signs. Nobody was going to improve the private spur of half a mile just for her and one other farmhouse. It was a waste of time thinking they would. She and Jack would have to pay for it between them; it would cost a fortune and take forever. Anyway, the hill accounted for only a fraction of the journey to Maxine. Just another fifteen minutes, all on the straight, and they would be there.

'OK Jess. Wake up. We've arrived and surprise, surprise, they're here to meet us.'

'Welcome to Tea Tree Flats.' Maxine even looked pleased to see them. To tell the truth, she was relieved they'd arrived in one piece. Ken added his welcome but he was more pleased to see Jess. He flung his arms around her and lifted her out of the truck. Angela was tempted to say 'mind your back' but stopped herself just in time. She didn't want a row as soon as she'd arrived and anyway she needed Ken to help her find a replacement for the Ute. She hoped they would be able to do that tomorrow.

'Hope you like the room, Mum. Ken finished the painting on Friday and we've had the windows open so most of the smell's gone. Here's your bag. I'll leave you to unpack while I make some tea.'

They'd done wonders with the room. It had been full of junk when she last visited. They'd even provided a kettle and a cup so she could make tea when she liked. Just like a hotel. There was a basket in the corner for Jess too. Angela was impressed that they seemed to have thought of everything. She might even enjoy these few days away from home. Then it suddenly occurred to her. She should've known. That's what it was all about. Make her nice and comfortable and she wouldn't want to go back up the hill. Well they were out of luck. She'd be bored to tears. It wouldn't stop her enjoying herself down in civilisation for a bit though.

Ken's friend, Bob Smaills, had a garage in Tea Tree Flats but he seldom had anything for sale, mostly doing repairs for the neighbourhood. To get anything decent to replace the Ute they would need to drive the seventy miles into Christchurch to Will Jackson's garage. Ken had known Will since school days and he knew they'd get a good deal from him. Will had been dealing in cars since leaving school, first with his uncle until he knew the ropes, then he'd branched out on his own. What he didn't know about cars wasn't worth knowing, so early next morning after a decent breakfast she hadn't had to prepare herself, Angela set off with Ken to see what was on offer. Neither had much to say, each busy with their own thoughts. It was almost two years since Angela had been in to Christchurch and she was amazed at the amount of new building. This reaffirmed her determination to stay as long as possible in her hilltop retreat.

Once at the garage, Will pointed her in the direction of the Utes he had and explained the features of the different models. 'If you find one you like the look of you can take it for a spin.'

Angela wandered around for some time, getting in and out of some of them, testing them for comfort and ease of controls. The price was on big cards in the window of each so she didn't have the embarrassment of asking 'How much.' Not that she was worried about the price. Most of them were within her range and she wanted to make her life easier to get about. The colour wasn't an issue either. It didn't make any difference to the performance.

Finally she found a dark blue one to her liking and she took Ken out on the highway for a quick run around. It was great on the open road with plenty of power and light on the steering. Tidy inside too. No holes in the upholstery or scratches on the doors. Still, that wouldn't last long, not with Jess and all the stuff she crammed in. Just to make sure how it would perform on the hill, they found a rough track on the outskirts of the city and put it through its paces. Angela was more than satisfied and Will was confident she had made the right choice.

'These Holdens are great vehicles and this one's only six years old, 1994 she is. That's nothing for a Ute, should last you years, that's if you get it serviced with me of course. We'll tidy it up and get you the WOF certificate and sort the paper work. Come back on Tuesday and it'll be ready for you. Nice to do business with you, Mrs Brook. Any friend of Ken's is a friend of mine.'

Ken was doubtful she'd call him a friend but they were related so he supposed that counted the same. Angela was pleased with her purchase and Will had agreed to take the Ford in part payment. It was so old she wasn't getting much for it but it was better than nothing. She could keep it till Tuesday when she collected the Holden. Ken asked her if she wanted to go shopping in Christchurch but she declined the offer. What did she need to buy? She certainly didn't need any more clothes and she could get any stores she wanted from the shop along from Maxine's. It was called Phillip's Hardware and General Store but it wasn't really Phillip's anymore. He'd long since died and his son had gone into the Army. He'd wanted more excitement than Tea Tree Flats could offer. Jo Mason ran it now and made sure it stocked everything but the kitchen sink. You could get that too, if you ordered it.

Sunday and Monday passed peacefully enough and Angela surprised herself she wasn't bored. On Sunday she didn't wake until 9am and her first thought was 'poor Jess, she'll want to go out'. She needn't have worried. Ken had pushed the door open quietly two hours earlier for Jess to slip out, eager to go with her friend on a long walk.

The lingering smell of bacon and eggs soon got Angela into the kitchen where Maxine was preparing the vegetables for lunch.

'Morning, Mum. Bacon and sausage are ready in the oven, how many eggs do you want?'

'Needn't have bothered with cooked breakfast for me. Don't want to be any trouble. Normally just have Weetabix.'

Maxine got out a couple of eggs and cracked them into the pan.

'No trouble, didn't do it just for you anyway. Ken and I always have a fry-up on the weekend.'

Angela sat down at the big table with its blue and white checked tablecloth, which matched the kitchen curtains. Maxine liked things to match, but she'd never cared one way or the other. She didn't use a tablecloth, just scrubbed the table everyday. She looked out the window and felt a pang of jealousy as she watched Ken coming up the path with an adoring, very wet and dirty Jess at his heels. Still, the dog gave her an enthusiastic greeting before flopping down in front of the warm Aga to dry off. Angela enjoyed her breakfast and Ken joined her for more toast and coffee.

'Good thinking to stay late in bed today. There was a heavy frost when I got up. It wasn't half nippy. Jess didn't seem to mind and was anxious to go out so I thought a good walk would do me good too. Went up Devil's Creek and Jess went bananas when she smelt the deer tracks and saw the odd rabbit.'

Maxine didn't want any help with the lunch so Angela retired to the lounge to see what was on telly and look at the papers, which Ken had picked up from the local shop. She never got a paper up at the house unless someone brought it up or she came down. Nobody was going to deliver up that road for two houses. Angela relied on the radio and TV for her news. She had to secretly admit that it was very nice not to have to get the wood in and chip the ice off the water butt for a few days. A TV that didn't need to be thumped every few minutes to get a better picture was also a bonus. She just hoped there would be no burst pipes when she returned. The water was turned off and all the outside pipes were heavily lagged so it should be all right. That was the trouble with leaving the place in winter.

Angela spent the rest of the day eating, watching the telly and taking Jess for another long walk. Monday was spent in much the same way but as it had rained all day and she hadn't been out, Maxine and Ken persuaded her to go along to the White Hart for a beer in the evening. Angela knew a few of the locals by name. Farmers she'd come across over the years, a few of Maxine's friends. One or two greeted her with surprise, 'Fancy seeing you down here, bit of a hermit these days, aren't ya? What brings you to the metropolis?'

'Not your blue eyes anyhow', she responded. 'Thought it was time I checked up on you all.' Jess determined where they sat, making straight for the fire, so they took their beers and joined a couple of locals, Fred and Bob, at a table in the corner. The easy chat and swapping of yarns reminded Angela of her first few years with Gary. She enjoyed the evening, lost in memories of times past. Still, she was happier now, on her own.

Tuesday there was the excitement of picking up her new Ute. It was a long way into Christchurch and would take over half the day so Maxine stayed behind again, to 'do things' for the birthday party the following day. Angela thought it a bit daft to try to hide things from her, a grown woman. It was only a birthday for Heaven's sake.

Ken and Angela left after breakfast and arrived at Will's garage soon after eleven to collect her new wheels. They called at the bank on the way so she could withdraw sufficient cash, which she stuffed into her handbag. It amused Angela to think nobody would guess she had $10,000 hidden in such a scruffy old purse. Maxine said she should treat herself to a new bag, but what for? She was attached to the old one and living where she did and at her age, she didn't need to worry about fashion. Not that she ever had. A car was different. When it came to it, she was sad to leave the old grey wagon in the yard. She supposed it would be broken up for scrap. Nobody wanted such big old cumbersome things these days, and it was heavy on the gas. Angela handed over the money and signed the necessary documents before she and Ken set off for Tea Tree Flats. She was delighted with the ease of steering and the turn of speed. It was a joy to drive, after the old one. Maxine and Jess had to be treated to a spin in the new vehicle when they arrived back. Both seemed suitably impressed. Maxine was particularly pleased that the Holden was so much easier for her mother to handle. Her daughter felt she'd had a satisfactory birthday already.

Angela awoke to the smell of bacon and eggs right under her nose.

'Wakey, wakey, rise and shine. Happy birthday Mum.'
Maxine was putting a laden tray on the bedside table as Angela struggled to wake up. God, she had been on this earth for seventy years. Where had they all gone? She couldn't remember half of them.

'Gee, this is a treat. Can't remember when I last had breakfast in bed. Thanks, Maxie.' Jess was sitting by the bed, nose eagerly sniffing the air. She was partial to a sausage or a piece of bacon if it was going spare.

'You'll have to wait, old girl. My turn first.'

Maxine had brought in her coffee too and was sitting watching her mother tucking into the food.

'Don't expect you feel any older, do you, Mum? They say you're only as old as you feel. There's some cards for you and the odd present which I'll bring in when you've finished eating – less you want them now?'

'What do I want presents for? Don't need presents at my age. Not that I feel old, well not most of the time.'

'Happy birthday, Angie. Jess bought you a present.' Pushing the door open, Ken laid a big bunch of flowers on the bed, retreating before she could say anything.

'What did he do that for? This time of year flowers are expensive.'

Even Maxine was surprised. Ken must have ordered them last week when he went into Christchurch unless he'd done it on the phone. She could see Angela was flushed with pleasure and probably some embarrassment, as she was often so horrid to Ken.

'I told you Ken was kind and he has a soft spot for you although I can't imagine why.'

'Get 'orf. He's probably giving them to Jess really.'

Maxine laughed and went off to get the cards and presents. When she came back her mother hurriedly put the flowers back on the bed.

'Just trying to decide what had the strong smell. I think it's the lilies.'

Maxine agreed but said 'Watch out for the pollen, it stains and you can't get it off.'

Angela had cards from Maxine and Ken, Jack from the farm, Bob from the local garage and even one from Will, where she'd bought the Ute. Ken must have told him. There was one too, with a dog on it, "from Jess." Ken again.

He shouted out now, 'You'd better get up, Angie. The neighbours have come to wish you happy birthday.'

'Hell's teeth! It's nearly eleven o'clock. I never stay in bed this late. Clear out you lot, I'm getting dressed and I need a shower.'

The day was a great success. Angela was relaxed and happy,

her cheeks flushed with excitement at being the centre of attention for once. She'd made an effort with her appearance too; clean jeans, sharp blue shirt and fancy multi-coloured jumper she'd knitted herself. It was too much to expect her to wear a skirt. It was doubtful she still possessed one. Maxine had not seen her quite so amenable for some time and she hoped nothing would be said or done to spoil it. The mobile phone had been graciously accepted and Angela had even paid attention to Ken while he spent some time showing her how it worked. Melanie and Grant from next door had come in with honey and a pot plant and they'd all had a beer and a lot of laughs.

Maxine just wished Angela would appreciate Ken more. He had a heart of gold but all her mother saw was the fact that he didn't do a proper job.

That evening, about six o'clock, Maxine started laying things out on the table. A large birthday cake with seven candles took pride of place. A big bowl of trifle and plate of éclairs, coleslaw and salads, napkins and cutlery followed.

'I'll put the hot things out later when the others come and we've had a drink.'

Angela's face darkened, 'I'm going if you're having a whole pile of people. You know I hate crowds.'

'It's OK,' Maxine assured her, 'There's just a few. Melanie and Grant from next door, who came this morning, your neighbour Jack, you like him, Bob from the garage and his wife Beryl. I could hardly leave her out. Then me and Ken, so that's it. You can't call eight a crowd.'

Angela cheered up. They were all people she liked although she had only met Beryl once. Still, she was probably OK if she was married to Bob. He was a decent bloke.

'Guess that's all right then. When are they coming? I could do with a drink, or aren't we having any?'

'You bet. Couldn't have your birthday party without some

booze. Ken, get your mother-in-law a beer, or would you rather have a glass of wine? We're going to crack open a bottle of bubbly later. Not every day you're seventy.'

'Quit reminding me of my age. I don't want to talk about it. Give us a beer to start with. When are the others coming?' 'Any minute now…' Maxine was interrupted by a knock on the door and a shout of

'Happy Birthday, Angie!' as Jack Flint let himself in. He looked quite handsome in a polo neck shirt and bottle green jumper and smart pressed trousers. His hair was neat and tidy and he smelt of after-shave. Angela hardly recognised him. She was so used to seeing him striding round the fields in muddy trousers and a thick leather jerkin, hair all over the place, his chin often sporting a thin layer of stubble. Jack had been a widower for several years and didn't usually bother with the refinements of life. He was a big fellow and seemed to fill the room. He enveloped Angela in a bear hug and planted a kiss on her flushed cheek.

'You don't look a day over 21, my girl. Have you had a good birthday? Is that a new wagon I see out there? You said you were going to get one. Sure it's not too nippy? Here, I bought you this for your big day.'

He produced a sturdy Hessian bottle bag containing two bottles of Oyster Bay Sauvignon. Angela couldn't tell one wine from the other but she could tell the difference between plonk and the better stuff. She'd heard favourable reports of this one and managed to look suitably impressed.

'After a bottle of this I'll race you in my new wagon.'

'Nah, I've got more sense but I might challenge you to a controlled test and see who can go up our hill fastest. Bob can be the referee.'

Soon they were all there and the beer and wine was flowing. Bob and Beryl gave her a powerful torch, which would be very useful. Fortunately they'd asked Maxine's advice and she had steered them rapidly away from a subscription to Saga magazine. Bob agreed to monitor a race up the hill but he said they would have to do it separately and he would take the time.

'Can't have you two racing together on that road. Don't mind if you kill yourselves but there're plenty of other nice people who use the public part of the highway.'

They fixed on the 1st November for the contest as the weather would be improving by then and Angela would have had a few months to get used to the new wagon.

Nothing happened to spoil the evening. The cake was ceremoniously bought in, the candles lit and Happy Birthday sung with gusto if not in tune. Even Jess enjoyed the party, revelling in all the unaccustomed attention. Gradually, the guests drifted away but it was nearly 1am when Angela, rather unsteadily, made for her bed. She thanked Maxine and Ken for a great party and the last thing she remembered was Maxine shouting, 'No need to hurry in the morning, we're not going anywhere.'

It was after nine when Angela woke but she was still the first to stir. She began packing up her things and stripping the bed. She'd warned Maxine last night that she was going back home today. Life here was getting too comfortable; she felt she was putting on weight, eating and drinking too much. Not that Ken and Maxine drank much but she was more inclined to have a couple of beers when she had company. Up at Whangata, she seldom bothered and besides, she felt healthier when she had regular exercise.

'Gee, you're pushing off early. Really fed up with us are you?' Maxine had appeared in her dressing gown and put the kettle on. 'I'd wait until the sun gets rid of the frost on that road if I were you.' She was quite disappointed her mother had stuck to her word and intended to leave them already.

'I'm not going quite yet and I've enjoyed my time here.

You've both been very decent to me but once I've decided to go I want to get on with it. I'll just give Jess a walk before breakfast.'

After breakfast Angela made her farewells and set off for home. She'd enjoyed her time at Tea Tree Flats but it was a soft and easy life and she could feel herself slipping quietly into old age. Maxine and Ken would 'do things' for her, there'd be no challenge, she'd be responsible for nothing, in control of nothing. When she became more feeble, difficult to look after, they'd be searching round for the 'right Home for Mum.' Well it wasn't going to happen. She'd be in control of her own destiny. Now she had her new wheels she might make a tour of the West Coast. She'd never been to Invercargill, or Milford even. She might take a helicopter ride, live a little. Now she was seventy she intended to take a few risks. She had in the old days but had got out of the habit lately. If there was any question that she could no longer look after herself, she'd find a way out. Her time at Mountain View had convinced Angela to make her own way out of this world when the time was right. She began singing in a loud tuneless voice, 'Pack up your troubles in your old kit bag,' ironically unaware that this was a favourite title of sing-alongs in old peoples' homes.

Chapter Ten

Three Months Later

The phone rang. It was Jack. 'Hi Angie. Hope you haven't forgotten the bet we made on your birthday?'

'The one where I said I could drink you under the table?'

'Na, you'd never win that. No, it was the one to see who was fastest up the hill.'

'Bugger, I'd forgotten that. When are we supposed to be doing it? I have to get in some practice.'

Angela hoped he couldn't detect the lie in her voice. She'd wasted quite a lot of petrol over the last few weeks, trying to reduce her time. She'd been very careful about taking her practice runs when Jack was unlikely to be on the road. Her time was improving and the Holden was proving better than she could have hoped.

'November 1st and that's next week, Tuesday. Should be a quieter day on the road, better than the weekend. If it goes well we could make it an annual event, call it the Whangata Hill race. What d'ya think? Are you still game?'

'Course I am. You'd better ask Bob when we should do it. He's gotta do the time. Is he going to ride with each of us? Poor bugger, we might frighten him to death.'

'You might, he'll be safe as houses with me.'

'We'll see, we'll see. You call him and let me know what time of the day we're going to do it. Glad you reminded me. See ya.'

Angela put the phone down, grinning to herself. She'd

got the journey down to twelve and a quarter minutes last week but was sure she could shave a half minute more off that. Mind you, that was meeting no other traffic. If she got behind a sheep truck or worse, a dozey old git, she could add ten minutes to her score. How were they going to allow for that? It wouldn't be fair if one had traffic and the other didn't. They could deduct one or two minutes for every vehicle they came across, but would that be too much? She didn't know. They'd have to decide before they started, and stick to it.

The 1st November dawned bright and clear and once the sun got up it was reasonably warm. At least it was dry. Jack had rung on Saturday to say they'd start at 2pm from Drybed Creek and Bob would drive with each of them in turn. They'd toss to see who went first. In the unlikely event of a tie they'd do a second run. Angela had wanted the best of two runs but Bob said he couldn't stand doing that hill four times in one afternoon, specially not with them driving like bats out of Hell. Jack was at the Creek when Angela arrived. She was more than a little annoyed to find Maxine and Ken there too.

'What are you here for? You're not driving with me.'

'Don't worry! I wouldn't dare. You're mad to race up this hill, especially at your age.'

Maxine could have kicked herself for mentioning age but she was wrought up and the words just tumbled out. She thought her mother was behaving like a teenager, showing off, trying to prove she was still young. When was she going to accept the inevitable?

'If you've come to try and stop me, you're wasting your time.'

Ken butted in, 'We're not trying to stop you but we're going to follow you in case you need any help. It makes sense, and we'll do the same for Jack. Somebody's got to take Bob back down for the next run anyway and it may as well be us.'

'I don't want to see you in m'mirror, you'll put me off. You've gotta stay well back.' Angela was in a bad mood now, which was likely to make for erratic driving.

'Come on then. Let's get on with it.' Jack didn't want any more argument and he produced a fifty-cent piece. 'What do you want to do, go first or second? Your call, Angie.'

'I'll go first. Tails.'

'Tails it is. Off you go then.'

'Do be careful, Mum.'

'It's a race for God's sake, I'm not pussyfooting around. I want to win so I won't do anything stupid. Don't forget, keep well back, I don't want to see ya.'

Bob and Angela got into the Ute and fastened their seatbelts. Bob checked there was nothing coming either way and had his finger on the stopwatch.

'Start when you're ready, Angela. Time counts from when you turn the key.'

Angela took a deep breath, started the engine and put her foot down. There was a hundred yards or so before the hill started proper and she wanted a good take-off. Although she recognised distances in kilometres, Angela had never got the hang of thinking in metres for short distances. She was brought up on feet and inches and she wasn't inclined to change now.

'God, this thing's got some power,' gasped Bob as he felt himself pushed back in his seat. Angela didn't answer. She was too busy concentrating. The bends and the steep gradient started almost at once and shortly there would be a sharp drop over the left hand edge as the trees disappeared.

A crash barrier had been promised but was not yet a reality on this section of the road. The road was well marked though, with warning signs to tell you how fast you should be going to take the corners safely. Angela never took too much notice of those. From long experience she knew she could exceed the limits by at least fifteen ks an hour. The road wound sharply to the right then into a steep left curve. She could straighten up for a few yards then into another right bend.

Ribbons of small rivers and creeks festooned the surrounding hills, most seeping under the road but occasionally washing across it. Only last month there had been a large slip on the next bend, partially closing the road.

Angela was muttering to herself all the time; *watch out for loose rock, brake just before the curve, accelerate round it, not too fast.* She managed that all right but then came the first hairpin. *Slower,* the sign said fifteen, *she must go slower, change down, for God's sake change down, don't brake, down again,* she felt the rear wheels loosing their grip as she took the corner too fast. Whew, that was close. She stole a quick glance at Bob. He was gripping the panic bar in front, his legs rigid on imaginary brakes, beads of sweat on his upper lip. A quick glance in the mirror. Good. There was no sign of Ken and Maxine.

All her attention was focused on the road ahead as another left hand bend was imminent. Angela found these worse than the right hand ones, the chances of slipping off the edge seemed greater. They were climbing steeply now and staying in second gear where she had more control; she put her foot down, causing the engine to roar. She couldn't risk third gear as the next hairpin was coming up. She talked herself through it. *Nothing coming, swing out, give yourself more room, pull the wheel round, not too far, straighten up, straighten up, the other way, come on, come on, respond you bugger!* God. She'd have to be more careful. Next time she might not be so lucky. This better not be a tie. She couldn't take another trip up here today.

At last, the turn off to their own road. The tarmac disappeared but she was unlikely to meet anything. She took the corner as fast as she dared. Bush on either side for a bit made her feel safer. It was an illusion. The road was narrower and unsealed and heavily rutted from the winter rains.

Angela had no idea how she was doing for time. Her arms were aching with the effort and her shoulders and neck were taut with tension. The suspension in the Ute was good but the surface was uneven and always damp from underground springs that veined the area. Bush had given way to a rocky bank on the left. The right dropped away, giving a magnificent view of the mountains if she'd had the leisure to look.

There was a fence of sorts that Jack had put up, with some white marker posts and the odd red reflector to guide them in the dark. Not that she made a habit of arriving back after dark. She was in second gear most of the time now she was on the final stretch. Steep and winding but widening out to the sloping plateau. At last she could see the house a quarter mile ahead. Angela, ignoring the strain she was putting on the Holden, changed up to top gear and roared up to the fence, stamping on the brakes at the last minute.

'Stop the clock! How did I do?'

'Eleven minutes and fifty one seconds and practically gave me a heart attack,' replied Bob, slumped back in his seat, relaxing his tense muscles. Angela was jubilant. That was the best she'd ever done.

'Jack'll never beat that. His Ute's heavier than mine, won't take the corners so well.'

'If he takes more risks on the corners than you I'll definitely have a heart attack. I don't know whether I can stand another run up here this afternoon.'

'Aw, don't be a wimp Bob, you promised. It won't be fair to do him on another day. What's another eleven or twelve minutes?'

'All right, all right. Of course I'll do it but I expect a beer, maybe two or three, when we get back. Here comes Maxine and Ken. They did what you asked and kept well back.' He broke off to shout,

'Do you two still want to make another trip? I think it is helpful to know someone is behind us if we have a problem.'

'Ken says he'll go but I'm a nervous wreck trying to keep up with Mum. Gee, you went like a bat out of Hell. I need a beer. Hope you've got plenty 'cos the others'll want some when they get back.'

'I got a load in last week and it's in the fridge. Get me one will ya, I'm collapsing out here where I can see the view.'

Angela sank into an easy chair on the veranda and put her feet up on a stool. Her pulse was racing and she felt a little short of breath. She had never driven up there that fast before and she didn't want to again. She'd probably taken some unnecessary risks but she'd been determined to beat Jack. He'd better not beat her. Maxine brought out beers for them both and joined her mother while they waited for Bob to return with Jack. Maxine could see that the effort had taken its toll on Angela. She had been amazed that they had only caught the odd glimpse of the Holden on a few of the bends ahead. Ken had his foot down and went as fast as he dared but they had never even got close. She was praying that her mother had won because she didn't want her having another go.

Angela sat up with a start. 'Here they come, listen. He's roaring up the road.'

Suddenly, Jack's wagon was in sight and he sped up to the fence, skidding with a flurry of stones.

'What's his time, what's his time?' She ran to the gate as Jack and Bob climbed out of the jeep.

'You can stop panicking, you beat him by seventeen, no, nineteen seconds and between the two of you, you nearly killed me. Never again. Any more competitions you can call on someone else.'

Angela was jubilant. 'I told you I could beat you. Men aren't always the best drivers.'

'I'd quit boasting if I were you, Angie. You might've beaten Jack but it doesn't mean you're a better driver and if you drive like that again you'll likely go over the edge and that'll be the end of you. Now what about that beer?'

Bob collapsed into Angela's chair and put his feet up. Maxine got them both a beer and found another chair for Jack, who seemed pretty subdued.

'Can't see how she beat me unless she was driving like a maniac.'

'Don't worry, she must've been. We couldn't keep up with her. Go on Mum, admit you took too many risks and promise you won't do it again.'

'Don't keep going on. I won, didn't I? Where's the congratulations? If it makes yer feel better I won't race up there again, all right? Now belt up and get on with yer beer.'

Chapter Eleven

England 2000
Living With Us

Derek was struggling with the crossword when Kristine got home. She never knew why he bothered. Mathematical problems were his scene but he hated to be beaten.

'How did it go?' he wanted to know.

'Well, I've found another one that's possible but they've no vacancies; at least, they have one but it's in a double room and your mother would never accept that, and we wouldn't expect her to. I've put her name down, just in case, but I must look at some more – if I can find them. I'll put her name down at Oakhurst too, although they already have a long waiting list. I think the clientele will be more to Evelyn's liking there. You know how she likes only to be associated with "people of quality".'

Derek put the pen down and gave Kristine his full attention.

'You must get all sorts in most of these homes. Mother will not be able to pick and choose her fellow residents.'

'Try telling her that. What's the matter Derek? You look as if you've something on your mind.'

'Well I have and I'm not quite sure how I should say this, but I've come to the conclusion you're right, Kristine. We should have Mother for a trial period, if you're really, really sure you don't mind. I realize you will take the brunt of it.' It all came out in a rush and Derek was rubbing his hand through his hair, something he always did when he was unsure of his reception.

'Oh no! We can't. You said it was impossible.' It was the last thing Kristine expected. She sank down onto the sofa. This was a bombshell she'd not seen coming.

'I've been bloody well wasting my time, trailing around homes for hours and now they're not wanted?' She seldom swore but the occasion called for it. Only now did Kristine realise how relieved she'd been that they had decided not to have Evelyn at home.

'Why have you suddenly changed your mind? It was her, wasn't it, the wretched woman. Evelyn has got her own way. I should have known. When it came to the crunch, you couldn't stand up to her.' She'd probably invoked the tears and all the sob stories she'd used on Kristine. In spite of her earlier insistence that they should try looking after his mother, she was devastated he'd come to this decision.

'It was you that said we should have her. That people would expect us to and I've now come to the same conclusion. I thought you'd be pleased.'

'But you said it was impossible. Nothing's changed. The house's still unsuitable, I'll still have to give up work, be at home all day. I've been going round these homes, trying to find something suitable. You could have told me before I'd bothered. Of course I'm not pleased.' Kristine was angry, upset, dreading the thought of having her mother-in-law, day in day out. She was fighting tears and her emotions were in turmoil.

Derek was exasperated. He'd agreed to what Kristine wanted so why was she so angry?

'All those things still apply and I'm not saying it will be easy but I'm trying to do what you wanted. Do what is expected of us, you said. Looks like I never get it right.'

'It's not only that, Derek, is it? Be honest, you let her

bamboozle you into having her here. You didn't take any notice of me before but you knuckle under to her.'

'All right, Kristine, that's partly true but I thought it was what you really wanted anyway so I gave in.'

Kristine knew that wasn't true. He'd given in to Evelyn but wouldn't admit it.

She knew she couldn't win but why couldn't he understand, there was a difference between what they should do and what she really wanted to do? Then there was the conflict of not wanting to put Evelyn in a home but dreading the thought of actually having her living with them. Kristine just knew she would be a bundle of anxiety most of the time. Derek had come to the conclusion, as she had originally, that it would salve their consciences if they gave it a try. She hadn't managed to convince him, but his mother, probably with judicious use of tears, had forced him into it. Evelyn had made up her mind that she wouldn't move unless she came to live with them. If they didn't have her they were selfish.

Kristine was sure Derek didn't want her there either, but if they put her straight into a home she'd punish them every time they went to visit. Kristine wouldn't be able to face her week after week. Well, they wouldn't have been able to put her in a home if she'd refused to go. Even so, her heart sank and she could feel the stress building as the enormity of what they were proposing came crowding in on her.

'Well, we can't do it immediately. Where are we going to put her? What alterations do we need to make to the house? There's all that to decide now.' Kristine was already trying to postpone the inevitable day. Derek tried to be helpful.

'Of course we can't do it immediately and we don't need to decide these things today, Kristine. Mother is all right at the moment so we can work out a plan coolly and calmly over the next month or two. How much notice do you have to give the hospital? I suppose you will have to give up work? Could you manage to stay on, perhaps part time?'

'Of course I can't stay working.' Derek must be mad if he thought they could have his mother living with them and then for both of them to be out all day. What would be the point? Sometimes men could be so thoughtless. 'I can't do part time and then do the house and be at your mother's beck and call when I'm at home.' Kristine got up and went out into the garden, taking her frustrations out on the weeds, crushing them in her hands and throwing them on the grass.

'Perhaps we should forget the whole thing. Forget I ever said mother should come here. We'll just find her a good home and be done with it.' Derek had followed Kristine into the garden, anxious to restore peace. He was determined his mother would not create a rift between them. Kristine did not answer for a few minutes, to all intents engrossed in her weeding. Slowly she straightened up, turning to face him.

'I'm sorry I got angry, Derek. I know I'm not making much sense but it's so hard to explain. I didn't want to put your mother in a home because I wouldn't want to put anyone in one of those places but the thought of having her here is very daunting. You know she and I don't see eye to eye on so many things. I'm afraid we shall have ructions in a very short time.'

Derek, as always, was inclined to be more optimistic. 'For a start, I don't think it will be as bad as you fear and anyway, what other options do we have? You won't be on your own, we'll all help and if it doesn't work out she'll have to go into a home. At least we'll be able to say we've tried. Who knows, Mother may well be more reasonable if she knows what the alternative will be. Come on, let's go inside. It's getting cold out here.'

Kristine wasn't so sure all would be well but she was as anxious as Derek to make her peace.

'I hope you're right. We'll have to try and make it work.

There will be a lot to do. We'll have to put handrails here and there where there is a little step. The study is the biggest room so perhaps we should clear it out and make it into a bedroom for her. What do you think? It'll be an upheaval but we could put the study upstairs. With the loo and the basin downstairs, she'll only have to go upstairs for a bath. If it works out, I suppose we could put a shower downstairs?'

'Oh God. I'll have to alter all the cabling for the computer and the phones and if it doesn't work it will have all been for nothing. It'll be bloody inconvenient having the office upstairs. To be honest, I haven't really thought this through. I suppose you've always known what an upheaval it'd be. Oh, I don't know. Are we doing the right thing?' Derek slumped back in his chair. Maybe it wasn't such a bright idea but now he'd got this far he'd have to go through with it. It was Kristine's turn to be positive.

'Come on, Derek. We've agreed it's the only alternative. We'll have to get on with it. Putting your mother downstairs will be the best solution. At least we won't have to clutter up the place with a stair lift.'

'I guess you're right, Kristine. We'll just do it. If the worst comes to the worst and she can't get up the stairs we can put a shower off the utility room. Can you bear it, love?'

'Now you ask me! Not really, if I'm honest but I think we have to. I just know it will be difficult. If we support each other, maybe we can make it work.'

'I'll start organizing it tomorrow. She's not going to be able to come here for about three months as there is more to do than I realized. Oh Hell, I forgot. You didn't say how much notice you have to give?'

'You might have forgotten but I haven't.' Kristine endeavoured to keep the resentment out of her voice. 'It's going to be quite hard to leave and be home all day. I only have to give a month's notice, but you're right, it will take at least three months before we're ready to have her here. We'd better both go and tell her, otherwise she'll think it's only you who wants her and I'm agreeing under sufferance.'

'Well, don't let's tell her until we're nearly ready or she'll get in a state.' Derek knew there would be other arrangements to make. 'She won't want us to sell the house although we may have to in the end. Perhaps we can let it on a short-term lease – we'd better not think about that yet but when she moves out, however temporarily, we'll have to make it secure. She won't like it. It's a wonder she hasn't suggested we move in with her and leave everything as it is.'

Kristine was horrified. 'Heaven forbid. I'll dig my toes in if she starts that caper. I mean it, Derek. There's no way I'm moving in there.'

'All right, don't panic, I won't either.'

Together they started a list of all the things they could think of that would need to be done as a result of their decision. Rebecca and Ralph would not be best pleased and would take some convincing that what they were planning was a sensible option.

'Oh, Heavens. I've forgotten about the supper. I should have put the meat on ages ago. We were going to have stew tonight.' At least Derek had a solution to that problem.

'Let's forget about it all for now. You and I are going to the Duke's Head for a meal, we deserve it.'

Chapter Twelve

Kristine and Derek never mentioned the move to Evelyn until nearly two months later, when they had made several changes to the house and talked to Social Services who had been surprisingly helpful. Evelyn expected it of course.

'My family's always looked after their own. We didn't go into homes. People of our standing don't go into workhouses.' However often Kristine told her they weren't workhouses, she wouldn't have it.

'What about Tiger? He'll have to come with me. I can't leave Tiger.'

'No, of course he can come.' Kristine had forgotten about the wretched cat. 'We'll have to get a room ready for you; bring over your own furniture if that's what you want, pictures, rugs, books and things. We need to change the rooms around so you can be on the ground floor. It will take a few more weeks to organize so you can be thinking about what you want to bring.'

'What about the house? You're not to sell it, Derek. Your father wanted me to live here for the rest of my life and you after us. Besides, I might want to come back here to live, and what about the garden, my lovely garden?'

Derek was ready for this. 'It's all right, Mother, We're not going to sell the house in the foreseeable future but we can't just leave it empty. We shall probably let it in the short term and then the garden will be looked after too. That can be in the terms of the lease. Don't you worry about it, that's my problem.'

That had been 20th June. It took Kristine and Derek until

the beginning of August before they were ready to receive Evelyn. Kristine had been sure she wouldn't sleep worrying about having Evelyn to stay but life had been so fraught with so much to do, she'd gone out like a light when her head hit the pillow. The house was almost ready so they were fetching Evelyn at eleven o'clock on Saturday. It had been quite an upheaval. They'd agreed to move the study to the guest room upstairs and put her in what had been the study, downstairs. Her favourite pieces of furniture had already arrived and her room looked much as it had in her own home. She wouldn't like the yellow curtains but she'd have to put up with them for the time being.

'Where are your friends going to stay when they come to see you, and what about us, when we come home? I thought you and Dad had decided to put her in a home,' Rebecca had been quite indignant when she phoned. She could see more clearly than Kristine, how things would have to change. Her mother had tried to explain that they had to give it a try.
Three months or so, perhaps six, and if it didn't work out it would have to be a home. There would be no going back.

Predictably, Rebecca said, 'Who are you trying to kid? You wouldn't have this huge disruption for just three months. Giving up work, hand rails everywhere, guards round this and that; all for three months. I don't believe it. More like three years. She'll drive you mad.'

Kristine knew she'd upset Rebecca, which was the last thing she wanted to do but it couldn't be helped. They had to do it and it was she that would have the hassle, not Rebecca. It was she that had the headaches, stomach aches too, and she'd never had headaches before. They started right after they'd decided to have Evelyn at Elmbrook Manor. Maybe they'd go when she had settled in, when they had a routine. They had to do it. God, it was so hard to please everyone – and do what was right.

Ralph was even more put out, which surprised Kristine. He always got on well with his grandmother, as he was her favourite. But then he often had friends to stay, especially Stephanie. She'd become rather a fixture of late. Kristine hoped it wasn't serious. He needed to finish his degree and get a job; girls were such a distraction.

She supposed they were better than drugs and Derek seemed to think Stephanie was a passing fancy, first love and all that. He should know, but then he never worried, the way she did. All mothers did. The young were inclined to be more selfish than they were.

Perhaps she and Derek had been the same at that age. She couldn't remember and never had the same problem. It was she who'd left home, nobody had moved in. It was only natural for the young to live for today and not think too much about tomorrow.

No doubt she and Derek would be put in a home pretty sharpish when their turn came. Not that she disagreed with the concept of a home, if a good one could be found. She just knew that life was going to be so difficult with Derek's mother sharing their house. It was like a black cloud looming over her.

Evelyn would be putting her nose into their affairs, even though she said she wouldn't. "I'll keep to my room and look after my own things, you won't have to do hardly anything for me," she'd said, but Kristine knew her better than that, "Why don't you put that lovely table, it came from my grandmother you know, over there out of the sun? The sun will bleach the walnut. Don't you think the conservatory needs new curtains?" On and on it would go. They hadn't really thought what they were going to do about meals. They couldn't both work in the kitchen. Kristine expected to do the cooking; it'd be easier that way. Perhaps Evelyn would have some meals in her room and she probably wouldn't get up for breakfast until after Derek had gone, as he left so early.

Be positive, you have to be positive, she told herself several times a day. If she didn't, they'd soon come to blows when Evelyn arrived.

Kristine had found it hard leaving her position in the operating theatre. She loved the work and was quite experienced, having done theatre work in several hospitals over the years. Every operation was different, even if for the same thing. Once the incision was made, you never knew exactly what you'd find inside. Different people; too fat, very thin, young or old, varying degrees of difficulty. Nasty surprises sometimes, too. It was something she had been able to do part time when the children were younger and she was barely doing full time now. As long as she was prepared to do her share 'on call' she could do less hours now but she would have had to juggle the hours around the lists and probably ended up hardly seeing Derek at all.

Kristine decided it would create more stress than she was prepared to cope with. She didn't need any more hassle. She knew she couldn't survive being on call to Evelyn all day and then possibly on call to the hospital at night. The staff had all been so kind, Julian, Mary, Justine, even crabby old Sister Evans. "We'll miss you," they said, sounding as if they meant it. Perhaps they did.

Kristine had been there ten years, full time for six. She hadn't enjoyed it all. Guts and chest, they were the best. Never knew what you were going to get. She hated doing plastics though. Pick, pick, put in a stitch; no, it doesn't look right, little to the left, fraction up a bit. No. She wouldn't miss those. Pity Millie McKenzie wasn't the general surgeon instead of pompous Pinkerton.

Well it would be a new life now, with Evelyn. Perhaps she could go back part time if Evelyn settled in OK but she doubted it. It wouldn't take long to lose the edge. Forget what instrument to produce next, what stitch to get ready. She'd left now; let that be the end of it. If she was bored, she'd have to get something else to do. God, she was dreading Saturday.

Chapter Thirteen

Rebecca couldn't understand why they had to do it. She wasn't unkind or she didn't consider herself so. She was just practical and she knew how much her mother worried about keeping everyone happy. She would end up being the unhappiest of all. It was going to be a real pain having Granny there all the time, bossing everyone around. Her mum said she wouldn't but she always had before, and Rebecca couldn't see why it would be any different now. She saw her grandmother as a queen bee, watching over the hive, directing the workers every which way.

She couldn't say anything to her mother. Whenever she tried, she got upset and said it was their duty. Rebecca couldn't see how it was her mother's duty. It was only very recently her father had thought it his duty and Granny was his mother. She couldn't see that it was her or Ralph's duty and certainly not poor Tom's.

Her father had bowed to pressure from the old bat. Couldn't he see how difficult it was going to be for Mother? She was convinced he didn't really want her there all the time either. She'd only cause rows between them, she always did. Her mum was too kind for her own good. She was too moral, too soft. She should have said no.

Rebecca knew she would have done in the same position. It wasn't fair, disrupting their whole life. Deep down, she didn't believe her mother wanted Granny there either. She'd been put upon by Granny, made to feel guilty. "Nobody in our family ever went into the workhouse, we always looked after our own, the young today are so selfish." She never let up.

It had nearly made her feel guilty but fortunately Tom had seen through Evelyn. "It's just emotional blackmail, take no notice," he'd said, so she hadn't. Besides, Rebecca knew her grandmother had not really looked after her own mother, although she always said she did. Great-granny had had a husband and all her grandmother had done was visited her mother for a chat every day. She'd be bored to tears and so would most people. Granny claimed to have done all this work in her youth but ever since she married she'd had servants of some kind and just sat about giving orders. Rebecca's grandfather had been too indulgent. He treated his wife like his beautiful doll and waited on her hand and foot. Rebecca couldn't think why; she'd bossed him around unmercifully.

Rebecca knew that Ralph didn't want his grandmother living with them either although he'd apparently told his mum on one occasion that it might be quite fun. Fun! It was not a word Rebecca would use about her grandmother, ever. Ralph told her she slipped him a fiver now and again. She'd never given her anything, except at Christmas and birthdays.

Rebecca was convinced it was because he was a boy. Her grandmother was hooked on this primogeniture thing and boys were more important in her eyes. Probably Rebecca was a disappointment, turning up before a son. And she didn't go to university. Still, she had redeemed herself a bit by working in a law firm and marrying Tom. A lawyer in the family was always acceptable.

Ralph was not going to be quite so chuffed when Stephanie came to stay. She would be at the other end of the house and it wouldn't be so easy for him to creep into her room. He didn't think anyone knew but Rebecca had seen him one night and she was sure her mother knew. She didn't miss much and she'd been young once. Rebecca thought it would be a hoot if he forgot it was granny in the study and paid her a visit. She'd probably die of shock.

She had rather hoped her mum and dad would come and stay with her and Tom some weekends but she supposed that wouldn't happen now. She would try and see that it did. Granny could stay on her own for one weekend. She'd been looking after herself up until now.

Chapter Fourteen

'I don't think you'd better come this weekend, Steph,' Ralph said. 'Gran's moving and it's likely to be chaos.' He had his arm round her and gave her a squeeze to tell her he really wanted her but it was just a bad time.

'But you said I could come the weekend after term started. What difference does it make if your Gran's there? If she's staying with you all the time are you saying I can't come and stay, ever again?' Stephanie was using her 'little girl's' voice, trying to wheedle Ralph into giving in. It irritated him when she talked like that but he didn't complain. Best not upset her anymore just now.

'No, of course not,' he replied, 'Don't be silly, but she is going to be in what used to be the study and the guest room will be upstairs at the far end of the passage and the old guest room will be the study. Mum will have to move furniture and make it presentable before she has anyone to stay.'

'Will she put in a double bed?' Her impish grin told him she was thinking the same as he was. A double bed would make their night-time trysts more comfortable.

'Of course you'll be able to come and stay, and no, I don't think she'll put in a double bed. It's a bigger room so she'll put twins in there I expect, so we might be able to improve matters.' He winked at her. 'Besides, it won't be so easy for me to sneak in without anyone seeing me. Perhaps you won't want to come under those circumstances?'

'Maybe I won't. That Richard Bedford tried to get me to

go out with him last week. Perhaps I'll take him up on the offer.'

She was just pretending, he could tell. Richard might look good but he was the meanest chap in the college, if not in the whole universe and Stephanie was high maintenance, as he well knew. Ralph considered he had a better physique than Richard and was an inch taller.

Having Granny at home should help his finances a bit too. She often slipped him a fiver if he buttered her up. She always said, "Don't tell your Mother, she wouldn't approve," and of course he didn't. It didn't take much; Evelyn was a sucker for flattery. In fact most women were, from Ralph's experience. Rebecca should try it and she wouldn't have so many arguments with Granny.

'Don't worry, I'll get you to stay as soon as Mum's fixed up the room. We could always go out for a spin in your Dad's car, find somewhere secluded in the country. What about it?' He found it a pain without his car but he couldn't risk taking it out without the MOT. Some of his friends had done so and got away with it but if he did, he knew he'd be caught. He couldn't afford the fifty quid, and it'd be more if something needed doing. Still, he'd better cut the beer to pay for it. He hated being without wheels.

'Ooh, yes! Lets!' She took out her mobile and proceeded to wheedle the car from her father.

It wouldn't take long. She was used to getting what she wanted. Ralph didn't know why she stuck with him as he was always short of cash. He put it down to his toned figure and blue eyes.

Chapter Fifteen

Saturday dawned and Derek yawned and turned over. He always enjoyed an extra hour in bed at the weekends. They both did, so why was Kristine up and gone when it was only 7.30am? Then it hit him. Today was the day his mother was coming to stay, not just to visit, but for keeps. No wonder Kristine had beaten him out of bed. She'd be in a right state, he'd better get up.

His mother's room was ready and her house was on the market. She'd been so angry with him when she heard he was going to sell, but it was just not practical to let it. He and Kristine were never going to live in it. They were fond of Elmbrook Manor and had no desire to move to a house that would require thousands of pounds spent on it to make it as comfortable as the one they had. Yes, the garden was lovely and Kristine liked gardening but it was too big for her to manage on her own and good gardeners were prohibitively expensive if you were fortunate enough to find one. Rebecca and Tom weren't interested in the house and a share of the money would be more useful to Ralph. Besides, when his mother eventually went into a home, they were going to need the finance.

As he washed and shaved, Derek reflected on the nightmare of the last few weeks, trying to clear out forty years of family life. Much of it was rubbish of course, but it couldn't just be thrown away. There were dozens of photographs, old letters, bills long since paid, old birthday cards, bank statements and old cheque stubs. Derek spent several weekends with his mother, trying to decide what she wanted to keep and what could go. Each photo and letter provoked memories, some painful some joyful, but all had to be commented upon and it was an extremely time-consuming process. Kristine had more patience for this kind of detail and she took her turn in sharing the reminiscences with Evelyn, proving more sympathetic over the items she wished to keep. But on some things Derek's mother was adamant,

'I don't want any of that furniture sold, Derek. Your father and I bought it together during our married life and it all has sentimental value. Besides, some of it is worth a fortune.'

'That's just it, Mother,' he'd told her. 'Some of it is valuable and we shall have to pay to store it. You may as well have the money for it. We've moved the best pieces to us anyway. The mahogany desk looks great in your room and you've got your bed and dressing table, oh and some of your best chairs. We don't have room for any more.'

'I might move into a sheltered bungalow or some such place and then I would need it.' (If only!) 'You are not to sell it, Derek, any of it.'

She did go through all the china and had given some nice pieces to Rebecca, who was quite touched. She didn't think her Grandmother cared. They'd never really got on – two dominant characters, he supposed. She'd packed up the dinner service and said Ralph could have it, if or when he got married, so that went into the attic. She wouldn't tell Ralph, it was to be a surprise when the time came.

She'd probably change her mind if he married Stephanie. She couldn't stand her. "Nothing but a gold digger," she'd said. Derek wondered what she'd do if Ralph didn't get married. Would he be allowed to have the things for a bachelor pad?

He'd worry about that when and if it happened and anyway his mother would probably be long gone by then. He had persuaded her to give Rebecca and Ralph a couple of the better pieces of furniture so she didn't have to sell them and she was reasonably content they'd be staying in the family.

At least the garden was a selling feature for the house. Having a gardener these last few years had made it a picture but old Bob was getting past it and had seized his opportunity to retire. Derek's mother had some good ideas and an eye for colour and he mused that she might turn her mind to their garden. It would give her something to do, but a moment's reflection told him it was a bad idea. Kristine wouldn't take kindly to interference in her precious domain.

Why did they ever agree to this? He didn't believe they had, it just evolved. Derek wouldn't acknowledge, even to himself, that it was his inability to stand up to his mother that they were having her to live with them. He was sure though, that they'd all regret it. His mother could be very difficult. Maybe she would be so grateful to have avoided an old peoples' home that she would be full of sweetness and light. Then again, she might not. Life wasn't like that. He just knew there would be problems.

The Social Services had surprised him, proving that you shouldn't always believe what you're told. They'd fallen over themselves trying to be helpful. They had looked at the house, sorted out where handrails were needed, and offered a booster for the loo when required. Kristine said they were so helpful because they hadn't any rooms in the homes and it was cheaper to get families to look after their relatives. Now who was being cynical!

He realised they would use more heating and hot water, but at least his mother had offered to pay her whack. In a lot of ways, his mother wasn't ready for a home. The trouble was, there seemed to be very few truly residential homes about. Probably sheltered housing would have been the best option at this stage. Somewhere where she could live an independent life but have meals cooked for her and washing done, things like that. There was nothing remotely like that in their area. Still, the die was cast. Poor Kristine was rather down; having to give up work and knowing she would be cheek by jowl with his mother all week couldn't be a cheerful prospect. But he was sure it wouldn't be too bad. Derek believed Kristine would be able to spend more time in the garden, go out with her friends, join a club or two. Things she had been unable to do while she was working. Ever the optimist, Derek thought that his mother would doze a lot of the time and if Kristine made an effort to get to know her and understand her better, he was certain they'd get on fine in the end.

Breakfast was rather like the condemned prisoner's last meal. They sat in silence, each with their own gloomy thoughts. Derek tried to read the paper but his mind kept throwing up future problems and he knew Kristine was a bundle of apprehension. He got up from the table and put his arms round her, giving her a bear hug.

'Come along, love. It'll be all right, you'll see. We're in this together. Don't let her get to us. Let's go now. The sooner we get her the sooner we'll find out if this is going to work.'

Chapter Sixteen

Evelyn was ready when they got there. Her precious Tiger was in the basket, probably thinking he was going to the vet. Not much else to bring. Just a small suitcase with a few clothes and toiletries. They waited while Evelyn went around the house having a last look at each room. She ended up on the patio, gazing at her beloved garden, tears rolling down her pale cheeks. Kristine felt very sorry for her. It must be very sad to leave the house you've lived in for so long, all the shared memories, the happy times, the sad ones too. Kristine put out her hand and gave Evelyn's arm a squeeze. Derek put his arm around his mother, picked up her case and guided her gently to the car. At least it was still summer. With the sun shining, nothing seemed so bad, for her or for them. Kristine took Tiger and put him on the floor beside Evelyn.

Derek tried to lighten the mood by speculating on how Tiger would get on with Buster. Big mistake. Evelyn had forgotten they had a dog and now she was terrified Tiger would run away when he saw him. Kristine glared at Derek and said she was sure it would be OK. Labradors were gentle creatures and Buster would probably run away from Tiger, not the other way around.

They arrived back at Elmbrook to find Rebecca had turned up. She'd put the soup on and set the table for lunch. Ralph had dragged himself away from Stephanie to lend family solidarity to the day. It was good of them to make the effort, especially as neither of them approved the new situation. However, the experiment was supposed to be a family affair so Kristine particularly, needed their support. Buster rushed in, wagging his tail, keen to show his enthusiasm for another family member who might offer him treats. Suddenly, he saw Tiger. What fun. Someone to play with. Tiger saw it differently. He hissed and spat from the safety of his cage, but not for long. Before they could stop her, Evelyn had removed Tiger from the cage to give him a protective cuddle. She was not quick enough. With a demented wail, he sprang from her arms, dashed into the garden through the patio doors and headed for the nearest tree, with Buster in hot pursuit. The first crisis. Why hadn't they made contingency plans for this? The truth was they never thought about the wretched cat. Evelyn was distraught.

Her beloved Tiger was about to be murdered by her son's dreadful dog.

Ralph and Rebecca were outside trying to control Buster and put him in his kennel so Tiger would come down from the tree. Kristine could see that they thought the whole episode highly amusing, although they were trying to supress their laughter. No doubt Kristine would find it funny tomorrow but right now it added to the tension. Derek sat his mother down and poured her a large sherry.

'Here, Mother, drink this and calm down. Ralph and Rebecca will shut Buster in his kennel and then Tiger will feel safe enough to come down. I assure you he'll be all right. Cats will always get the better of a dog. Buster is a wimp really and once Tiger learns to turn on him I know who will be the boss.'

'Why don't we have lunch? Rebecca has been good enough to get it ready. Buster is now away out of sight and I'm sure Tiger will soon be down to see you. Perhaps you should keep him in your room for a day or two until he has settled. We'll get him a litter tray. I promise you, they will get used to each other.' From past experience of introducing a dog to a cat, Kristine felt quite confident that all would eventually be well.

Evelyn was still tearful and anxious but readily agreed to lunch and another sherry as she confessed to not having had any breakfast. They managed to make it a cheerful meal. Ralph regaled his grandmother with stories of university life, much exaggerated, Kristine hoped. Evelyn was soon smiling and joining in the conversation. Derek sneaked out to see if Tiger had come down from the tree. He managed to catch him and bring him to Evelyn who clasped him to her bosom, murmuring endearments and sympathising with him about the 'nasty doggie'.

'You go to your room, Evelyn, and have a rest. I'll bring you some coffee, or would you prefer tea? It has been a traumatic time for you. I'm sure Tiger would like to join you. You wait and see. He'll be perfectly at home by tea time.'

'I hope you're right Kristine. I think I will have a rest, it's all very strange and unnerving. I should like a pot of tea if it's not too much trouble.' Ralph took her arm and led her down the passage to her room. He always managed to cheer her up. He probably reminded her of Derek when he was a boy.

The first fortnight passed uneventfully. Tiger managed to achieve an uneasy stand off with Buster after giving the poor dog a nasty scratch on his nose. Buster looked soulfully at him, "why can't we play and be friends?" It might happen eventually but it could take a while. At least he didn't chase Tiger any more. They just kept a wary eye on each other.

One morning about a month later, before leaving for work, Derek observed,'How's it going? Doesn't seem so bad.' Kristine saw it differently. 'Your mother is always hovering, wanting to do things. I don't know what to give her to do.' She had given her some light dusting and she kept her own room tidy. 'I don't like to ask her to do "chores" like peeling the potatoes, in case she thinks I'm exploiting her, you know, just making use of her.'

'Oh, Mother would never think that. She's always

remarkably cheerful when I see her. I do believe this experiment of ours is working,' he replied blithely.

'If you say so.' Kristine wished he hadn't brought up the subject of his mother's happiness or otherwise, before he went to work. He was always in a rush and she couldn't tell him what it was really like. He didn't understand. Men didn't, or perhaps it wasn't just men, it was anyone without her sort of conscience. Perhaps she was worrying too much about whether Evelyn was happy or not. If only she could be relaxed about it but she found it so difficult. She felt pressured at every turn.

'You don't see her as often as I do or for so long at one stretch. It'll be murder in the winter when we are in the house day in and day out.'

'For Heaven's sake, Kristine, why think about the winter now? It's only August. Who knows what will happen next week, let alone three or four months from now.' Gathering up his things for work he kissed Kristine and asked, 'What exciting things have you got planned for today then?'

'Oh I thought we might slip over to Paris and climb the Eiffel Tower,' sarcasm flowed unbidden from her mouth. Derek started to shake his head in exasperation so she relented, smiled cheerfully and told him they were taking an excursion to the garden centre for a few plants and to have lunch. It would be an outing, a change of scene. He looked relieved, waved and was away, thoughts of his mother sliding from his mind. That was typical of Derek. Deal with now and let tomorrow look after itself. She should have smiled and said things were fine. She didn't want Evelyn making trouble between them. She knew he cared about whether the arrangement was working or not and didn't want Kristine to be unhappy but he just didn't see it from her perspective. He never had to listen to his mother, "Have you got a button to match this cardigan, Kristine?" Or, "Have you got a dictionary? I can't find mine."

"Have the papers come yet? They seem very late today. Mine always came early." "When you go to town will you get me the Lady magazine? I cancelled my order because I felt sure you'd have it. I'm surprised you don't. It would have been wasteful to have two copies." On and on she went.

Kristine had to explain that she didn't get any magazines because she seldom had time to read them. She would occasionally buy one if she saw something that interested her. Derek wasn't there to feel the vibes of criticism emanating from his mother. Kristine felt them when she forgot the napkins or the butter knife when setting the table. It wasn't necessary for Evelyn to say anything and mostly she didn't but Kristine could just feel the disapproval. That was a woman's thing. Rebecca felt it too but Ralph didn't and couldn't understand what they were on about. Derek never noticed anything, but of course Evelyn doted on him. Daughters-in-law were fair game but Kristine couldn't say that to Derek. He'd just laugh and say either that she was imagining it, or she should just ignore it.

As Evelyn wouldn't be up for an hour or more Kristine could get on with the washing, making the beds, doing the ironing. The hoovering would have to wait until she got up. The noise might wake her. There she was again, worrying about making a noise. Most men wouldn't think about it, they'd just make the noise and if it woke her, too bad. Kristine couldn't bear the recriminations. She decided there and then that she must find something more interesting to do with her life. Go to a class, learn something different and leave Evelyn to her own devices a little more. She had been looking after herself until now so a few hours on her own wouldn't hurt her. Perhaps Evelyn was bored too. She had very little to do now she was living with them. Maybe she'd like to have some friends round once a week or fortnightly, to play Bridge? Kristine could make sandwiches for them, set out a tray with tea and coffee, and then leave them to it. Evelyn had always liked her Bridge. It certainly wasn't Kristine's thing. She thought how awful it would be to be tied into playing with the same people week after week. Some of them took it so seriously too, almost World War Three if you played the wrong card. If she could persuade Evelyn to have her Bridge friends round on a Thursday then Kristine could join that new NADFAS group in Bilston. That only met once a month but she could go out somewhere with Janet, or Sue on another Thursday, even join a class at the Tech. Kristine felt quite cheered up with these thoughts. Now all she had to do was to convince Evelyn that she would like to resume her weekly Bridge afternoons.

'Evelyn, I've been thinking, would you like to have some friends round now and again to play Bridge? You used to love it. Just because you've moved here doesn't mean you have to give up the things you liked to do, or to stop seeing your friends.' Evelyn was taking her time over her cornflakes and yogurt. She didn't have a great deal for breakfast but didn't like to be hurried. Kristine had stopped for elevenses and felt it was a good opportunity to try out her idea.

'I don't know whether I would, Kristine. I've never been so keen since dear Brian died.'

'Well we could ask some of your friends and try it.' Kristine was desperate that her brilliant idea wasn't lost before it got started. 'This is your home now and you must feel free to ask your friends to tea or whatever. Perhaps you'd like a small lunch party occasionally?'

'That would be nice. I should quite like that but I'm not sure about the Bridge. You see, now I've come to live here with you and Derek I don't see the same need to socialize. I've got you for company you see. I did tell you that's what I needed.'

Evelyn got up and made herself some toast. Kristine's heart sank. She must say what she was thinking or she would regret it and be resentful. She took a deep breath and launched forth. She knew she was talking too fast but she didn't want to sound as if she was complaining.

'That's all very well, Evelyn, but I like to go out sometimes and see my friends. Now that I'm not working I might like to join a club or Arts society. I've never been able to attend anything on a regular basis because I was working and if I'm out I want to know that you have some company, not always sitting here on your own.'

Evelyn looked up in surprise. 'But you go out now, quite often and I'm perfectly all right. Besides, Rebecca could come over for a day and be with me if you want to go gallivanting off.'

'I don't want to go "gallivanting off" as you put it, but I'm sure we should both benefit from a day here and there with our friends. Have you forgotten that Rebecca works four days a week? Don't worry about it now. When we come back from our outing you can ring two or three of your friends and they can come to lunch next Thursday. If it's a warm day we could have it outside and perhaps you could ask your friends what they think of the Bridge idea. Now don't forget, we're off to the Garden Centre as soon as you're ready. We'll have lunch there which will be a change for both of us.'

'I'd forgotten. I'll go and get my things. Will I need a coat?'

'I shouldn't think so. Rain wasn't forecast and we shall be in the car'.

Perhaps the Bridge idea wasn't such a good one. Maybe Evelyn and her friends would rather just sit and gossip but Kristine was determined to check it out. She'd have to think of something else if it didn't work. Rebecca might come and stay with her grandmother one day a month while Kristine went out. That wasn't really too much to ask. They were supposed to be sharing the care of Granny although Rebecca had been dead against the idea of Evelyn coming to Elmbrook. Thinking about it, they were bound to fall out. Evelyn was so critical and

Rebecca so outspoken. Kristine doubted Rebecca would want to be tied to the same day each month though, and her one-day a week off work was precious to her.

Kristine wanted to do a little more for the Red Cross too now that she wasn't working and she was determined to join the Conservative Lunch Club. Not that she was particularly political but she had been to one or two of their talks as a guest and had found they had a variety of interesting speakers. They happened once a month and she would only go when the subject appealed to her. She should be able to manage that. Evelyn might like to go too occasionally, although Kristine was really looking for things they could do separately rather than together. It was so difficult, everyone had agreed to help with the experiment, but they didn't always remember that it involved the odd sacrifice, particularly of their time.

'Well, did you buy out the Garden Centre, Mother?' Derek was in jovial mood when he joined them in the garden.

'The place isn't like it used to be, Derek. They have rabbits and parrots and masses of exotic fish now. Almost hard to find any plants. Then there's a craft section, glassware and even books. They should call it an emporium or department store. It can hardly be described as a Garden Centre.' Evelyn was quite dismissive of the updated "River Meadows." When she used to visit to stock her garden, there was a huge choice of plants and trees and terracotta pots but that was it. Nothing else. Still, there was a pleasant restaurant now, with tables overlooking a lake and well laid out gardens. Derek was astonished. It had obviously changed dramatically since he'd last been there.

'But I'm sure you enjoyed your outing and your lunch?'

'You make me sound like a school child, Derek, talking about outings as if they were a treat for being good.'

'Don't be like that, Mother. It wasn't what I meant and you know it.'

'More tea, Evelyn?' Kristine butted in quickly before they got to bickering. Evelyn was so touchy and on her dignity you had to be careful what you said. She was surprised she had snapped at Derek though; it was usually at her. Perhaps she was trying to get at her for taking her on her outing. No, she was being far too sensitive, reading in meanings where there were none. Heavens, she was becoming like her mother-in-law.

'Your mother did buy a pretty mauve Streptocarcus for her room. They have some very good house plants and we had a healthy lunch of avocado salad.' Kristine left them to chat and enjoy the evening sun while she did all the things she hadn't done because they'd been out. Tomorrow would have to be an 'at home' day. Kristine decided she would have to organise their outings like she used to for the school holidays. One outing a week, one day when her friends came, and if she was lucky, one day when Evelyn went to see a friend. Kristine smiled at the irony of Evelyn's complaint of being treated as a school child. It was a similar situation.

Chapter Seventeen

The experiment had worked fairly well for the last three months. Evelyn got herself up and dressed and got her own breakfast. She managed the stairs when she wanted a bath but only when Kristine was about to help her in and out should she need it. During the summer months she could walk in the garden or sit in a sheltered spot and read a book, but winter was fast approaching. It was becoming dark earlier and earlier with cold winds and the occasional frost discouraging Evelyn from venturing out. Fortunately, the Bridge idea had eventuated. Three of her friends, Rose Burnley, Julia Carter and Fiona Dedham came to Elmbrook Manor once a fortnight. Rose and Julia were just as forgetful as Evelyn when playing cards but Fiona had the patience of a saint, which made it work. They also came for lunch once or twice a month and they took it in turns to invite Evelyn to their homes. The best thing about that was that Rose and Fiona still drove so they picked her up. It wasn't so bad. Kristine did get time for herself. She'd managed one lunch out and two Red Cross events even though she'd had to put up with, "Oh are you going out again today Kristine? You're out nearly as much as when you were working."

She was learning to ignore Evelyn's niggardly complaints and bite her tongue rather than retaliate. Her mother-in-law did sometimes dry the dishes and she dusted her room. She even peeled the vegetables occasionally. Rebecca said she'd settled because her mother gave in to her all the time but it was easier that way. And it wasn't all the time. If she felt it was important, Kristine didn't give way. It was the little things she found so annoying. The daily suggestions that various pieces of furniture might be moved, for example. Kristine had forgotten how often Evelyn had moved the furniture in her own home. Whenever they'd turned up they would notice that she'd moved everything around. She would swear it had always been in its new situation and next time it would be somewhere different. Kristine wasn't like that. She would find a place for something, and if it was convenient and it worked, she'd leave it there, maybe forever. She'd changed the curtains in Evelyn's room. Derek's mother hadn't actually complained about them; just mentioned not once, but almost every day, that yellow was not her colour. It was easier to move them to the new guest room and get her the dark green ones she wanted. Sometimes, even before her breakfast, Evelyn would criticise Kristine's clothes.

'You know, Kristine, you shouldn't wear pink, it doesn't suit you.'

'Oh, don't you think so? I wear it because I like it and Derek does too.'

'You shouldn't listen to Derek on colours my dear, he never could tell one from the other. No I think blue or green would suit your colouring better.' Kristine chose to ignore Evelyn on this one. She'd be rude if she answered and that would spoil the whole day. She would wear what she liked.

The other bugbear was that when Evelyn wanted something she wanted it at once. It was seldom convenient, as Kristine was usually doing something else. If she wanted a new towel, it must be now; if she couldn't find the book she wanted, Kristine would have to find it now, this minute. If she didn't, Evelyn would keep asking every few minutes until Kristine felt she would explode. It was some time before it occurred to Kristine that perhaps Evelyn's short-term memory was starting to go. If that was the case she would have to make allowances for it and be more patient. At least Evelyn would not remember she'd already asked for something so Kristine could provide it when she had time. Evelyn's short-term memory would prove to be much more irritating for Kristine than her mother-in-law.

Chapter Eighteen

Living at Elmbrook Manor was not as bad as Evelyn had feared and she felt she mustn't criticise. Not that she believed she did of course but she feared that if they thought she was being difficult, her son and daughter-in-law would put her in a home. She didn't think Derek would but she believed Kristine might and that Rebecca certainly would. Evelyn considered that her granddaughter had developed a hard shell from somewhere. It certainly hadn't come from her side of the family and even given her lack of breeding, Kristine was gentle and soft-hearted, Evelyn could see that.

Her 'girl friends' as she called them, were coming over the next day for their fortnightly Bridge. Derek called them the Alphabet Club because their surnames spelt ABCD. His little joke. She never would have thought of it. Evelyn thought it was tomorrow they were coming. She would have to ask Kristine. She found it distressing to be so forgetful.

Kristine had confirmed that her Bridge friends were coming on Thursday, which was tomorrow, but she was mystified as to why her daughter-in-law was so short with her? It was probably because she asked if she'd got that nice brown bread from Mansfield's for the sandwiches and not the plastic tasting rubbish from the supermarket. Well she might have forgotten. Evelyn didn't believe she was the only one who forgot things.

She decided to keep out of Kristine's way for awhile to allow her to get over it. Most days it was too cold to be in the garden but it was quite pleasant that morning. She'd better get some fresh air before the rain came. Next week it was Evelyn's turn to have the girls' lunch. She must plan the menu this time. Kristine should be able to cook something other than flan, which was so every-day. Perhaps she could manage salmon with a lemon and asparagus sauce. Evelyn didn't want to let the side down. Fiona was such a good cook and Julia always bought in something exotic because money was no object.

Evelyn put on her jacket and stout shoes to take a wander around the garden. The first leaves were turning, changing the multiple shades of green to the yellows and bronzes of Autumn. Buster was eager to join her on her walk, hoping she would take him over the fields to look for rabbits. Thank goodness he no longer chased Tiger now that the cat had shown him who was boss. Tiger had settled very well, better than she had hoped. Kristine had said they would but Evelyn had never quite believed her.

Oh, she must remind Kristine that it was time to cut back some of the summer growth in the garden as it was beginning to look very untidy. Perhaps she'd better wait until tomorrow before mentioning it, considering Kristine had been a little off-hand earlier.

Ralph had grown into such a charming boy, just like his father. It'd be quiet now without him. Evelyn had enjoyed the rides in his car although he did go very fast. He said he didn't but he made her quite nervous. Her stomach knotted up and she could feel the perspiration running down her back.

She had insisted on sitting in the front even when Stephanie had been with Ralph. She knew Stephanie resented it but she aimed to show her the proper way of doing things. In Evelyn's eyes the girl was a right madam. She hoped the liaison was not serious but it had been going on for some time.

Evelyn had thought Ralph would settle into one of the

professions when he left university next year but he didn't intend to.

'I'm going off round the world on a gap year, Gran,' he'd said. 'I didn't go away before Uni so I'm going now.'

She didn't know where he was going to get the money. 'It will cost a fortune,' she'd told him, but he replied 'No it won't, Gran, you do things on the cheap and take casual work when you can get it in the countries you visit. You don't have to eat much, carry everything on your back and even sleep on the beach in hot places.' He was so confident, but to his grandmother it sounded very irresponsible – and highly dangerous. She hoped he was not planning to take that Stephanie with him but she doubted he would. She was used to the soft life; thoroughly spoilt, it was time somebody said no to her.

Evelyn knew that living with Kristine and Derek was supposed to be on a trial basis but she was relieved not to have heard any more about going into a home. She hardly caused any disruption to their lives so, in her opinion, there was no reason to turn her out. Her fear of a home had been reinforced with what she had read in the paper only yesterday. The article said that half the elderly people in care homes were sedated to make them easier to look after and to save on staff. She knew it happened in the prisons too but was prepared to accept that there it might be necessary.

Evelyn's imagination was working overtime. Imagine it. If she was in a home she'd be a zombie by now. It was disgusting. No, she was quite sure they had changed their minds about putting her away. Besides, if they tried it, she would just refuse to go. Still, she wouldn't mention it unless they did. Her friends could come to Elmbrook and she could go out and about; Kristine even took her to church in spite of not going much herself. Because of her, she probably went more than she used to and that must be good for her soul if nothing else.

Evelyn was convinced Kristine had seen the light about these homes. Fiona told her that two of her other friends were in homes and they hated it. Most of the staff were black and some were so foreign, they didn't even speak English properly. Often nobody came when you rang the bell and you hardly got any food in some places. Fiona did say many of the black girls were kinder than the others but, even so, Evelyn was sure she would die at once if she went into a home.

'Would you like a coffee, Evelyn? I'm just making one and I expect you're cold now. The sun's not as warm as it was. Oh Buster, what a mess, your feet are so muddy.'

'Yes dear, thank you, it is rather chilly. I've been thinking while I've been walking round the garden, the oblong bed by the magnolia could do with some more interesting plants.' Evelyn had quite forgotten her resolve not to make any suggestions until the next day.

'Oh. What do you suggest?' There was always something that wasn't quite right or Evelyn felt could be changed. Kristine felt compelled to add, 'Bear in mind we can't do much about it until the spring.'

Evelyn was exasperated. Really! Anyone would think she didn't know anything about gardens.

'Of course, I know that, but now's the time to be planning for next year. I always did our garden plan in the autumn. If you order your plants now then they come at the right time. I can do a plan for you. It could be like that border we had in Church Close. The one down the south-facing fence. That was such a lovely garden. I do miss it and being in charge of my own affairs. Of course, I chose flowers for their colour co-ordination, much the best way. So much more satisfactory. I don't know what criteria you use. Perhaps you just do random planting?' Oh dear, it was obvious she had upset Kristine again. She couldn't imagine why. She was only trying to be helpful.

'I choose flowers for their scent first and colour second. Besides, I think any colour goes together in nature. God didn't colour co-ordinate the Universe. As to doing the ordering, I usually do it in January when the catalogues come out. That's been quite soon enough up till now.'

'There's no need to be so sharp, Kristine. I'm only trying to give you the benefit of my long experience and I thought you might be pleased if I took over some of your tasks.'

'It's very kind of you, Evelyn but the garden is something I enjoy and choosing the plants is all part of it. Perhaps we can look at the catalogues together when they come.' Kristine knew she'd have to pour oil on troubled waters now. She had been rather abrupt but she did love her garden. Elmbrook was her garden and she would organise it in her own way.

'Just as you like. I'm not one to interfere. I'm going to my room to read the paper.'

Kristine groaned inwardly. Oh Hell, she thought, I've upset the old thing now. We'll have frost all day but I'm blowed if I'll apologise. She could scream with the frustration of it all. She never got an apology from her mother-in-law. Kristine wouldn't have snapped at her about the garden if Evelyn hadn't already given her instructions that very morning about what Kristine should cook for her friends when they came next week.

'I wonder if you can manage something other than quiche,' she'd said. 'I always think quiche is so common, so everyday. Would you be able to manage some poached salmon with a tasty lemon sauce, or something of that order?'

She'd even offered to go to the supermarket to buy the fish so Kristine just knew she would have to find a recipe and make the effort. It would be something else next month and obviously she couldn't ever give Evelyn's friends quiche again. Kristine called any such dish, flan, because it could be made with a variety of ingredients and her friends often had flan. She didn't realise she was so common!

Evelyn never criticised the food when Derek was there. She always said how delicious everything was. That's what made it so difficult. If Kristine told Derek what his mother said he would say she was too sensitive. 'I'm sure Mother didn't mean it,' he'd say. 'You probably imagined her tone if you were a bit fraught. You suggested Mother had her friends to lunch. It's only reasonable that she gives them what she thinks they would like.'

Kristine knew she was snappy and unreasonable that morning. It was such a small matter but since Evelyn arrived, all these little things achieved gigantic proportions when she was trying to run the house to please everyone. Derek always made excuses for his mother and Kristine worried too much. She knew she did but she couldn't help it. It was her nature. Perhaps she should just ignore Evelyn or say yes, of course, just as you wish? But why should she? It was her home too and she, Kristine, should be able to do some of the things she wanted to do. Sometimes, she longed to tell her to shut up but then the vision of Angela shouting at the patients in Mountain View would spring to mind. But perhaps she could relieve her feelings another way, without hurting Evelyn.

That evening, Kristine hunted around in the study and found a small tape recorder Derek had bought for some project. She checked the tape was empty then sitting in the bedroom where she couldn't be overheard, she poured all her frustrations, complaints and even swear words against Evelyn, into the tiny machine. Oh, the relief! Why hadn't she thought of it before? This would be her safety valve when things got too much for her. Nobody else would ever know.

The days passed. Kristine tried to put her mind into neutral and get on with the housework. It was still fine enough to put the washing outside and she could pick some spinach and pull a few leeks for supper while she was out there. She loved her garden. She didn't want Evelyn taking over her domain, imposing her ideas. She'd had her turn, now it was Kristine's time to grow what she wanted, in her garden. Gradually, she had found scented plants for most months of the year, with hellebores and early snowdrops to cheer things up in the winter. Besides, Kristine had other things weighing on her mind. It would soon be Christmas and there was so much to do. Evelyn had already been chuntering about buying her cards and presents. When was she going to do it? Was Kristine going to take her? Could they go somewhere further away where there was more choice and some more up-market shops? Well, the cards could be bought in Bilston. Evelyn, like Kristine, always bought charity cards and there was usually a complete selection on sale in the library. Perhaps they could go to Bath for the day to buy presents? It would be an outing and she would enjoy browsing around some smarter shops They would have to go in the next week or so or the crowds would be impossible.

A list beforehand was essential too, as Evelyn was excruciatingly slow at making up her mind. She would make a date for next week and take Evelyn to Bath, or Cheltenham, she could choose. They would try and get the cards this week and do them over the weekend.

Chapter Nineteen

The following Tuesday dawned clear and bright so Kristine and Evelyn set off for Bath, complete with the present list. That was one good thing about not working. Kristine could choose what day she went out rather than have to go when she was off, rain or shine. They had bought the cards last Friday and spent the weekend writing them. Evelyn had been rather tiresome trying to decide whom to send to. She didn't seem to have a list from last year.

'Well I always send to the relatives and you must have a list of those, and then I send to all my friends, but of course some of them have died and I'm not sure about who has and who hasn't. Oh dear. I can't go sending to people and saying happy Christmas to Mary and Bill if Bill has died – but then it might be Mary who's died and I wouldn't send to just Bill as I never knew him like I knew Mary.'

Kristine did feel sorry for her. She was in a muddle over it but wanted to do the right thing. Derek came up with a satisfactory solution in the end.

'Why not just sign the ones you're not sure about? Say "Happy Christmas, much love Evelyn". You could even add "Hope this finds you well" if you wanted to be more chatty.'

'Derek, you're wonderful,' she'd beamed and got on with the cards at her own pace. They were able to look up the addresses for her and all were ready to post by Monday. Another task Kristine could tick off.

Bath still had some interesting independent shops as well as the usual chains and they managed to get a car park reasonably close to the main shopping centre. Kristine was able to get through her list quite quickly. Evelyn took considerably longer, not only because she couldn't decide which sweater or which piece of jewellery to buy, but she couldn't believe the prices. Although she had bought similar gifts last year she was thinking in terms of 1970s and 1980s prices, when she had shopped regularly. They broke up the day with lunch in the Regency restaurant, which served traditional food in a 'refined setting,' as Evelyn put it.

Kristine remembered to buy plenty of wrapping paper and gift tags and by four o'clock they were both worn out and ready to go home. It had been a successful day and Kristine knew that she would be able to pick up anything they had forgotten in the local shops.

On the way home, Kristine was mulling over Derek's proposal. Last night he had suggested they go on a short holiday in early December. Somewhere warm, and not too far away. Perhaps Cyprus or Tunisia. It would be nice to get some sun before the winter set in. He said she needed it, would give her a break.

'I think it's a lovely idea but could we make it February? There's always so much to do before Christmas and I'd much prefer having something to look forward to when the weather is cold and gloomy. Besides, what shall we do with Evelyn? We can't just leave her, especially in the winter when the fires need seeing to and what about the dog? Oh, and Tiger. Both will have to go into kennels.'

Kristine was torn. She was pleased Derek had suggested it as she'd love to have some sun and a time away but the difficulties seemed insurmountable, not least Evelyn's objections.

'Give me some credit for thinking it through before suggesting it. It was Mary, saying she was coming over and asking to stay for a week or two that gave me the idea. She could stay for three weeks if she wanted to but one of those weeks she could keep Mother company while we took a break. What do you say? Mary often stays with us and I know we're glad to have her but I'm sure she would do this for you. February is probably just as convenient for her if she has plenty of notice.'

'Are we going to ask Evelyn or are we just going to tell her? I suppose she has met Mary and she seemed to like her. Of course it all depends on whether Mary is prepared to do it. Mother doesn't need much looking after, except her meals and seeing she takes her medication. It would save putting Buster and Tiger in kennels. Mary loves dogs.' Kristine was beginning to think it was possible after all.

'Oh, I think we just have to tell her we are going away for a week and Mary is coming to stay with her. Can you email Mary tomorrow and see if she'll agree? Will we need to pay her? She'll get her keep of course and the use of the car. What do you think? We shan't say anything to Mother until Mary has said she can come.'

'Ooh. I feel quite excited already. I shouldn't as I don't want to be disappointed. You are a dear. Let's go to Tunisia, it sounds exotic. We haven't been there and I'm sure it will be quite warm in February. I'm certain Mary would be offended if we offer to pay her but we'll buy her something nice.'

Kristine had emailed Mary first thing that morning before they went to Bath and was then on tender hooks in case she didn't agree to come. She told herself that of course Mary would come but her temperament was such that she never believed treats for herself would eventuate. Mary was unlikely to reply instantly, she may only check her emails every few days.

Contrary to her expectations, Mary replied promptly. She'd be delighted to keep an eye on Evelyn for a week. If it was all right with them she would arrive about two days before they went away to receive instructions. Evelyn was sure to be on some sort of medication and it would be wise to know the doctor's number and so forth.

Instead of reassuring Kristine, it set her worrying about Evelyn getting sick while they were away. What if she took ill? Would they have to come back? Was it worth going just for a week if they might have to come back? 'For Heaven's sake,' Kristine told herself, 'just be thankful Mary is coming. She is perfectly competent and will be able to deal with any eventualities, better than you, probably!'

Derek went ahead and booked a hotel and the flights for the third week in February before Kristine thought of any more difficulties. He also undertook to tell his mother of the arrangements. Kristine knew Evelyn would make fewer objections if Derek told her. Ralph and Rebecca were delighted that they were going away and Rebecca and Tom agreed to act as next-of-kin in an emergency. They only lived an hour away and could help Mary should she run into any problems.

It was probably the thought of a holiday during the worst of the winter that made Christmas surprisingly less fraught than Kristine had expected. Ralph arrived the week before, mercifully without Stephanie. Her parents were taking her to some exotic location, he said. Kristine had finished the spare room but wanted it for Rebecca and Tom. They lived so close but she'd asked them to stay a few nights over the Christmas period and they had been delighted.

'Otherwise we can't partake of the Christmas spirit,' said Tom, 'and I hope Father Christmas is going to leave me a stocking.'

They turned up two days before Christmas and both were a great help entertaining Evelyn while Kristine coped with the usual preparations. They got Evelyn to help sort the cards into sizes so they could put them in the card tree and she tied new ribbon on the tree decorations.

Christmas morning Kristine was up early to get the turkey

in the oven. She had prepared and stuffed it late the night before and had even peeled the potatoes and rolled up the sausages in bacon to ease the pressure in the morning.

She took the opportunity to ring some of her family in New Zealand before the others were up. Hearing them all, sharing the laughter and the chat, always made her a little homesick but her life was here now. Having Derek and Ralph and Rebecca at home was all she really wanted although she wouldn't have minded a basketful of New Zealand sunshine. Katherine had told her they were having the warmest Christmas for many years.

After breakfast they all went to church and Evelyn was made very welcome by the vicar and the rest of the congregation. One or two of the older ones said Evelyn must come to tea with them over the holiday, which was an unexpected bonus. Kristine hoped they wouldn't forget to ask her. Rebecca helped with the lunch and the three men did the washing up.

After watching the Queen's speech, which Evelyn insisted upon doing, Ralph played Father Christmas and distributed the presents from under the tree. Evelyn joined in telling stories of past Christmases, trying to remember the best presents they'd ever had, and the worst. Evelyn recalled when, as a girl of ten, she had longed for a signet ring like several of her friends had. Receiving a tiny box, she had been overcome with excitement, only to be plunged into disappointment when she discovered a silver thimble nestling in the tissue paper. After tea and cake, Evelyn dozed by the fire, oblivious to a rather noisy game of Trivial Pursuits. At last, Kristine was able to relax and enjoy having her family around her.

Chapter Twenty

As the plane raced down the runway Kristine slowly exhaled and gave a sigh of contentment as she felt all the tension ebbing away. She had made it. They were on holiday with nothing to think about, nothing to worry about for a whole week. She wouldn't think of Evelyn, of Tiger and Buster, of Mary and how she would cope. She wouldn't have to think what to have for lunch or dinner or satisfy Evelyn's sudden desire for chocolate cake for tea. She would forget about the cold grey days and not getting the washing dry. She squeezed Derek's hand in gratitude for suggesting the holiday and accepted a glass of wine before lunch. They'd had an early start to be at the airport by ten o'clock for the flight at twelve fifteen and she knew it would not be long after she'd eaten that she would doze off.

The four-hour flight seemed amazingly short and after minimal formalities at the airport they were transported by coach to Hammamet, further down the coast from Tunis. Shielded from the searing heat by the air conditioning, Kristine was fascinated by the totally different landscape, alien to her experience. Sand coloured houses with a staircase up the outer wall to the flat roof; goats browsing the inedible-looking cacti she had only previously seen in the Snoopy cartoons. Colourful blankets on the occasional camel added splashes of interest to the general, rather monotonous fawn and brown of the desert.

Kristine unpacked as quickly as possible and changed into her swimsuit. She'd been tempted to buy a bikini but decided her figure wasn't quite up to it. She was glad Ralph and Rebecca weren't there to pass disparaging comments about her cellulite.

'I'm going straight to the beach. I want to have a swim before the sun goes down. Ugh, my body is so white. Makes me look unhealthy. Oh,' she giggled, 'You're even whiter than me.'

Derek had emerged from the bathroom in his trunks. All visible flesh smothered in factor 15 sun-cream. 'Will you put some cream on my back? I don't tan as well as you.' Kristine smeared the lotion on his back and a little on her face but she didn't bother anywhere else.

'Right, that's done, are you coming?'

'Try and stop me. I've got my book, my glasses and a towel and I see we can get drinks at a beach bar. Let's go and enjoy ourselves. I forbid you to think of home for the entire week.'

Kristine was in Heaven. Lying in the sun, book in one hand, drink in the other, the clear warm sea lapping gently on the shore a few yards in front of her. What more could she want? Derek and she had made a pact that they would have the first two days doing absolutely nothing. They would get up, have breakfast and spend the rest of the day on the beach. If this proved as relaxing as expected then they may have another day doing nothing, before exploring the markets and the old town. They might even take an evening excursion on a camel to the edge of the desert. On Thursday they would take a day trip to Tunis then they would have all day Friday and part of Saturday on the beach. Then it would be back to reality.

It was day five in Heaven when Derek's mobile woke her. They'd both collapsed into deck chairs on the beach, intending to get some pictures of the sunset. Neither of them had meant to doze off but they'd had an exhausting day in Tunis wandering around the souk, fighting off the hawkers trying to sell them everything from carpets to brass camels, carved chests to leather belts and handbags. At first it was fun trying to secure a bargain but Kristine soon tired of bartering for every item and preferred to go without. Who could be ringing them? It had to be Mary, or Rebecca.

'Hi, Rebecca, is there a problem? Oh, God. That's all we need. Where is she? How did it happen? No, no, she shouldn't blame herself, she can't help it if Mother falls over. Is she there? Put her on and your Mum will have a word.'

'Mother's fallen in the house and broken her leg and Mary feels it's her fault. You'd better have a word with Mary and get the full story. Rebecca's there with her. Tell her we'll try to get an earlier flight but it might be difficult.' Derek took his hand from the mouthpiece and handed the phone to Kristine.

'Mary, hello. What happened? Hmm. How is she taking it? Yes, of course. No you couldn't possibly. Derek says we'll try to get back soon, tomorrow if we can. We're not sure how easy it will be. We'll give you a call when we've talked to the Travel Agent and don't worry, it's not your fault.'

'Well, we can't help that, we've had a lovely five days, thanks to you, so we're very grateful. Yes I'll have a quick word with Rebecca, see you soon.'

Kristine reassured Rebecca that they would get back as soon as they could and they'd call her when they had a firm flight number. She sent Evelyn their love and handed the phone back to Derek.

'Poor Mother. I hope she's not in too much pain. Did Rebecca give you any details?'

'She said she was in Mowbury Hospital and was on pain relief. They are trying to decide what to do with the leg. It's a fairly straightforward fracture, so they might just pin it. She probably won't need traction. Apparently it happened in the night. Evelyn was going to the bathroom and slipped on that rug she insisted on having by the bed. Mary heard her cry out and was able to get the doctor and ambulance quite quickly. She and

Rebecca were really reluctant to call us and spoil our holiday but thought they had to. Besides, Evelyn was asking for you. Poor thing, she'll be very upset and disorientated in hospital.'

'I'll go in and see if I can get hold of the Rep. They usually appear in the bar in the evenings. You can stay there a bit longer if you like.'

'No, the sun's gone and the midges will be out so I may as well get a shower. We'll still need to eat this evening. I doubt they'll be able to organise a flight before tomorrow.'

They gathered up their things and returned to their room, each busy with their own thoughts. Derek knew his mother, at eighty-three, was vulnerable to a heart attack or stroke from the shock of the fall but at least she was in the best place and being professionally looked after. He tried not to think about what might happen and put his mind to getting back as soon as possible. Kristine's mind had leapt forward. What would happen when Evelyn came out of hospital? Would she be able to come back to Elmbrook? How mobile would she be? Was now the time to think again about homes? It was too early to think of post-hospital. Evelyn would have to have an anaesthetic if they were going to pin her leg and if they did she might be up and about quite quickly. There was no doubt she would want to go back to them.

The Rep wasn't there so they had an early supper, neither saying much. Kristine tried to reassure Derek that his mother was a tough old bird and would be fine. They sat in the bar until Megan appeared. She was suitably sympathetic and made a few calls on her mobile.

'Can't confirm anything until tomorrow but we think we can get you on a flight at two o'clock. Will that be OK?'

'That'd be fine, Megan. When will you know for sure?'

'About nine tomorrow, so you'd better be ready as the transport will have to leave almost at once. I'm afraid there'll be a charge, Mr Arnold, for the transport.'

'I expected that. We'll be ready and many thanks for your help. See you here just before nine then. Won't you join us for a farewell drink? We have had a splendid holiday and we're sorry to be going back early.'

Everything went according to plan and it was not long before they were on the flight home. Rebecca and Tom agreed to meet them and take them straight to the hospital to see Evelyn. She was very tearful when she saw Derek and held his hand so tightly he said afterwards he thought she'd stopped the circulation. She was in a four-bedded bay on the surgical ward and mercifully there were no men in the beds next to her or Evelyn would have had a fit. Kristine preferred the layout of the old Nightingale wards where you could keep an eye on all the patients as you walked up and down. The bays offered more privacy and didn't seem so stark but in some, with bays in odd corners, patients' needs could be overlooked. Still, this was better than most, with a straight central corridor, the bays on one side and a variety of service areas off the other.

Evelyn seemed bright enough but rather confused and kept asking Derek why he hadn't been there at once. The sister explained it was a simple break and they would put a plate in and she'd be up and about fairly quickly. They had waited to do the operation until Derek had returned. It would be done first thing in the morning and once she had recovered from the anaesthetic, Evelyn would start physio to help her walk and regain her confidence. Rebecca had seen that her grandmother had everything she needed so they kissed her goodnight and promised to return the next day when she came out of the theatre. When Kristine and Derek got home they spent some time reassuring Mary that Evelyn would be fine and the fall was certainly not her fault. She'd been great, thinking of everything they would need when they got back and making preparations for supper. Kristine unpacked and put the washing in the machine. She would have Evelyn's washing to do tomorrow.

Kristine, Derek and Mary turned up at the hospital at visiting time to find Evelyn still sleeping off the anaesthetic. Sister said all had gone well and if there were no hitches Mrs Arnold would be out of bed the following day. They sat with her for half an hour and were just about to leave when Evelyn opened her eyes and wanted to know where she was.

'You broke your leg, Mother, do you remember? You're in the hospital and have just had an operation to pin it together. How do you feel? Are you in any pain?'

'I thought you were abroad somewhere. Why didn't you come before? What am I doing here?'

'I've just told you, Mother. You've broken your leg. You have to be in here.'

'Sssh, Derek. Don't get cross with her. She's still recovering from the anaesthetic and is likely to be a bit confused, at least until tomorrow. We were away, Evelyn, and Mary was with you. She has been so good getting you to hospital straight away.' Kristine went closer to the bed and patted Evelyn's hand.

'It's all right. We are back from our holiday now and will be in to see you every day. Hopefully you won't be in here very long. They'll have you up and walking very soon. Is there anything you want?'

'Yes. I want to know why I'm here. My leg hurts and I want a drink. They wouldn't give me anything to drink when I asked before.'

Kristine checked with a passing nurse whether Evelyn could have anything to drink. She didn't seem particularly bothered or offer to get anything for her so Kristine found the kitchen, found a glass, filled it with water and took it back to Evelyn, who then said she'd prefer a cup of tea. Derek persuaded her to make do with the water for the moment and they'd try and rustle up a cup of tea but staff looked to be in short supply. Kristine and Mary sat with Evelyn while he wandered along the corridor looking for someone who might make some tea. There were two nurses bent over one of the computers at the work-station. Well, he imagined they were nurses. It was so difficult to tell these days with such a variety of uniforms. When Derek first met Kristine, he was a patient on her ward, in the days when nurses, staff nurses and sisters could easily be identified by their uniforms and their caps or veils. Nobody wore a hat of any description now, some were in trousers, some had stripes of varying colours, some plain colours and of course, quite a number were men.

There were so many gadgets and electronic devices to monitor that there didn't seem much time for actual nursing. Derek was defeated. He went back to his mother and suggested Kristine or Mary went into the kitchen and made a pot of tea. The staff could hardly complain as they were not prepared to do it. Between them they found what was needed and took Evelyn the tea, staying with her until she'd finished it.

Over the next few days they shared the visiting between them. Kristine enjoyed Mary's company over the weekend and was sorry when it was time for her to go. Evelyn was making good progress but Kristine was not impressed with the state of the ward. The floor didn't look as if it had been swept recently. There was a short piece of bandage under a trolley in the corner by Evelyn's bed and it was festooned with dust. It had obviously been there for some time.

The physiotherapist saw Evelyn every day and soon had her on a walking frame managing a few more yards each day. A week later Sister rang to say Evelyn was being transferred to the rehabilitation ward that afternoon. She could stay there for two weeks prior to her discharge. The hospital was anxious to free up the bed and Evelyn was desperate to get home. 'Probably afraid we're going to put her in a home,' was Kristine's observation as she came off the phone.

'Do you think we'll be able to manage her after this?' Derek was doubtful Kristine would be prepared to cope with his mother when she was visibly more frail.

'Let's wait and see what she's like in two weeks. It's only a week since her fall and she's probably still a bit shocked. She'll get more sleep and feel more relaxed away from all those really sick people and should get more intensive physio in the rehab ward. They'll assess her before she's discharged and we'll have a better idea how she can cope.'

Chapter Twenty One

Evelyn was discharged two weeks later. She had made considerable progress since leaving the main hospital but needed to regain her confidence. She was still using a walking frame for longer walks but should be able to manage with a stick around the house. Kristine noticed Evelyn had become quite subdued and was inclined to be tearful. She was fearful of being left alone and Kristine was afraid to leave her.

Although Dr Nicholls had arranged some physiotherapy for her at the hospital twice a week, Kristine was resigned to the fact she would need to be with Evelyn for the next few weeks while she was learning to walk properly again. It was irksome not being able to go out unless someone else was in the house but she knew it was necessary.

Gradually, Evelyn gained more confidence. She used a stick while inside but she preferred to keep the frame for use in the garden. However, she became querulous whenever Kristine said she was going out, even for just an hour. Occasionally, Evelyn's Bridge friends would take turns to spend the afternoon with her but Kristine did not like to ask them unless she had something essential to do. Going out for pleasure was becoming a thing of the past. One day she nipped out to the butcher and met Sue, by chance.

'Come and have a cup of coffee and catch up on the gossip.'

'I shouldn't really. I told Evelyn I wouldn't be long.'

'Well you won't, what's half an hour? You have to have some time to yourself. Just tell the old battle-axe you'll put her in a home if she doesn't stop moaning.'

Kristine laughed, 'Oh, Sue, you are terrible. All right then, a coffee would be nice but I really must be quick. Half an hour at the most.'

Of course, they got chatting and it was nearly an hour later when Kristine arrived home. Evelyn complained bitterly that she'd been left alone for such a long time.

'I thought I was going to have to find my own lunch, you were gone so long.'

'Now, Evelyn, you know I wouldn't leave you to do that. I always make arrangements and tell you if I'm not going to be here for meals. I met a friend and we had a chat, that's all.'

Kristine found herself snapping at Derek over minor matters. She was aggrieved he didn't seem to notice that their whole situation had changed. To him, Evelyn had broken her leg, she'd had it mended and now they were back to normal. For Kristine, everything had changed. Shouting into the tape recorder still helped but not quite as much as before.

Trying to spend any useful time in the garden was hopeless. Unless it was really warm Evelyn wasn't keen on sitting outside so Kristine, every twenty minutes or so, would have to remove her gloves and wellies, to go inside and check on her. When Derek was at home, he and Evelyn chatted away, often about when his father was alive and Derek was still a boy. This gave Kristine some respite but she just wished Evelyn would be so amenable when she was alone with her. Derek genuinely believed that because his mother was well and apparently happy, Kristine must be doing a good job and therefore she would also be happy. Job satisfaction and all that. Perhaps, if Kristine had been able to see her care of Evelyn as a job well done she might have been more able to ignore the countless minor irritations that were blighting her life. But she couldn't and she worried endlessly about everything. The weeks turned into a month and then two and the strain was beginning to tell.

Rebecca arrived unexpectedly one afternoon and found

her mother near to tears. Fortunately, Evelyn was having her nap so Rebecca made Kristine a coffee and sat her down for a heart to heart.

'She's too much for you, isn't she? You've lost weight and you never get out these days. What does Dad say?'

'I haven't bothered him because he's been quite busy at work. And anyway, he doesn't think there's a problem because his mother is perfectly charming to him and always seems happy when he's around. But that's only at weekends unfortunately and he just doesn't understand what she's like when it's just the two of us.'

'You worry about her too much. You should go out and leave her more often. I'm sure she'd be perfectly all right.'

'Oh. I know I worry unnecessarily but she picks at me all the time and forever wants me to do things for her. If I don't, she puts on such a sorrowful act that I have to spend the next hour or so making amends. I do feel tired, and not being able to go out without worrying that she'll fall again is quite a strain. It sounds pathetic though; one old lady who gets up and can feed herself and walk about, what's so difficult about that? I should be able to cope. Hundreds of others do and for much longer than I've had to, and under worse conditions.'

'That's not the point. She might get up but you have to help her, do her meals, and it's not as if she eats what you put in front of her. You do the shopping, help her bath, do her clothes and on top of that you have to be constantly on the lookout in case she falls or has a diabetic turn or whatever. I expect she moans all the time too.'

'No, she doesn't moan exactly, it's more niggardly criticisms, such as, "Are you going out again, which lunch is it this time, not another coffee morning," that sort of thing. Makes me feel as if I go out all the time, which I don't. She's very subdued otherwise and we hardly have any normal, chatty conversation. I think she chats away to her Bridge friends but then I usually leave them to it and take that opportunity to do what I have to do. At least they still come, usually weekly but sometimes only once a fortnight. It makes me more anxious than cross, worried that there might be something I should be doing that I'm not.'

'Have you spoken to the doctor? He should be able to advise you.'

'I shall have to speak to Dad about her first. He'll say she has to go in a home and I expect the doctor will too. Maybe that's what she is afraid of. Perhaps if I reassured her that we are not going to turn her out she might pick up?' Rebecca was horrified,

'You can't tell her that! You might have to, eventually. One thing's for sure, you can't carry on like this. I'll try and come over for a day a fortnight and give you a break. I know I said I was going to and I haven't done it but I'll start on Monday. Perhaps you could get a carer in for one day on the alternate week then you could be sure of one whole day a week to yourself; it's bound to make a difference.'

'If you could that would be great, it would help enormously. I'll talk to your father this evening and see what he can suggest. I think we have to try the carer route before we consider the homes. I might just make enquiries at Lakeside and Oakhurst to see if they have any vacancies. There's another option of course, respite care. Julia Stuart looked after her mother-in-law for about two years but she only agreed to do it if the old girl went in for respite two weeks in six. It seemed to work very well but then her ma-in-law may have been more accommodating than Granny.'

'That wouldn't be difficult....:' 'Kristine, are you there.' Evelyn's querulous voice echoed down the passage.

'Speak of the devil. I'll go and see what the old bag wants while you finish your coffee'

'Oh do be kind to her, Rebecca. You'll be old eventually and you'll want someone being nice to you.'

'Don't worry Mum, I'll be charming,'

'Kristine, where are you?' They could hear her muttering, 'I expect she's gone and left me again.'

'I'm coming, Granny. Nobody's gone and left you,' Thinking, *It's a pity they didn't once in awhile.* She said, 'Mum is having a sit down. Now what can I get you?'

Kristine relaxed back in the chair and contemplated her next move. She was relieved she'd shared her worries with Rebecca and she must now talk to Derek. The situation had to change or she'd go mad. Evelyn was marginally less demanding than before her fall but was doing less and less for herself. Even at night Kristine had to get up and see her to the loo. Maybe Derek could persuade his mother to have a commode in her room. It needn't stay there all day, just at night. When Kristine had mentioned it to Evelyn she'd dismissed the idea as disgusting. That evening, once Evelyn had retired to bed Kristine broached the subject of his mother to Derek. He was expecting it.

'I was going to talk to you about Mother. Why didn't you mention the difficulties? Rebecca told me how upset you were. I should have noticed the problems but I've had other things on my mind, I'm sorry.'

'She needn't have mentioned it. I told her I would speak to you but it was because I knew you were busy that I didn't say anything. I'm afraid it has all got too much for me, especially having to get up in the night to take her to the toilet. I don't sleep properly as I'm on edge in case I don't hear her and she falls again.'

'Surely you can get a commode or whatever it's called, to have in her room. You'd have to empty it of course but wouldn't it be better then getting up in the night?'

'Of course it would. Don't you think I haven't thought of that, but your mother won't hear of it, says it's disgusting having a loo in your bedroom.'

'I'll talk to her. It's unreasonable, expecting you to get up in the night and look after her in the day.'

'Perhaps we could get respite care for her. A week here and there would help enormously and would break her into homes gradually so it won't be so bad when she eventually has to go into one.'

'What does that entail? Do they go into a home for a bit and then come out? Isn't that rather unsettling and disruptive? After she's been in the first time she wouldn't want to go in again.'

Derek was quickly putting Kristine off the idea. Would Evelyn be worse when she came out? Oh God. It was all so difficult. They should have put her in a home in the first instance. Kristine said it was an interim solution and she realised it wasn't ideal. She'd ring a couple of the homes in the morning and see if they had any rooms available for respite but first of all Derek would have to have a serious discussion with his mother.

'I've had enough tonight. I'm taking a cup of tea and an early night as I'm bound to have to get up at least once. I feel better now I've talked to you and Rebecca. She's promised to come over and be with Evelyn one day a fortnight and if we can get a carer in for another day or get some respite care things will be better.'

Next morning Derek took his mother into the garden. Early May was one of the nicest times of the year. The sun was pleasantly warm and the garden was full of flowers. Evelyn was always more mellow when surrounded by flowers and trees. The daffodils were over but the wisteria and the honeysuckle were glorious, their perfume enough to put anyone in a good mood.

'Mother, we need to have a serious discussion about your care. You have slowed up a lot since your accident and Kristine is not sure that she is adequately meeting your needs.' Derek was secretly pleased with that sentence. 'Meeting your needs' showed that his mother's wishes were foremost in their minds. Evelyn thought no such thing as Kristine could have warned him.

'She's tired of keeping an eye on me, I suppose. After all, that's all she does. I mean it's not extra to cook a little more for me or wash a few clothes when she's doing the washing for both of you. I still dust my room, dress and feed myself and keep myself occupied. What's difficult about that?'

'There's a lot more to it than that, Mother, and you know it. She worries about you constantly, knowing she can't be near you all the time. She doesn't like going to the shops and leaving you in case you fall; you're not very steady on your feet these days. She can go into Bilston but never further afield unless she gets someone to sit with you. Then there's the business of getting up in the night.' Derek found this embarrassing but he plunged on. 'It would be so helpful to Kristine if you had a commode in your room, just at night of course, not in the daytime. Nobody else need know it was there.'

Evelyn's lip trembled. She sniffed loudly and fished out a handkerchief from her pocket. 'I think it's disgusting having a commode in the bedroom, like having a chamber pot under the bed. People of our standing don't have such things. While I can get to the bathroom I intend to do so.'

'You're talking rubbish, Mother. Before they had bathrooms like they have today, everybody, and I mean everybody, even the Royal Family, had chamber pots under the bed for night-time use. It's nice if you don't have to but there is no shame about having a commode in the bedroom. Some of them, especially French ones, were very elegant pieces of furniture. I've seen them reported in antique magazines as going for thousands of pounds. Besides, it's dangerous for you to go down the passage in the night and Kristine can't sleep properly, listening out for you.'

'I thought so. It's all about Kristine and what she wants, it's not about me at all.'

At that moment Kristine came round the path with a tray of coffee and a cheerful smile.

'I'm sure you two are ready for some coffee. Have you put the world to rights?'

'I hear you want to get rid of me, Kristine. I thought it was only a matter of time before you tried to put me in a home. It's always been your intention.'

Derek jumped in before Kristine could say anything she might regret.

'That was a terribly hurtful thing to say, Mother, and I'm sure you didn't mean it. Kristine has always had your well-being at heart and wants to do the very best for you, as I do. I said this was a serious discussion and I meant it. You must agree to a commode in the bedroom and then we shall see if we can get a home help or a carer to come in a few hours a week to give Kristine a break. She'll be able to relax if she knows someone capable is looking out for you. Failing that I'm afraid it will have to be a week or two's respite in a residential home. Let's face it, if Kristine didn't care for you she wouldn't get up in the night to you and she would go out in the day without worrying whether you were OK or not, so I think you owe her an apology.'

Kristine was grateful for Derek's intervention. She would have loved to say, '*You're an ungrateful old woman and should go in a home tomorrow*' but she realised life would be a lot easier if Evelyn didn't lose face. She patted her arm and said,

'It's all right. I know you didn't mean it. We are both trying to make life as comfortable as possible for you. If you will allow me to get a commode to put in your room for the night, life will be much easier for both of us.'

'If I must, I will have it. I do appreciate what you're trying to do but my life is so different and undignified these days. I don't think either of you realise just how galling it is to have to rely on other people for help with personal things which should be private.'

Kristine and Derek accepted that this was the closest they were going to get to an apology. They had broached the subject and cleared the air. It would be easier now to introduce a few changes to make life more agreeable all round.

'Come on, Mother, if you've finished your coffee, take my arm and we'll have a walk around the garden before lunch. It must be warm as I see Tiger has ventured out.'

Chapter Twenty Two

Carol, the cheerful woman from Social Services whom Kristine was used to dealing with, was happy to provide a commode. It could be delivered if they were unable to pick it up. Of course it was standard issue and most unattractive but Kristine dealt with that. An old piece of floral material made a skirt for the legs, with enough left over to make a cover for the whole thing, effectively disguising it when not in use. Evelyn accepted it with bad grace but agreed to use it during the night.

Life went on much as before for several months. Kristine was getting much more sleep so she could cope better during the day. Rebecca managed to come for the best part of a day every two or three weeks, enabling Kristine to see her friends or just browse the shops if that's what she felt like. The weekly Bridge sessions had finally become fortnightly but Evelyn and her friends were still meeting for lunch every few weeks.

When Ralph finished at university in the summer he provided some respite for Kristine by ferrying Evelyn to her various social appointments. He also took her on several drives into the countryside before he sold his car to improve his cash flow. Kristine begged him not to drive too fast as Evelyn always looked decidedly pale on her return from these jaunts.

Ralph planned to go into banking where he was blithely confident of making huge sums of money, but first he and a friend were taking off round the world for six months, going where the spirit took them. He would be visiting his aunts and uncle in New Zealand and getting to know his cousins a little better. He couldn't really find out what people were like from photos and letters although he was in email contact with two of his male cousins.

His parents had taken him and Rebecca to see their mother's family fourteen years before but he couldn't remember much about them. From memory, the best thing about New Zealand was the beaches. He discussed his plans with his grandmother, tracing his probable itinerary on the map and making hair-raising claims that he was going to bungy jump, do free fall parachuting and white-water rafting. All of this alarmed Evelyn greatly and she kept telling him not to take risks. However, there is no doubt Ralph had a beneficial effect on Evelyn because she looked on him as another Derek.

The downside came when it was time for Ralph to leave. He and Edward waited anxiously for their results before setting off. Fortunately, they both got a 2-1 and went off in a wave of euphoria, first stop Thailand, to relax on the beach.

The house was quiet without him and Evelyn more cantankerous than usual. She was eating less and her diabetes, previously under control, showed signs of instability. Several times in the last month Kristine had had to call Dr Nicholls or the nurse to adjust her medication. When it happened a third time the doctor took Kristine aside and said he felt it was time Evelyn had more full time nursing care. She was not eating the right food or not enough of it and her diabetes needed closer monitoring.

Kristine was indignant. 'Are you suggesting I don't know how to feed her properly? She demands some special food and then when I go to the trouble and expense of preparing it, she says she doesn't want it. I don't see how a nursing home, even the best one, could cope any better, faced with that.'

'Certainly not. I know the difficulties but she is less likely to question or refuse food given her by those she sees as professionals. All right, I know you are a nurse but she doesn't see you as that. You must remember, I have known your mother-in-law for many, many years and it is not an idle boast that she usually listens to me when I say, "Mrs Arnold, you must do this for your own good." Besides, it has taken quite a toll out of you these last two years and you should not continue to do it, for your own good. If it would help, I will suggest it to her, as a trial at first and see how it goes.'

Realising she had been unduly touchy, Kristine thanked him. 'That would be helpful. She will only think I am trying to get rid of her if I do it. I'll talk to Derek when he comes home. I'm sure she will need to be assessed and we shall have to let her see a couple of homes. I promised she would choose if it ever came to that.'

Doctor Nicholls went to have a private chat with Evelyn. It was agreed that Derek and Kristine would take her to see Lakeside and Oakhurst and she could choose. Providing they had a vacancy, it would be up to the selected home to assess Evelyn for admission.

She was adamant that it would only be for two weeks, a month at the very most but Dr Nicholls warned her she would have to stay until her diabetes was stabilised. Each home had a single room available so Kristine made an appointment for the following Saturday to take Evelyn to inspect them.

When the day finally arrived Derek had difficulty keeping a straight face as he came from his mother's room. 'You'd think she was going to see the Queen, she's dolled up to the nines, make-up, jewellery, the lot.'

'I expect she wants to make a good impression. Won't want them to think she needs to go into a home and she'll want to be superior to the other residents and the staff of course. Is she ready? We'd better go, or we'll be late and get a black mark.'

Oakhurst was the first port of call and it was certainly impressive. The place had been purpose built four years previously and was modern and functional. Unobtrusive ramps, attractive polished wood handrails, light, airy sitting rooms and tasteful furnishings. Immaculate lawns and flowerbeds surrounded the building. No wonder it was so expensive. A pleasant, cheerful member of staff showed the three of them to Matron's office before asking if they'd like tea or coffee. Derek whispered to Kristine, 'I didn't think you were supposed to call them Matron these days.'

'I think it's OK in a nursing home and that's what this is.'

'Good morning, Mrs Arnold, Mr and Mrs Arnold. My name is Freda Perkins. Do sit down.'

They had all agreed before leaving home that Evelyn would ask and answer the questions as she was the one having the care. Kristine and Derek would intervene only if necessary. They had been over the questions they needed to ask and didn't see any difficulties.

'Perhaps you would start with your questions, Mrs Arnold. By the way, what do you prefer to be called, Mrs Arnold or by your Christian name –let me see, ah here it is, Evelyn.'

'Oh, Mrs Arnold of course. Only my intimate friends call me Evelyn. I would have to have my own room you know.'

'No difficulties there, Mrs Arnold, all our rooms are single occupancy. Nobody wants to share a room with a stranger in what is to be their home.'

Kristine gave an agonised glance at Derek as she waited for the predictable response from Evelyn.

'I think you are under a misapprehension, Matron. This is not to be my home. If I come here, and I have yet to decide, it will be to get my diabetes properly stabilised as my doctor has advised, and then I shall be going back to live with my son.'

Kristine gave Matron full marks for her quick recovery.

'Of course, I quite understand. You must forgive me, we don't often have respite patients because we are usually full and I am normally assessing permanent residents. However, when charming Dr Nicholls asked if we could accommodate one of his special patients we were glad to be able to help.'

Suitably mollified, Evelyn went on with her questions and seemed satisfied with the answers. The coffee arrived at this point, creating a break in proceedings. Kristine could see Evelyn noting the fine china, the silver coffee pot, the good quality biscuits. Calculated to impress and succeeding very nicely.

'Now, Mrs Arnold, there are some questions I need to ask you. You will find some of the questions very elementary but I assure you they are necessary so we can give you the care you expect and deserve while you are spending some time with us. That is always assuming that you decide to come here of course. Are you able to dress yourself and attend to your own toilet?'

'I would have thought that was obvious.'

'I did warn you, Mrs Arnold, that these questions are basic. I can see very clearly that you can do these things but the girls who will be looking after you need to know what you can do without having to ask you all the time. Anyone who stays with us for however long, needs to have a care plan and the answers to these questions are part of that plan. I see you have a stick. Do you need it all the time or can you walk unaided?'

'I could manage without it but since I broke my leg some months ago, I prefer to have it with me for confidence.'

Kristine was about to intervene at this blatant stretching of the truth but Derek nudged her just in time. The staff would find out soon enough that she was telling fibs. She might not even come to Oakhurst so it was kinder to let her keep up a front while she could.

'That's excellent. I imagine, though, that you would need a little help to take a bath? To have someone with you so you don't fall.'

'Yes, well my daughter-in-law is usually about when I have a bath so it would help to have someone nearby.'

Miss Perkins pressed on. 'I see you wear glasses. Do you have different ones for reading?'

'Oh no. These are the latest kind that allows me to read and to see in the distance. They're graduated I believe. Very expensive they were too.'

Matron was quick to concur. 'Indeed they are. Mine are varifocal too but I think they justify the expense.'

Derek was getting very bored and rather embarrassed at having to listen to this close questioning of his mother's personal habits. He would have preferred to wander around the garden and leave the details to the women but he'd promised Kristine that he'd stay as backup in case his mother became difficult. He wandered over to the window and tried not to listen to the discussions; about her teeth, her own or false, how many times she got up to the loo in the night, and whether her bowels were regular or not.

Finally the questions were finished. Matron seemed happy with the answers and declared herself satisfied that Oakhurst would be able to provide the care that Evelyn needed. Dr Nicholls would be changing and reassessing her medication, if and when she came in. Then it came to the question of the fees. Here Derek was all attention. This was the difficult part.

'Our weekly fee for those on respite is £600 but that does include almost everything. I say almost because the hairdresser is extra but £5.50 for a wash and set is extremely reasonable, I'm sure you'll agree. Oh, and a newspaper would be extra if Mrs Arnold wants her own, although we do have a few copies of the Times for shared use.'

'I would have to have my own because I do the crossword every day.'

Another exaggeration. Kristine couldn't remember the last time Evelyn got more than two words of the crossword. Matron offered to show them around the home.

'You'll want to see what the bedrooms are like and look

at the dining room and sitting areas. We do have our own laundry so the washing is done in house although I advise you to give your daughter-in-law any special woollens or delicates, to wash at home. With the best will in the world we cannot do the washing as well as you would yourself.'

They were able to peep into one or two of the residents' rooms. They appeared to have good furniture and carpet with attractive curtains. One even had a small fridge, which excited comment from Derek.

'Is that for the gin and tonic, Matron?'

'Not exactly, Mr Arnold, although residents can keep a small amount of drink in their rooms, if permitted by the doctor of course. Those who opt to have a fridge use it for fruit or cheese and butter or other treats that their relatives bring them. Permanent residents usually bring their own furniture too.'

Derek muttered to Kristine that he thought, for the price, Evelyn should get a gin and tonic every evening.

Half an hour later they took their leave of Freda Perkins, promising to let her know within the week if they required the room. It had taken longer than they expected so they went to The Wheat Sheaf in Bilston for lunch, before going to repeat the process at Lakeside in the afternoon.

Evelyn was rather quiet during lunch and had to be encouraged to eat her salmon salad. She had found the whole performance dispiriting, which was rather what she expected. She didn't want to go into a nursing home, even if it was only for a few weeks. She couldn't help thinking about her friend Elizabeth who had gone to live in a home in Scarborough, to be near her daughter. For a while she had sent Evelyn letters, most of them complaining about the home, how she felt neglected, how miserable she was, but soon there was nothing.

Finally, Jane Weston had written to say her mother's

memory was failing and it was pointless to write to her any more. She couldn't remember any of her old friends.

Evelyn couldn't bear that to happen to her and she felt sure it would, once she got into one of those places. Would Julia, Rose and Fiona visit her or would they just forget about her? Even in Oakhurst, the residents who were sitting in the lounges did not appear to be talking to each other, just staring into space. Matron had said there were various forms of activity laid on but it was probably that frightful bingo or community singing.

'Come along, Mother, eat up your strawberries. We must get to our appointment at Lakeside. This shouldn't take quite so long because you know what the questions are likely to be and you also know what to ask.'

'It's all right for you, Derek, you don't have to go into one of these awful places.'

'You can't possibly call Oakhurst awful, Mother. It looked like a luxury hotel to me.'

Kristine thought her mother-in-law unusually perceptive when she retorted, 'I agree that's what it looked like but don't forget, that was "front of house", it's what happens behind the scenes that you want to know about and you don't find out that until later.'

Kristine did her best to cheer her up. 'Try not to get too despondent about it, Evelyn. Just as soon as your diabetes is under control you will be able to come back to us. Try and keep a positive attitude, it will help. Look on it as another of life's experiences.'

'I don't need new experiences at my time of life, Kristine, I need familiar routine', retorted Evelyn.

Kristine was taken aback to find that the Care Manager had changed since she had visited Lakeside eighteen months before. The new woman, Ruth Stevens, introduced herself and explained that Eileen Rogers had left because of illness.

However, she was able to find the information relating to Evelyn that Kristine had provided on her previous visit. Kristine briefly brought her up to date, explaining that they were just looking for a few weeks respite care where Dr Nicholls could stabilise Evelyn's diabetes.

'I think last time you came you were looking for a permanent place for Mrs Arnold. Is that not the case now?'

'Oh no. Mrs Arnold came to live with us in the end and I think it has been a happy arrangement, hasn't it, Evelyn?' Kristine was grateful Rebecca wasn't there to witness her blatant lie. 'There is just one thing, my mother-in-law fell and broke her leg last February so she is slightly less mobile than she was. Still, she will be able to answer any questions you have.'

'Before we begin, I must tell you that we are now dual registered which means we are a nursing home as well as residential. This does mean that if someone initially does not need nursing care but subsequently does, then they do not have to move out.'

Evelyn was quick to point out that this did not affect her as she was only there for respite and would be gone in a few weeks. The questions followed much the same pattern as at Oakhurst and the answers seemed equally satisfactory to Kristine and Evelyn. Derek felt utterly redundant and this time he excused himself and took a walk in the garden. Evelyn made no protest, as she was as embarrassed as Derek, detailing her personal habits in front of her son. They met up with him again on their tour of the home.

It was an older building than Oakhurst but in a charming setting with an oval lake flanked by rhododendrons at one end and several benches nearby. Two benches were occupied by residents and a member of staff, all happily chatting together. Kristine could see the glint of goldfish near the surface of the lake. It helped seeing both homes on a lovely sunny day as it gave the best possible impression.

If anything, the rooms were slightly larger than those in Oakhurst and the decoration a little more faded. However, permanent residents could take in their own furniture, carpet, curtains and even bed linen if they wished, although they had to comply with the fire retardant legislation. The whole atmosphere of both homes was such an improvement on Kristine's past experience, she felt sure Evelyn would be safe and well cared for in either place. It was ironic that it was the hospitals these days that offered such poor care, with endless reports of super-bugs and general neglect.

They thanked Miss Stevens for her time and assured her they would be in touch as soon as possible as to whether or not they wanted the room. Just as they were leaving, a rather sprightly old lady came round the corner of the house. She was wearing a pretty floral dress, a large straw hat and carrying a voluminous canvas bag.

'Why it's Nancy, Nancy Jackson. Whatever are you doing here? I haven't seen you for ages and why aren't you in Surrey?' Evelyn was delighted to see a familiar face and they clasped each other warmly with both hands.

'I might ask you the same question, Evelyn Arnold. Not about Surrey of course but why are you here? I am here because when my Frank died, my daughter Jocelyn, you know the one who lives near Bath, insisted I came to be nearer them. Less distance for them to come and see me, you know, with the children and everything.'

'But in a home! Don't you hate it? Why couldn't you live with them?'

'Oh no, that would be worse. I should hate it. Actually I don't mind it here, they're very kind and Jocelyn and Richard take me out and I stay with them for the odd weekend. I don't drive any more but the home has a minibus and I can go to town if I want to. But tell me, what's happening to you?'

Evelyn explained that she had been looking at nursing homes for brief respite to sort out her diabetes. 'I was supposed to decide whether I would go into Oakhurst or here. Seeing you here, Nancy, has settled it. Having someone I know to talk to will make all the difference. Derek, I must come here. Do you want to tell Matron while we're here? I should hate for her to give the room to someone else now that I've made up my mind.'

'Are you sure, Mother? I don't want you making up your mind on the spur of the moment and then regretting it tomorrow. Kristine, did you ask about the fees? I should have remembered but I had to get out. It's just not my scene. I'm sure you got all the details.'

'Yes we did. They've gone up since I last came here of course but they're still cheaper than Oakhurst at £520 for residential and £580 for nursing.'

'What will Evelyn be, for respite?'

'She'll be residential but there will be a bit extra for any nursing care she has in connection with the stabilisation of her diabetes. I should go back and tell Matron now. It will be nice for Evelyn to be here while her friend is here.'

Derek went back inside and made the arrangements. Dr Nicholls had said he would organise the necessary treatment just as soon as Evelyn had found a place so they booked the room for Wednesday of the next week. Evelyn said goodbye to her friend, waving and saying she would see her soon. It was a very much more cheerful lady they were taking home than they had brought out that morning. Kristine could not believe their good fortune. Instead of tears and reluctance to go into 'one of those horrible places', Evelyn was quite looking forward to it.

'Of course I'm not staying in there, so it will be quite like a holiday. I haven't been on holiday for years, as you know.'

'You must make the most of it, Mother. I'll order the Times for you to be delivered every day and you must take in some books to read, although I rather fancy you and Nancy will be gossiping all day and won't have time for anything else.'

'We don't gossip, as you call it, Derek. We catch up on the news and I haven't seen Nancy for, oh it must be six or seven years. I feel very sorry for her that Jocelyn and Richard don't have her living with them. I can't imagine why they don't. Long Meadow is a large establishment and I know they are not short of money.'

Kristine felt she must defend Jocelyn although she didn't know her well, or her circumstances.

'Well she does have four children, Evelyn, and they are quite a lot younger than ours and still away at school. They are at different schools and have different holidays. It must be very hard to juggle the terms and the holidays and run the farm. I would think Nancy is better off where she is, with the family coming to visit her regularly.'

'Well, I'm just glad it's not me. I shall be very pleased to get back to Elmbrook Manor after my little holiday.'

On the Tuesday evening Kristine helped Evelyn pack a small bag with everything her mother-in-law deemed necessary. She had to dissuade her from taking her entire jewellery box with her. The Care Manager had specifically asked Kristine to see that Evelyn did not bring valuable items into the home. Kristine assured Evelyn she would bring in anything she had forgotten or found she needed. Next morning, armed with Evelyn's current medication, they drove the half hour journey to Lakeside, arriving in time for coffee. Kristine declined the offer to join them, left Evelyn in Matron's capable hands and drove in to Bilston to have coffee with her friend Sue. She could not believe the relief she felt. A huge cloud had been lifted from her shoulders.

She was free. Her life was her own again for two, possibly three precious weeks.

'One half of me feels elated and the other half feels guilty as Hell.'

Sue was incredulous. 'Why on earth do you feel guilty? You've looked after the old bat for nearly two years, it's time you had a rest. Besides, she's there at the request of the doctor so guilt doesn't come into it.'

'Yes it does, as I'm so pleased she's not with us any more, at least for the moment. Years ago when I worked in an old peoples' home I thought children were terrible, palming their parents off into institutions so they could enjoy life.' It was the first time Kristine had voiced her guilty feelings to anyone else. 'Now I'm no better than them.'

Sue couldn't see where the guilt came in. 'When we're young we all have these idealistic views of life. It's only when we grow up that reality kicks in. It's only natural to be pleased that you've some time to yourself. She's been nothing but a thorn in your side since you've had her there, all your married life in fact. I should be over the moon.'

'You sound just like Rebecca. She calls Evelyn an old bat too, but she isn't that bad. Her selfishness is partly her upbringing and partly Derek's father's fault for indulging her all the time. I'm to blame too because I worry too much about her; worry if she's happy, worry if she's safe, worry if I've upset her. I should let it all wash over me.'

'Kristine you are the limit. You're too moral for your own good. You've given the woman a safe, warm home for Heaven's sake. You're not responsible for her personal happiness. That has to come from inside herself. She'd be a lot happier if she wasn't so self-centred and critical of everyone else.'

'I'm sure you're right, Sue. She depended totally on Brian for everything and they did everything together which has made me realise how important it is for wives, and husbands, to have their own friends and develop their own interests. Well, now that I am free, let's go and do some shopping and then have a nice lunch at the Olive Branch. It's on me today and don't let's mention Evelyn again. I'll just enjoy my freedom.'

Chapter Twenty Three

The three weeks went all too quickly. Kristine made the most of her freedom, going to lunch with her friends or shopping in Bath, even having a dinner party. Of course she could do that whether Evelyn was there or not but somehow she never had the energy or the incentive. She called in to see Evelyn once a week, as Derek did and Rebecca even made the effort. It was as well Evelyn returned when she did or Kristine would have found it very difficult to have her back. She had had time to herself because she wasn't working and she didn't have Evelyn. Life had suddenly become very pleasant.

Evelyn had not found it such a disagreeable experience as she had imagined, largely because Nancy was there. They had been able to have meals together, watch the odd TV programme in Nancy's room and talk over old times. They even had a sherry together before lunch. Kristine and Nancy's daughter, Jocelyn made sure they took treats to them both. Dr Nicholls professed himself pleased with Evelyn's progress in stabilising her diabetes. She had been sticking to her diet and eating what was put in front of her. Again this was Nancy's influence. Nancy wasn't particularly fussed about food and said as long as she had enough that was all that mattered. Kristine felt it was a pity that some of Nancy's outgoing nature and lack of snobbery had not rubbed off on Evelyn. Nancy mixed happily with the other residents but Evelyn thought herself a cut above most of them and was very choosey about whom she'd speak to. She made no secret of the fact she thought the other residents were boring and vulgar, much to Kristine's embarrassment. Evelyn made no attempt to get to know any of them so how could she judge?

For several weeks after Evelyn came home she asked to go and visit Nancy so Kristine would drop her there for an hour or so while she did her shopping. Christmas was fast approaching and it was time to do the cards and buy the presents again. Evelyn didn't seem quite so keen to go on a shopping expedition this year. Bilston would be quite far enough. Nancy had confessed that she just gave her daughter Jocelyn a list and she did it all. So much easier. For Nancy maybe, thought Kristine, but what about her daughter? Jocelyn probably didn't find it so convenient, with a home, a husband and four children to contend with. It was beginning to dawn on Evelyn that there were advantages to being in a home. Not having to think about what to do each day or what to buy and she rather enjoyed being waited on. It was like old times when she'd had plenty of help in the house. She began to think she might like to go back for a few weeks and keep Nancy company. She was sure Kristine wouldn't mind, just for a few weeks. Not permanently, of course.

'You know, Kristine, I would quite like to go back into Lakeside for a few weeks to keep Nancy company. I think she's rather lonely. Of course, I don't want to go in permanently, but perhaps for a month or so. What do you think? You wouldn't be offended would you?'

Kristine was almost lost for words. It was as unexpected as it was welcome but she was careful not to show her delight at this development.

'I'm certainly not offended. I am very pleased that you and Nancy got on so well. But would you want to go before Christmas? Wouldn't it be nice to have Christmas here with us?' Secretly, Kristine would have loved to have Christmas on their own, not have to worry about whether Evelyn was happy or not. But on second thoughts it would be better to have Evelyn at home with them. If she was in Lakeside they'd still all have to go and visit her which would break up the day. When would they have Christmas lunch? They'd probably have to have it in the evening and they wouldn't be able to relax. Evelyn might decide at the last minute she wanted to come out for the day. No. Better to have Evelyn until after Christmas. Besides, Kristine reminded Evelyn that Nancy would probably be going to her daughter's for Christmas too.

'You could go in for a few weeks in the New Year. The only difficulty I can see is that Lakeside doesn't normally take respite residents, only if the doctor recommends them and if they have room. They much prefer permanent residents because it helps their funds and makes staffing easier. We can ask Derek his opinion this evening and I'll ring Miss Stevens in the morning.'

Kristine warned Derek to show suitable sorrow, but not too much, at his mother's wish to leave them again so soon. He was as flabbergasted as Kristine that Evelyn had come to this idea on her own. He did think it would be better after Christmas to avoid having to fetch and carry his mother on Christmas Day. Evelyn did stress several times that it would only be for a month or so, then she would be back. Derek and Kristine assured her that they would support her if that was her wish. They were sure that Nancy would love to see her.

The following morning Kristine rang Miss Stevens to check on the availability of a room in the New Year. It was as she had thought. They might have one in January or February, but should it be required for a permanent resident Evelyn would have to leave.

'Of course, your mother-in-law could have the room permanently with pleasure, then there would be no need for any future upheaval.'

'I understand, Miss Stevens, but at the moment, Mrs Arnold senior is adamant that she does not want to leave us for good. It

219

may of course come to that and I shall certainly tell her that she may have to move out at short notice. May we say yes to a room after Christmas when or if one becomes available?'

'If we have a room available then we could confirm it for a month, and she would not have to leave within that time. It would take that long to process any new resident. Is that satisfactory? Perhaps we shall be able to convince her to move in full time. We won't have to assess her again as it is such a short time since she was last with us.'

Kristine confirmed that the arrangement was ideal and she would be in touch after Christmas. Rebecca was delighted to hear that her grandmother was going back into the Home. 'I shall visit her regularly and tell her how marvellous the Home is and how lucky she is to be there.'

'Well don't overdo it or she'll think we're trying to get rid of her and demand to come back like a shot.'

'Never fear, I shall be tact itself. While she's got Nancy for company she's not going to miss us. I'm surprised she doesn't drive Nancy up the wall but perhaps she doesn't boss her about. But be honest, Mother, you'd be able to get your life back if she stayed in there and you could even go back to work if you wanted to.'

'I don't intend to do that. It will be just so good to have my days to myself. Your father and I can come and stay with you and Tom for the weekend now and again or go away for a few days without having to worry about anyone else. There's always Buster and the famous Tiger. I've grown quite fond of Granny's cat, now that he and Buster rub along together. He's no trouble.'

Kristine sent an email to Ralph that evening to tell him the latest news. He was somewhere in Australia so when he picked up the message he would send his grandmother a card. She loved to show off that she had cards from her grandson in all these exotic places.

Chapter Twenty Four

Christmas passed relatively painlessly, with Evelyn happy for Kristine to buy the presents she requested and even to choose suitable cards. It was strange without Ralph but Rebecca and Tom came, bringing with them the happy news that Kristine and Derek could expect their first grandchild in July. Kristine was over the moon but Evelyn was doubtful about the great age and decrepitude associated with being a great-grandmother. Still, it was pleasing to think that the Arnold line would be carried on, although it would be much more satisfactory when Ralph had a child and she could be sure the name would continue. Evelyn was dying to tell Nancy the news but had to curb her impatience as Nancy went to Long Meadow for ten days over Christmas and New Year.

It was hard to believe it was now 2003 and she had been born in 1922. So much had changed in the intervening years. How Evelyn longed for the bygone age when Brian was alive and everything in the world was just right. It made her tearful to think of the past but it was more bearable when she had someone near her own age to share her thoughts. Well she would be with Nancy next week if Kristine could get a room.

Monday 10th February dawned bright and frosty, the same as most days that week when Kristine took Evelyn her early morning tea. She had left her until later that morning to get some of the household chores out of the way. Today she would ring Lakeside and see if they had a room for her.

Kristine knocked gently on Evelyn's door but there was no answer. She pushed open the door and was immediately struck by the powerful smell of urine. Lights were a bit harsh when you were only half awake and Kristine usually walked round the bed and pulled the curtains. Not this morning. Something was wrong. Quickly she put the tray on the floor and turned on the light. She was horrified to see that Evelyn was perched precariously on the edge of the bed. The lid was half off the commode and her glasses and book were on the floor. Evelyn was struggling to say something but nothing was coming out and there was a look of fear in her eyes. The left side of her face was contorted and she was plucking at her useless left arm. Evelyn had obviously suffered a stoke, but was trying desperately to get to the commode. It was too late for that as the bed was sodden and the pillows were damp with saliva.

'Oh, my dear Evelyn, don't worry. I'm here now and we'll get the Doctor straight away. Here, let me get you somewhere safe before I go and ring him.' Kristine moved Evelyn's glasses and her book from the floor, put the lid back on the empty commode and moved the large armchair nearer to the bed. She grabbed Evelyn's towel from the rail to cover the chair and holding Evelyn round her waist and under her left arm, she managed to manoeuvre her gently into the chair. Fortunately, she was not as heavy as she used to be.

'I'll have to leave you for just a minute, Evelyn, while I ring Dr Nicholls. He'll need to come and see you straight away as you appear to have had a little stroke.'

Kristine had no idea whether it was a little stroke or a big one but she didn't want to frighten Evelyn any more than she was already. She picked up the tray by the door and dashed along the passage to the phone in the kitchen. Fortunately Dr. Nicholls was still at home. He promised to call at once and said he'd also call the ambulance as it was certain from Kristine's description of Evelyn's symptoms that she would need to go to hospital.

Kristine went back to Evelyn and explained the position,

critical of the home and those around her. Kristine visited twice a week but tried to vary the days she went in. She didn't want Evelyn to expect her always on a Friday or any other particular day of the week. Derek usually went on the weekend, often a Sunday morning, when he joined Nancy and his mother for a sherry before lunch. Kristine never ceased to be amazed at the residents enjoying a sherry with their relatives. This was unheard of when she was first involved with residential homes. Rebecca popped in about once a fortnight and was able to share with her grandmother little anecdotes about the trials and joys of being pregnant. She reported that Granny seemed to be quite interested and was kinder to her than previously.

Derek collected his mother for lunch on Easter Sunday and two of her Bridge friends, Rose and Fiona, were invited. As they were widows too, they appreciated roast turkey, which they never made for themselves. Evelyn went back to the home laden with chocolates and several Easter eggs.

It was five weeks before the telephone was connected. Derek made out a list of phone numbers, printing them in large type and laminating the page. He pinned it up by the phone and they had a trial run with Evelyn ringing Kristine while Derek was there.

'Well you can see it all works, Mother, so you'll be able to call your friends and have a chat. Don't worry about the bill, it will come to us, so unless you're ringing Australia every week it won't break the bank.'

'Who would I be ringing in Australia, Derek? Ralph is the only one I know there but I don't know his number. Do you have it?'

'It was only a joke, Mother and I don't know Ralph's phone number. He only has a mobile to use in emergencies. It's too expensive for regular use. I expect you'll get another card from him soon. Next month he goes on to New Zealand.'

Chapter Twenty Six

Evelyn came out for the weekend of the 4th May to celebrate her birthday with the family. For eighty-five she was doing very well; still in full command of her faculties, although her short term memory had deteriorated considerably. Apart from her diabetes, a slight limp following her broken leg and a still weak left arm, she was remarkably fit. Kristine had made and iced a cake and provided a few other culinary treats that she didn't think would have much effect on her diabetes. Rebecca and Tom joined in the celebrations and the highlight of the afternoon was a specially timed phone call from Ralph in New Zealand. Evelyn was most impressed that he'd set his alarm so he'd wake up to make the call. So was Kristine, as Ralph was normally very difficult to prize out of bed.

It was one Sunday a few weeks later that Derek returned from the Home in a rather thoughtful frame of mind. Kristine noticed it straight away.

'Is anything the matter, love?'

'I don't know. Mother seemed fine, quite chatty today in fact. No, it was the atmosphere in the home more than anything. I can't quite put my finger on it. The bells kept ringing, on and on, for ages. Nobody seemed to be answering them and when I commented on it both Nancy and Mother said, "Oh that often happens when they're short of staff." I must say, I only saw one member of staff all the time I was there.'

'Perhaps they were getting the lunch, or feeding those that needed to be fed.'

'They must do that every week and I've never noticed the lack of staff before. I think we should keep an eye on it. I hope they're not cutting corners to save money.'

'Can't get the staff more likely, especially on a Sunday. Most staff members are married these days with their own families and they all hate working on a Sunday, even if it is double time. I'll keep an eye out when I go next.' Kristine knew just how hard it was to get staff, especially at the weekends.

It was Wednesday before Kristine visited and she did think there were fewer girls about than usual. She made a casual remark to the girl bringing round the drinks at teatime.

'Are you very busy these days? I expect you're always busy.'

'It's been murder the last couple of weeks. There's never enough staff and some of these foreigners are OK but you have to explain to them in words of one syllable what to do or they get the wrong end of the stick.'

'Do you have a lot of foreigners then? I have noticed two nice kind girls who said they come from Ghana.'

'Yes, there's a lot of them. About three from Ghana, then two from Poland, two from Latvia and one from Portugal. We did have some French girls as well but they've gone back home now.'

Kristine murmured a sympathetic response and when the girl had gone she asked Evelyn if she had any problems understanding the staff. She realised instantly that it was probably a mistake to give Evelyn an opportunity for complaint. However, she was quite positive.

'Well the coloured girls, I never remember where they come from, are quite the kindest of them all but they are sometimes difficult to understand. They smile a great deal which cheers one up. There are some from those Eastern Block countries and they are very kind too but know very little English. They go to school in their spare time and of course I correct them if they don't get it right. That's if I understand what they are trying to say.'

Kristine felt sorry for the girls. She knew exactly what they must feel like. Her mother-in-law hadn't hesitated to correct her when she was first married and English was her native language!

'I'm sure they will appreciate any help you can give them and it is an interest for you too, to see them progress.'

Kristine thought it would give Evelyn something to occupy her mind to help the staff with their English. She might suggest to Nancy that she and Evelyn run a short conversation class, in the girls' spare time of course.

Next time Kristine went in to Lakeside her nostrils were assaulted by a powerful smell of stale urine. Instantly she was back in Mountain View all those years ago. Dear God. Was this home going to go the same way? Until now, the lack of unpleasant smells had been one of the plus points of Lakeside but today it was terrible. Evelyn was full of it.

'This place smells, I can't bear it. Nancy and I have been forced to sit outside, even though it's not really warm enough. We can't put up with the smell.'

'Have you made a complaint to Matron?'

'Oh yes, we've both told her and she uses the excuse they're short of staff but it just isn't good enough.'

'I'll have a word with her, but your own room's all right isn't it?'

'Yes, if you keep the door shut, but you can't do that all the time, it's too stuffy.'

'Well you could do that for a short time and you can always open the window.'

Kristine was sympathetic about the shortage of staff but perhaps there was more to it than that.

'I'll ask Matron what the problem is but it is hard to get staff out of nowhere. People just don't want to do cleaning much these days.'

Kristine spoke to Matron on the way out. She apologised about the smell but two of the domestic staff had reported in sick that morning and they were consequently way behind with the cleaning. She hoped it would be sorted in a day or two. Things did improve for a few weeks but there was a gradual, barely perceptible decline in the standard of the home. Evelyn did not seem as happy as she had been at first but Kristine was unsure how much was due to the decline in standards or to Nancy's deteriorating health. Her friend was inclined to spend more time in her room and occasionally she retired to her bed for the day. Kristine hoped she was not getting fed up with Evelyn; Heaven knows, it wouldn't be difficult. She dismissed this negative thought. Nancy may have some illness Kristine knew nothing about and she prayed silently that nothing would happen to her as she knew it would have an adverse effect on Evelyn. This had been one of the best homes available so what was she going to do if things got worse? Where could they go and could she bear to put Evelyn through the agony of moving yet again? Lakeside must be due for an inspection soon so they would make sure they had a copy of the report. Meanwhile, they would have Evelyn out to lunch on Sunday.

Kristine was not sure that Sunday lunch had been a good idea. It would have been better if Nancy had been well enough to come too but she hadn't felt up to it. Evelyn enjoyed the roast beef, "cooked properly and not over done. I must say you're a good cook, Kristine." Praise indeed. Kristine had made Evelyn's favourite pudding of chocolate roulade and there was even enough to take back for tomorrow to share with Nancy. Now the fridge was installed, little treats like those were possible. Just as she was about to go back to the home, Rebecca and Tom turned up. Rebecca was now heavily pregnant and the baby was due in two days time.

'I'm having the baby in hospital, Granny, but as soon as I'm home and organised I'll bring it in to see you.'

'I should like that. I do hope it's a boy, they're so much easier than girls.'

I'm sure you do, thought Rebecca. As Evelyn had never had a girl, what did she know about it? She'd always preferred Ralph to her but Rebecca contented herself with saying,

'I can't promise a boy but as long as she or he is healthy I don't mind.'

'Come along, Mother. I'm afraid we must go back now or you'll miss your supper. It's a nice evening, perhaps you and Nancy can sit outside for a bit if she's feeling better.'

Going back was the problem. Evelyn didn't want to leave the family group where she was the senior member. She felt shut out and abandoned.

'I really don't see why I have to go back. I have managed very well here for lunch, fed myself and been to the bathroom without help. Why do I need to be in that place?'

Kristine looked helplessly at Derek. She was useless in the face of this kind of pleading. Everything Evelyn said was true but she had been there for one meal, all of five hours. All day, every day, every week, that was something quite different. Derek was never going to be influenced by this kind of talk. He smiled and gave his mother a hug,

'You know that's impossible, Mother. You need twenty-four hour care, a suitable bathroom, regular physio, all those on-going facilities. Come along, we'll get you back in time for tea and we'll make this lunch a more regular event so you'll have something definite to look forward to.'

Nancy had felt well enough to get up for tea so Derek and Kristine left the two of them catching up on the day's news. Again though, there seemed very few staff in evidence.

Chapter Twenty Seven

Two days later, on 22nd July, Rebecca produced Luke Thomas, the great grandson Evelyn wanted. He weighed in at a respectable eight pounds and was fit and healthy. After telling Kristine and Derek, Tom rang Evelyn with the happy news, promising to bring Luke in to see her as soon as possible.

Evelyn hurried off to tell Nancy. Now she was a great-grandmother she was ahead in seniority as Nancy's grandchildren were still at school.

Kristine and Derek couldn't wait to see their lovely grandson and to take some photos. They would have to send some to 'Uncle' Ralph.

It was three weeks later when Kristine was visiting, that the home seemed to be in a state of upheaval. There were plenty of staff and everyone was rushing about 'doing things'.

Evelyn was full of it. 'The inspectors are here. They came early this morning and are going to be here all day. They even interviewed Nancy and me and asked us what we think.'

'What about? What did they ask you? Did you give a good report?'

Calm down Kristine, she told herself. What are you afraid of? She didn't rightly know but she had a sudden irrational fear that the home might close and then what would they do? She wished she didn't have such an over – active imagination.

Evelyn was in her room and had quickly switched off the television so she could better fill Kristine in on the excitement. Kristine made a mental note that Evelyn was watching the television during the afternoon. "I never watch television during the day as there is nothing but rubbish on," was a favourite refrain.

'Of course we said the staff were very kind and tried their best but we had to mention that sometimes we couldn't understand some of the foreign ones. Oh, and we did say that when they were short of staff the place smelt very bad. Well we had to, they'd want us to be truthful.'

'What did they say? There's no smell now and there seems to be plenty of staff today. They can't have known the inspectors were coming, as I understand all their visits are unannounced these days.'

'The lady who spoke to us just said thank you for our comments and then she moved on.' Evelyn was quite confident her comments would be included in the report.

Just then, a tall fussy-looking man knocked at Evelyn's door 'Excuse me, Mrs Arnold, is this your daughter-in-law? I'm Joseph Pickard, one of the Social Care inspectors and I wonder if I might have a word.'

Evelyn introduced Kristine who agreed to accompany Mr Pickard to the relatives' sitting room for a 'confidential chat'.

'How do you find Lakeside, Mrs Arnold? Do you feel that it provides the care that you expected for your mother-in-law?'

Kristine wanted to be honest but she also wanted to be fair to the home. The last thing she wanted was to cause trouble for them but she didn't want the standards to slip or for Evelyn and Nancy to receive poor care.

'Yes, on the whole, I think it does. The staff seem very kind and are always pleasant when I, or any of our family visit. My mother-in-law is always clean and neatly dressed, although she does most of that herself. She says she gets plenty to eat and of course we bring her treats.'

'Do you find the home clean always?'

'There was a spell a few months ago when it smelt badly

of urine but I think that was a one off. Several members of the domestic staff had been off ill and they were behind with the cleaning. It has been fine lately. I think they are short of staff sometimes but then these places always are, don't you think?'

'That is perfectly true but it is unacceptable to have the staffing below a certain level, Health and Safety, you know. Homes at all times are required to have a certain ratio of staff to residents and they must not fall below that standard.'

Oh, how pompous he sounded. Kristine was thankful she'd never had to deal with this kind of person in the course of her work in the operating theatre.

'Now tell me, Mrs Arnold, do you or any of your family have any problems with the foreign staff? There are several here who have limited English. Does that cause you a problem? Not in a discriminatory sense you understand.'

'It doesn't cause me any problems, but I can see there may be a communication problem, especially with someone who may have had a stroke and have difficulty in making their wishes known.'

'I think Mrs Arnold Snr. has had a small stroke at some stage, hasn't she? Are you saying she has difficulties with the foreign staff?'

'No, certainly not. My mother-in-law has no difficulty in making herself understood, very clearly too. In fact she helps the staff with their English sometimes. Besides, they take English lessons, I believe, so they should be getting better all the time?' Kristine felt that the big-headed Mr Pickard was hoping to elicit different answers to those his colleague had got from Evelyn.

'Yes, yes they do. Well, I think that is all I have to ask you, Mrs Arnold. Do read our report when it comes out next month and feel free to contact us any time you have any queries. Here is my card.'

Kristine took the proffered card and noted the long list

of initials after Joseph Pickard's name. Pompous twit. She wouldn't be ringing him with any complaints. He gave Kristine the impression that he was there to find fault if he possibly could. Perhaps he saw it as a justification for keeping his job. She went back to Evelyn who was all-agog to find out what Mr Pickard had said. Kristine reported that he had asked her much the same questions as the lady had asked her and Nancy. She had probably given much the same answers. Kristine joined Evelyn and Nancy for a cup of tea before leaving, promising Derek would come at the weekend.

One Monday in the middle of September Kristine arrived at the home and had to step over the builders' electric drill and various other tools by the door to one of the main sitting rooms. She signed in but before going to Evelyn's room, she called at the office to find out what was going on. Matron was apologetic for not having notified relatives of the necessary work now in progress.

'Fire regulations. Following a fire at a home in Scotland last year, much more stringent fire precautions have to be put in place. You may have read about it in our last report. Doors to the main rooms have to be fire-proofed, fire retardant glass has to be put in the windows overlooking the fire escapes and a new switchboard linked to the fire station. It is going to take some time, I'm afraid, Mrs Arnold, so there will be a certain amount of disruption in the home. Another thing that is causing some consternation to the residents is the regulation that all bedroom doors must be kept closed. We are not allowed to prop them open any more.'

'Why ever not? I should hate to be sitting in my room with the door closed all the time.'

'Another part of the fire regulations, Mrs Arnold. The reasoning is that if a fire started in a particular bedroom and the door was open, it would quickly spread to the rest of the home. With the door shut, it would be contained.'

'It seems very unkind, Matron. If you're in your own home you don't keep the doors shut. What if they fall? You wouldn't notice them, maybe for several hours.' Kristine thought it was a very short-sighted policy.

'We have thought of all that and we are going to fit special stoppers to the doors that will allow them to be held open, but they will close automatically when the fire alarm is activated. I think everyone will be satisfied with that but it will take some time to get them all fitted. We have fifty rooms as you know. In the meantime, we have done a risk assessment on everyone and will prop the doors of those who are more prone to falling. Obviously, we shall fit the device to those doors first. It all takes time.'

Kristine remembered reading about the fire and thinking how dreadful it must have been. Seven or eight residents had lost their lives so she could see how important it was to have adequate safety measures in place.

'I expect it will be very expensive too?' Kristine wondered just how long it would be before the fees went up.

'Oh, it's certainly very expensive but I'm sure you'll agree that the safety of the residents is paramount, Mrs Arnold. A letter will be going out this weekend. I do hope you'll bear with us.'

How would Evelyn be taking the additional noise and upheaval? So far she wasn't complaining. Her friends had been in on Saturday for a game of Bridge and apparently Rebecca and Tom had called in yesterday with Luke. He was two months old now, smiling and taking an interest in his surroundings. Evelyn had nursed him for a photograph, which would have to be added to the collection on the wall. It was Kristine's greatest joy these days to be able to visit Rebecca regularly and watch the progress of her grandson. She was so glad she was free to do so.

The promised explanatory letter arrived on Thursday but

as yet no mention of increased fees. However, the building work was expected to take at least three months, probably longer, as some of it could not be done during the winter. The external doors and changing of the glass would have to wait for the warmer weather. There was also a note saying the latest report from the inspectors was now available in the home or on line. Derek down-loaded it that evening and they examined it carefully. Overall, it was a good report but staffing levels were mentioned as a concern, particularly the domestic staff. There would need to be an improvement before the next inspection.

Chapter Twenty Eight

Christmas came and went with minimum fuss. In addition to being able to coo over her great grandson, the highlight for Evelyn was Ralph's return from the other side of the world. She had not asked after him for some time and Kristine was concerned that she might have forgotten him. It soon became clear that she'd been afraid he would find the Southern Hemisphere more attractive and never come back. He had originally gone for six months but had been away for almost a year. Because of this, Evelyn had been trying to come to terms with the fact that she might never see him again.

'How could you possibly think that, Gran? I just had to come back and see your lovely face.'

'You are a flatterer, Ralph and you don't mean a word of it but I am delighted to see you. You must tell me all about your adventures.'

'Better than that, I'll show you all the photos when we've had lunch.'

Evelyn had definitely perked up now Ralph was home and possibly because Rebecca and Tom had had a boy. Derek commented to Kristine that evening that his mother seemed to have a new lease of life.

'Yes, I hadn't realised how despondent she was. I suppose it is inevitable that she will be coming institutionalised. We must make sure we get her out more but latterly she has seemed less inclined to want to make the effort because of the trauma of having to go back. Perhaps it will be different now that Ralph is back and Luke will sometimes be here when she comes out.

She'll feel she is in on his progress, you know, when he sits up, when he gets teeth, all those sorts of things.'

'So she can boast to Nancy, I suppose. Well, we'll have her out each week while Ralph is home but I hope he'll get a job soon and then he'll probably be living in London. Still if he's in this country and can ring her up occasionally that will help.'

Derek was of an era when one trained for a profession before taking off around the world, not afterwards.

'Oh, I know one thing that'll cheer her up. I saw in the paper yesterday that Stephanie was engaged.'

'Who's Stephanie?'

'Derek, you must remember Stephanie, Ralph's girlfriend, the one your mother couldn't stand, said she was a gold digger? Although what gold she thought she could get from Ralph I can't imagine.'

'I remember now. Does he know yet? Do you think he'll be upset?'

'I haven't told him but I shouldn't think it'll worry him, he's probably had three or four girl friends, maybe more, while he's been away. I seem to remember you were sure that she was just a passing fancy.'

Life settled back into a pattern with Evelyn coming out most Sundays. Nancy came too if she felt well enough but she was slowly declining and was spending more time in bed. At first Evelyn tried to badger her to get up and 'pull herself together' but when it had no effect she gave up. She didn't want to alienate Nancy as she was her only friend in the home. Evelyn did not consider the other residents as having the same social standing as herself and Nancy.

'Mostly riff-raff, I don't know how they come to be in here,' she would say and Kristine had to hush her up on more than one occasion. Judging by the newspapers, Lakeside was a model home compared with many around the country. Every other week there were reports of appalling neglect and ill treatment, with the offending homes forced to close.

'Nobody comes in to a nursing home because they want to, they come in because they have to. Their circumstances are such that they need full time care.'

'Well they should put like minded people together then everyone would be much happier.'

It was no good trying to reason with Evelyn by telling her that everyone chose the best home they could afford and all had the same entitlement to be there. Kristine was often acutely embarrassed listening to Evelyn going on and on about the poor quality of the other residents. She hoped most of them were too deaf to hear her.

It was the end of May before the fire regulation improvements were finally completed and Derek and Kristine were not surprised when the fees went up in June. They were now nearly £530 per week, which Evelyn thought was a scandal.

'If you had kept me at home you would have been so much better off. Now all my money is being eaten up in this place.'

Derek saw it differently. 'Mother, it's rather like living in an hotel and you have no other outgoings. Your heat, light, food and washing are all taken care of and you're waited on as well. Your pension pays part of it and the Government meets a portion of your nursing care so it's not too bad really.'

Kristine had been inclined to think the fees were extortionate too, but for peace of mind and safe care of her mother-in-law, not to mention her own freedom, they were well worth it. She just hoped they would not go up too much more. Over £25,000 a year would soon eat up any capital Evelyn had. Kristine didn't know how people without a private income were able to manage. Of course when your finances fell below a certain level, the state paid but you then had to go into whatever kind of home the local authority was prepared to pay for. It could be something like Mountain View, which she remembered with dread and obviously, if the papers were to be believed, there were still some places as bad as that. Sometimes she wondered what had happened to Angela and Sandra, and the Matron and Sister Johansen. Well Matron was probably dead by now and Helen had written several years ago saying that Mountain View had closed. Kristine had not even been able to find it when she was last in New Zealand. Angela would be nearly seventy, always supposing she was still alive. It would be interesting to know what she felt now, about being old?

Chapter Twenty Nine

New Zealand 2002

Angela braked sharply to avoid the pukeka ambling across the road. Bloody birds. Stupid they were, always getting run over. Visitors liked them because they were a pretty blue with a red beak and legs. This one had a lucky day. Just as well it hadn't been there two years ago when she and Jack had staged the hill race. They had been going to make it an annual event but she'd cried off. Jack called her chicken but she wouldn't budge. She'd told him she was happy being the champion of the last century. He could claim victory in the new one, as her heart wasn't in it. Besides, who would adjudicate? Bob refused point blank and said only an idiot would drive with them in race mode. Although the schools had gone back and many of the locals had had their holidays, there were still plenty of tourists about, many of them foreign. They were the worst, used to driving on the other side of the bloody road, often causing accidents.

But that wasn't the only reason Angela was driving slower than usual. She was finding it difficult to concentrate on her driving while her mind kept mulling over Dr. Richard's verdict. They could give her tablets to delay the onset, which would give her a couple more years of useful life, if she was lucky. God, she wasn't old. She didn't feel old. Inside, she felt about forty. Bloody Agnes probably thought that too. Shit, why did she have to think of her. Angela pushed the unbidden thoughts to the back of her mind. She was nothing like Agnes. OK, she wasn't as agile as she used to be, couldn't walk quite so far, had the odd aches and pains, but old – never. What was she going to do? Grin and bear it? Wait until she was really trembling and shaking, even falling about? No way. She didn't want to think about the dribbling. Mind you, when she'd mentioned that to Dr. Richard he didn't seem to recognise it as a symptom. Said it might have been a problem in the old days but not with the modern drugs. Perhaps she could wait a year or so and see how it went. If the tablets he'd given her put paid to the mild tremor she could hang on a bit longer. She wasn't going to tell Maxine or she'd have her down the hill like a shot. No. She could hide it quite easily from Maxine. If she did notice, Angela could say she felt a bit fluey or she'd been doing too much. Anyway she didn't see her that much and it would be even less as winter approached. She was glad she'd done some touring last year; up the Kaikora Coast to Nelson and even down to Queenstown the year before. God, that was a fantastic place. She couldn't believe the scenery. She'd thought it was good in Whangata but Queenstown was something else again. Every time you went to buy a loaf of bread or a pint of milk you had those fantastic mountains for a backdrop. No wonder they were called the Remarkables.

By the time she reached the house, Angela had decided to give herself until March next year then reassess the situation. Providing she didn't deteriorate any more of course. If that happened, she'd have to do something sooner. As she put the Ute in the shed Angela told herself that apart from remembering to take the pills Dr Richard had prescribed, she would think no more about her condition. She'd asked him to post them every couple of months to save her going down. The poor chap nearly had his head bitten off when he suggested Maxine could collect them and take them up to her.

'Don't you dare mention this visit, or any other visit, to

my daughter. Patient's health is supposed to be private. When I come here it's my business, nobody else's.'

'All right. I've got the message, but you might need to tell her at some stage.'

'Well I'll do it when I'm good and ready, not before.'

She would have to hide the tablets in her bedroom so there was no danger of Maxine or Ken noticing them.

It was easier said than done, not thinking about what might happen to her. Visions of Agnes, and sometimes crusty old Bill, would appear before her when she least expected it. Out walking the dog, cooking a meal or when she was trying to go to sleep. That was the worst, at night, just as she was drifting off, there would be Agnes, a shaking, dribbling figure coming back to haunt her. Trembling and agitated, Angela would get up, turn on all the lights and sit by the stove sipping a cup of tea, laced with whisky, until sleep drove out the demons.

As the weeks and months passed and she didn't get any worse, Angela got into her old routine and the visions faded. She found she drove less but she used her mobile phone more. That way she kept Maxine happy and she wasn't all the time badgering her to come down from the hill.

Chapter Thirty

'Mum sounds quite cheerful these days. She gives us a call nearly every week now she's got the new phone. A brilliant idea of yours, love.'

'I have them sometimes,' responded Ken modestly. 'I had noticed she was ringing more often. She doesn't bawl me out when I go up there as much as she used to either, Perhaps she's mellowing in her old age.'

'For God's sake don't tell her that, she'll have your guts for garters.' Maxine knew any mention of age to her mother caused ructions.

Ken was reading the paper. They didn't get it every day as it was usually the same old boring stuff. He liked the sport though and turned to the back pages first. Disgusted that NZ had lost again to the Aussies, he was glancing through for any other news when something caught his eye.

'Just as well you're not looking for a nursing home for your mother, I see another one's closed down. That's the second one in a fortnight.'

'Where? Let me see?' Maxine moved round to read over Ken's shoulder. 'Oh, it's in Riccarton. The posh area. We couldn't afford something like that anyway. Don't forget, Mum said she wouldn't go in a home. We'd have to have her here. She wouldn't be much trouble I don't suppose.'

Ken wasn't so sure. 'That's all very well while her lift goes to the top floor but if she's doolally it'd be a different story.'

'I can't imagine Mum, doolally. Difficult yes, but she's

always been that. Ah well, we'll just have to take it as it comes. She seems OK at the moment; not complaining of any aches and pains or other ailments. No. She'll probably die in her bed, just because she said she wouldn't.'

Chapter Thirty One

Two Years Later

Angela had walked a long way. She got the rug out of her backpack and spread it on the ground. She'd brought her lunch and a couple of beers out into the wilderness to try and lift her spirits. She was sitting about a hundred yards from the edge of a sheer drop into the valley a thousand feet below. The view was fantastic, worth millions if it wasn't up that bloody road. Laid out before her were the Southern Alps, remnants of snow glistening on the peaks in spite of the summer sun. Another Christmas had been and gone, when she'd been forced to spend a week with Maxine and Ken and that was the problem. Maxine had seen her taking the tablets. She'd managed nearly two years without her finding out. Oh, she'd been careful, taking them before the others got up but she was supposed to take them with food and Maxine had come in while she was trying to get a biscuit out of the tin. Her hands were shaking more than usual that morning and she'd dropped the tin, shedding broken biscuits all over the floor. Jess had thought all her birthdays had come at once.

'What are you trying to do Mum? Don't tell me you're hungry? Thought you said we'd fed you too much last night. Here, what's these tablets, what are you taking tablets for?'

'Nothing. They're just vitamins.'

'What do you take me for? Since when've you taken

vitamins? You don't believe in them. Come on, out with it, what are they for? I'm your daughter, you can tell me, otherwise, I'll go and ask Dr Richard.'

'He won't tell you, it's private. I'll bloody kill him if he does.'

That was it. The cat was out of the bag and she had to tell Maxine that she had Parkinson's. She had to go over the whole sorry saga. How long have you had it, what are you taking, what made you go to the doctor in the first place, what are your symptoms? Why does she want to know? She doesn't know a bloody thing about it. On and on she went. Questions, questions, questions until Angela shouted at her 'Shut up, for God's sake. Why do you think I didn't tell you? Do you think I want to talk about it, 'cause I don't and I'm not going to. You know about it now so let that be the end of it.'

That had been over a month ago. Angela propped herself against a rock, put her face to the sun and closed her eyes.

Out here she could think. The air was perfectly still and the sun's rays seemed to penetrate through to her soul. Not that Angela believed she had a soul. No, you lived and you died. You didn't know anything about before you were born and you wouldn't know anything afterwards. Nothing. That was the end of it. She might as well get it over with, finish it now. What did she want to hang on for? She didn't have any grandchildren and anyway she wouldn't want them to see her gaga. She didn't want Maxine and Ken to look after her, and it'd be a relief for them not to have to do it. Angela popped a beer and had a long drink, straight from the can, as she always did. Jess nuzzled her leg expectantly, looking for a drink too.

God. She'd forgotten Jess. What to do about Jess. She couldn't take her with her, it wouldn't be fair. She'd had quite a good life. Plenty of food, lots of exercise. Angela poured some water she'd bought for Jess into a plastic dish and the dog drank noisily, slopping much of it on the grass.

What could she do? She couldn't take off in the Ute without her. Jess went everywhere with her. Perhaps she could ask Jack to have her for the day, say she was going into Christchurch and it wasn't fair on the dog to take her all that way. But she'd taken her before. She could take her to Maxine's and leave her there, say she was going to a friend's who didn't like dogs? No. Too many questions. "Whose your friend? You don't have any friends, not ones that don't like dogs anyway." Jack might swallow that story, Maxine certainly wouldn't. It need not be as far as Christchurch. Ashburton say, or Rakaia. Long time friend who'd just moved there and always hated dogs. Yeh. That'd do, but when, when was she going to do it?

Jess tugging at her jeans woke Angela. She was stiff and cold as the sun had gone down behind the mountains.

'God. I must have dropped off. Thank goodness your belly told you it was time for tea, Jess or we'd bloody well be here all night. Come on old girl, we've quite a walk back and we must make it before dark.'

Angela packed up her things, slung the rucksack over her shoulder and trudged after Jess who was racing ahead, anxious for her food. It took them nearly an hour to reach home and Angela was exhausted. It made her feel old and she hated it. She fed the dog first and was tempted to fall into bed without any tea but she needed food to take her tablet. She put the TV on while she boiled an egg and cut some chunks of bread. There was nothing much to watch but it was company and stopped her thinking. Funny, worrying about taking her tablet with food when it didn't matter any more. She could take it with beer or whisky, maybe not even take it. Who cared? Angela reasoned that she had to go on taking her medication until all her plans were in place. She didn't want to deteriorate so much that it was impossible to go when she wanted to and in her own way. Her meal finished, she got up, turned off the TV; she couldn't see it properly anyway, tears kept blurring

her vision. Not tears for herself but for Jess. It'd be better if
the dog went first but she couldn't afford to wait. Jess might
live for years and by then Angela would be in a home. No.
The thought terrified her. She poured herself a large whisky,
skipped the water and took herself off to bed, glad that Jess
chose that night to sleep on her feet. She didn't always, but
perhaps she felt that Angela needed her company. Tomorrow
she would make her plans and by the end of March she would
be gone. Why put up with another winter? She'd always hated
the cold.

Angela spent all the next week cleaning her house. She
started on her bedroom, tossing out birthday cards from thirty
years ago, holey jumpers and a few skirts she never wore.
Angela lived in trousers. They were the most practical for the
life she led. The odd ornament and picture she would leave
for Maxine. She could throw it if she didn't want it. The spare
room was cluttered with twenty years of things that might
come in useful; empty boxes, plastic bags, several pairs of old
gummies, probably had holes in by now, odd tools, Ken might
like those, several old jackets, two battered suitcases, ancient
newspapers, a box of candles for power cuts and dozens of
other bits and pieces. She would have a bonfire as most of it
could go.

Angela didn't know when she decided, but sometime
during the week she made up her mind to visit Maxine. Just
for a night or two. She wanted to see her one last time. Soppy
old fool. Why did it matter?

'Maxine, it's me. Thought I'd come down for a day or two.
You're going to be there aren't ya?'

'Course we are. We're always here. Anything the matter?'

'No. Should there be? Can't I come and see you without
something being the matter?'

'All right, all right. Don't lose your rag. We'd love to see
you. I'll have the kettle on. See you later.' Maxine put the

phone down, deep in thought. She wandered into the garden to find Ken.

'That's a turn up for the books. Mum's coming down for a visit, without being asked. A day or two she said. I wonder what's up? You don't mind, do you?'

'Na. S'pose she wants a bit of pampering. Probably tired of cooking for herself. Be nice to have Jess.'

Ken could put up with his mother-in-law as long as she brought her dog. Ken had lost track of his parents years ago. They'd never bothered with him so he'd returned the favour. Meeting Maxine had been the best thing that ever happened to him and at least Angela was civil to him these days, quite pleasant sometimes.

'Hey, maybe she wants to come for good?' Ken wasn't so sure about that idea.

'No chance, she's too bloody independent. I guess she just wants a change, we'll soon find out, says she'll be here about coffee time.'

In the end Angela stayed four days. She was lying in the lounger in the garden, enjoying the sun. Jess was dozing nearby. Maxine and Ken had had to go to Ashburton for the day and she declined to go with them. Towns didn't interest her and it was too hot to be in a car. Life was comfortable. She was well fed, she had company and didn't have to bother about anything. Jess was contented too. Plenty of long walks with Ken, new smells and even a trip to the beach one day. Angela went too that day as she had a hankering to see the sea one last time. Her thoughts were taking a dangerous turn. She was looking for a way out, a reprieve from the course she'd set herself. Perhaps she could give in, say she'd like to come down from the hill, ask them to put up with her, permanent? She could pay her way. She had savings and her pension of course and neither Maxine nor Ken had mentioned anything about her going back. Is this why she'd come down? Had she known the visit would weaken her resolve, make it easier to give in? She'd go back tomorrow, see how she felt, back in her own surroundings. She had to admit the shaking was worse down here but then Dr Richard had explained that the shaking would be worse when she wasn't doing anything. Another good reason for looking after herself, doing things, not sitting about getting stiff and gradually not being able to do anything. She'd been struggling to control the tremor so they wouldn't notice, wouldn't feel sorry for her, help her, make her feel like a baby.

To give her her due, since she first found out about her mother's condition, Maxine hadn't mentioned it, hadn't asked any questions. But no. She must go back and think it through again.

She'd promised to put the tea on so it was waiting for Ken and Maxine when they returned. Getting the meal gave her something to do, helped control the shaking. When they'd finished eating and chatting over a couple of beers, Angela announced she'd be leaving in the morning.

'Just as you like, Mum, but you know you're welcome to stay as long as you want.'

'Yeh. Well, I'll have breakfast first, it's better than what I make for m'self.' Angela's attempt at a joke lightened the mood and they watched an old film on television until quite late. It amused Maxine, when she went in with the coffee, to find Ken and Angela snoring during the most exciting part of the film. The only one watching with interest was Jess.

By midday, Angela was back at Whangata. She was shocked to find she was shaking much more than usual after the drive and stumbled twice between the Ute and the house. She'd forgotten to take her tablet in the anxiety to get away without an emotional farewell. She'd experienced rising panic when Maxine had leant over and given her a hug and a kiss on the cheek as she was leaving.

'Drive carefully, won't you Mum.' She'd managed to mumble 'Course I will, I've been doing it long enough haven't I', before slamming the door and roaring away. She pulled over a mile down the road to blow her nose and wipe her eyes.

Chapter Thirty Two

The trembling and lack of co-ordination had helped Angela come to a decision. She now knew what she had to do. The fall she had a week after she returned from Maxine's confirmed it. Although she hadn't done more than scrape her hands and knees, it had shaken her. She had taken it easy that afternoon and the next day she finished cleaning the house.

It was a calm warm day so Angela took all the rubbish from the bedrooms out to the yard, well away from the house and prepared a bonfire. She then turned her attention to the out-buildings. One 'building' was really only a lean-to which held an old copper with a grate underneath and a couple of concrete tubs where some poor mutt of a wife had had to do the family washing. A washing machine was one of the few luxuries Angela had provided for herself. The other building was probably some previous owner's garden shed. Apart from a few basic vegetables like potatoes, onions and carrots, Angela hadn't done much gardening. She couldn't be bothered with flowers. She liked the wild ones and preferred to leave them where they grew.

Once the fire was burning strongly she started bringing old crates from the sheds and the back of the garage. Why had she kept all this stuff? Thought it might come in useful, she supposed. End rolls of mouldy wallpaper, odd pieces of timber, empty paint tins, and an old car seat, little left but the springs. The rats had had the rest. Angela tossed it all on the fire. She gingerly picked up a rotting piece of carpet and a family of mice ran out. Jess half-heartedly chased them but it was too hot and she flopped back on the grass. Angela got the hose and washed out the garage. It had never been so clean. She swept out the worst of the rubbish from the shed, transferred the things she'd salvaged for Ken and shut the door. By now it was teatime. Lunch had passed her by. She was filthy and very tired. She would soak in a hot bath, have some tea and watch the telly. Tomorrow she would tackle the kitchen.

By the end of the week everything was ready. The house was clean and tidy. She'd checked on the insurance for the Ute, found the deeds of the house in case Maxine wanted to sell it, though God knows who'd want to buy it. Then again, some of these smart city people might like a country house. Anyhow Maxine and Ken might like it themselves, especially in the summer; could tell everyone they had a 'mountain retreat'. She'd called in to see Jack and asked him to have Jess next weekend when she was going off to see her friend Sandra, who doesn't like dogs. Sandra was the only one she could think of that nobody round here had heard of. Goodness knows what had happened to her. Years ago Angela had seen her wedding photo in the Wellington paper. Spivvy looking guy if she remembered rightly, probably didn't last. Sandra was always the dumb blonde. Jack was delighted to have Jess but he couldn't understand how anyone disliked dogs. 'How come she's a friend of yours then?' Why did he have to ask questions? What did it matter how she knew her?

'Knew her years ago, haven't seen her for ages. Had a postcard a couple weeks ago. Said she'd moved just south of Greymouth. Thought I'd go and see her before the winter.'

'God, that's a hell of a way. Given yourself quite a hike. Not the best of roads either if it's wet. Yep. Just bring Jess along, Friday you said? Lucky she gets on with Joe and Nell. When're you coming back?'

'Sunday evening or maybe Monday, depends on the

weather. Come to think of it would you put up with her until Tuesday if I needed a bit longer? It is quite a drive. Weather's been OK up till now and the forecast is good.'

Angela felt herself going pink at the lies. Not that she was averse to lying when it suited her but Jack was a good friend and she was going to leave him in the lurch. He'd have to tell Maxine when she didn't come back.

'Thanks anyway, see ya Friday about 10.'

Angela determined to enjoy her last week. She and Jess went for long walks over the hills. She was grateful for the clear, warm, sunny days with a crystal sky arching over the incredible scenery of bush-covered foothills, barren, scree-scarred slopes leading to snow-covered peaks in the distance, deep valleys, networked with creeks and bigger rivers. Much of the time she argued with herself; was she doing the right thing? What about Maxine? She didn't need to worry about Maxine, she had Ken to keep her company. Oh, she'd miss Mum at first but let's face it, she'd hate to have to look after her when she became old and doddery. Perhaps she wouldn't get much worse? Just go slowly down hill, no trouble to anyone? No. She knew that wasn't true. Most days she tripped or stumbled and she couldn't stride out like she used to. Her hands were trembling nearly every day because she wasn't doing anything.

Visions of Agnes floated before her; urine dribbling down her legs, her lip quivering, eyes pleading; Bill Harkness, accusing, leaning forward from his wheelchair, pointing his finger. Just like the dreams. Night after night these images graphically illustrated her inevitable decline.

Angela yelled, 'No! No! No! Go away.' She was so over-wrought, she wasn't watching where she was going. The scree-covered ground suddenly sloped away and she lost her footing, sliding twenty or thirty feet. A clump of scrubby tea tree saved her falling any further. Angela lay where she was for several minutes, gingerly trying to assess the damage. Nothing appeared to be broken but her arms and legs were skinned and bleeding. Trousers would have given her more protection but then she hadn't expected to throw herself down the hill. The bruises would appear later.

Fortunately, either side of where she fell, the ground was ridged and sloped more gently and Angela knew she would be able to get back to the track even if it was on her knees. Jess had bounded up whining in sympathy with her mistress. Angela put her arms around the dog's neck and sobbed into her coat in sheer frustration.

Slowly Angela picked her way back, taking her time and watching her step. At least the fall had banished the visions for the moment and she could concentrate on where she was going. Once she was safely home she threw her torn shorts and T-shirt in the bin. She washed and cleaned her cuts, dabbing them with iodine although she didn't know why she bothered. They wouldn't have time to get infected. She'd wear trousers and a long sleeved shirt till Friday. Not that anyone was likely to notice, she never saw anyone except Jack and that was only occasionally. Just two more days.

Friday dawned bright and clear. The kind of day Angela loved best. Fresh and damp in the early morning, gradually becoming warmer and drier as the day wore on. She dressed carefully in dark tracksuit with a clean white T-shirt. She wouldn't want anyone who found her to say she was dirty. Mind you, if she made a good job of it and they didn't find her for ages it would hardly matter that she'd started off clean.
She threw a spare set of underclothes and her pyjamas and toilet gear into a small suitcase. She was supposed to be going to stay with someone, wasn't she?

Angela made some strong coffee, liberally lacing it with whisky until it was almost half and half and filled a large thermos. She made several doorsteps of cheese and Marmite sandwiches for her lunch. She might not eat them but it had to look right. She'd be expected to take provisions on such a journey. These days, four, four and a half hours should see her to Greymouth but bad weather or slips on the road could make it significantly longer.

Jess was getting excited thinking they were going on an outing together. Angela pulled Jess to her on the sofa and gave her a big hug, fighting back the tears, whispering her goodbyes and assuring Jess Ken would look after her and give her the best of treatment.

The poor dog was puzzled. 'Come on,' she seemed to say, 'let's get going.' Angela pushed her away, wiped her eyes and took her things out to the Ute. She checked everything was turned off, locked the door and stood, for one last time, breathing in the clean fresh air and gazing at the spectacular view. Jess was already in the back of the Ute, excited to be moving at last.

'Not for long I'm afraid, old girl. This time you're staying with Jack.'

Angela drove the two hundred yards down the track to Jack's driveway giving several beeps on the horn as she pulled up at the side of the house. Jess leapt out to throw herself at Jack for a hug and a fussing, much to the distain of Jack's own two dogs. Joe didn't mind but Nell was inclined to be jealous and after all, she was top dog in the Flint household.

'Well, you're off then. Wondered if you'd go, when the time came.'

'Yer well, I need a change. Change's as good as a rest, or so they say.'

Jack was unconvinced. 'A trip to the West Coast is a change I could do without. It's OK with me if you don't come back till Tuesday but if you're not back by drinking time on Wednesday, I'll send out a search party.'

'You do that – and thanks for having Jess – and everything.

See ya.' Angela gave one last pat to Jess, climbed into the Ute and drove away fast, before she could change her mind.

'Don't drive so bloody fast or you won't make it to the West Coast,' Jack shouted after her but she was gone. She didn't see Jess' sorrowful face or hear her whimpering at being left behind.

'Never mind old girl, she'll be back soon.' Jack's gentle tone comforted the dog and she soon joined Nell and Joe arguing over some juicy bones.

Chapter Thirty Three

Angela drove for two hours before stopping for a break. She had joined route 73 which skirted the Craigieburn range as it wound up towards Arthur's Pass where the road was twisty and steep. There would be little traffic, nobody to notice what she intended to do. Most of the tourists had gone and the skiing season had not begun.

She pulled into a lay-by just north of Paddy's bend and consulted the map. She noted with wry amusement that the view to her left was of Mount Misery, idly wondering how it had got its name. Very appropriate, but it just served to deepen her gloom. Soon, she would find a suitable unprotected drop. It had to be high and steep enough for there to be no possibility of recovery or survival.

Angela was nervous. Her heart was racing and as soon as she'd stopped driving her hands began to shake. Hurriedly she unwrapped the sandwiches she had brought and poured some of the coffee from the thermos into a mug, trying not to spill it in her lap. The food and hot drink, not to mention the alcohol, served to calm Angela's nerves. She hadn't realised how hungry she was. Breakfast had been a rather skimpy affair, she had been so anxious about taking leave of Jess and Jack. She refilled her coffee mug but then thought better of it and poured it back into the flask. She needed to get nearer her destination before she was incapable of driving.

Angela drove on. Now that she felt warm and comfortable, the shaking had stopped; she got to thinking. Maybe if she had coffee laced with whisky every day instead of the tablets, she could get by for another year or so? She could go on to Greymouth, have a couple of nights by the sea and reconsider. She had some money and her credit card so she could stay in a motel under another name; have time to consider her new plan. Yes, that's what she would do. Burying the thought that this was just another delaying tactic, she would press on to the coast today, decide if her new plan was feasible and come back on Sunday whatever the outcome. She could always do the deed on the way back if that was her final decision. The road was just as steep in the opposite direction, with many tight bends needing all her concentration. It was becoming noticeably cooler in the cab the nearer she came to the summit of the pass and Angela turned up the heating. Having made her decision, she began to enjoy the journey, stopping several times to admire the view. Jack was right, it was a long drive and by the time she reached the coast Angela was exhausted. The sea, an unattractive battleship grey, did nothing to improve her mood.

Oh God, she thought. Why did she come? It would have all been over by now if she'd stuck to her original plan. It was three o'clock so she must find somewhere to stay and a liquor store for more whisky. The road followed the sea to the town, some twenty minutes to the north. On entering Greymouth, an aptly named town if ever there was one, Angela came across a supermarket near the station where she bought a loaf of bread, some cheese, an apple and two bananas. She hummed and hahd over whether to buy a half or a whole litre of whisky then decided on the latter. It was her medicine after all and would help her sleep.

Angela retraced her route out of town until she found the isolated motel sporting a vacancy sign that she'd spotted on the way in. Only the road separated the rather rundown complex from the wild and rocky shore.

'Have you got a room for the night?'

'Sure. No 3, on the front. You can park right outside. Good journey?'

'Yes, thanks.' She took the key and the offered third of a pint of milk and went straight to the room. It ideally suited her purpose. The owner wasn't exactly welcoming which was probably why so few people were staying there. It amused her to sign in as Sandra Spencer, her old friend from New Plymouth and the one she was supposed to be visiting. The unit was basic but had the usual bathroom, bedroom and cooking facilities with a few sachets of tea and coffee and a television. It was enough.

It was 8.30am before Angela stirred from a whisky induced dreamless sleep, which she had badly needed. She showered and changed into clean underclothes before having a simple breakfast of a cheese sandwich and a pot of tea. She made some more sandwiches with the rest of the bread, half filled her flask with sweetened coffee, topped it up with whisky and put it with her few belongings into the Ute. She would not touch it until her return journey. Traffic police were few and far between in this area but Angela could not afford to be arrested for drunk driving. She was probably still over the limit from last night's binge so she would just drive the half mile back to town and park up somewhere by the sea for the day. She paid her bill and left.

Once in town, she bought a sticky bun to have with her sandwiches and fruit. The floodwall walk along the town side of Grey River had been built to prevent the town from flooding but she had heard it was not a hundred per cent successful. She crossed over Cobden Bridge and turned left down to the beach, one kilometre further on according to the sign.

Angela found a sheltered spot and sat watching the waves crashing on the shore. The turbulent surf matched her thoughts, tumbling and spraying round in her head. Gradually though, the mesmerising surge and ebb of the tide brought a calmness to her mind and Angela knew what she had to do. It was no good. The shaking had returned with a vengeance now the whisky had worn off. How long would she last on a diet of whisky? She would become so befuddled she wouldn't know where she was or what she was doing and Maxine would have to put her in a home. She had made her decision. She would take her final journey that afternoon.

On her way back to the Ute, Angela passed an old fellow in a wheelchair, being pushed with difficulty by a woman she took to be his long-suffering wife. He'd obviously had a stroke as he was muttering incomprehensibly to himself and Angela could see that one side of his face and his right arm were paralysed. She swore to herself as she hurried on, that she would never, ever be in that condition.

Feeling hungry again and knowing she had at least two hours driving ahead of her, Angela stopped long enough to buy a warm meat pie. She topped the Ute up with diesel, taking advantage of the toilets at the garage before setting off, back the way she had come, eating the pie out of the bag as she drove along. Once she was well away from civilisation and had started the climb into the mountains, she pulled over and poured herself a coffee from the flask. God. She needed that. Her shoulders and back were aching and she cursed the shaking when she took her hands from the wheel. She pushed on until she had passed the small hamlet of Otira and pulled over at the first available spot. It was almost dusk now and she hadn't seen any other vehicles for some time. If she remembered correctly there was a missing section of crash barrier on a particularly steep bend just below the summit of the pass. Exactly what she was looking for. Where the road curved round in a tight loop, a sheet of orange plastic netting afforded the only protection from the sheer drop to the valley below. As it came into view she decided to go past it, pressing on to the lookout point at the summit where she could turn around. She needed to be driving down hill to gain the necessary momentum. Good as the Ute was, Angela didn't think she would be going fast enough from her present direction, to do a proper job. Going uphill, she would also have time to pull back if she lost her nerve again. Teetering on the edge and being rescued didn't bear thinking about.

It was dark and reluctantly she put the inside light on just long enough to pour the last of the coffee and whisky into her mug. She drank quickly as she didn't want anyone stopping to see if she was OK. This was it. No turning back. There were no lights in either direction so she started the engine and drove off the way she had come. Yes, there it was, two bends ahead. The barrier had probably been swept away by a rock fall and not yet repaired. It was the perfect place. Maybe the Government would be blamed for her death, for not having repaired it sooner. Serve them right. Angela had no time for Governments of any complexion.

The alcohol was having its effect and Angela felt she could do anything. She even started singing, songs from her youth, the one of Elvis,' how did it go? 'I can do anything…' Her driving was more erratic now and it was harder to keep the car on the road. Ah. There was her corner, speed up now, faster, faster, 'Goodbye Cruel World' Angela shouted as she crashed through the orange plastic at nearly 60 miles an hour and plunged into the ravine.

The pick-up hit an outcrop half way down, mercifully rendering Angela unconscious before it landed in a burst of flame 800 feet below.

Chapter Thirty Four

England

Matron was finding it a struggle to explain to the owners of Lakeside that they needed to increase the wages of the staff. Not her own, she wasn't asking for a pay rise. The home was chronically short staffed and the inspectorate had said they must recruit more before the next inspection in December.

Although it was only September, Ruth Stevens had asked Harry and Phyllis Bailey to come into the office to advise them of the difficulties she was having in finding staff, let alone recruiting them. The owners did not live on site and left the day to day running of the home to Miss Stevens.

She began conciliatorily enough by acknowledging that Lakeside paid as well as most and as Matron, she tried to be accommodating with the hours the staff worked. Most of the staff were female; they had families and if their children were still at school there were the holidays to cope with, and the inevitable illnesses. It was the nature of the work that was the problem, together with the responsibility required.

'What have you tried? Have you been advertising in the right places?' Harry Bailey was a large bluff man, who liked to project himself as brisk and business-like but often came across as a bully. The last thing he wanted to do was increase the wages. It had been bad enough when the minimum wage came in and they'd made sure they paid above that anyway.

'I've advertised in all the local papers and the Carer

magazine and on the relevant websites. It's very expensive, as I'm sure you know. You must've had the bills.'

'It's damned expensive and if it's not producing results we must think of something else. And you should know, that's not the only expensive thing. Now we've done the fire regulations, the latest dictat is we have to reduce the temperature of the hot water in all the basins. This means fitting a device on all the taps in every basin. At fifty quid a time, that's expensive. I sometimes think the Government is trying to drive us out of business.'

Matron was astonished. 'Why are they insisting on that? We haven't had anyone burnt with hot water. Perhaps we won't have to do it if the temperature of our water is OK?'

'Well it's not. They tested it last week and it was nearly ten degrees hotter than they stipulate. The poor old dears will be washing in luke-warm water. Bloody interfering bureaucrats, they wouldn't want to wash in tepid water.' Harry was really angry now but Ruth felt she had a solution to this problem, which perhaps wouldn't cost them so much.

'Why don't you just reduce the temperature of the water in the header tank, then that would be just one operation rather than dealing with all the basins? It would be cheaper overall too, if you don't have to get the water as hot.'

'Listeria, bloody Listeria, that's why we can't do that. Don't you think I'd have thought of that? Apparently the water has to be heated to a higher temperature initially to kill any possible Listeria germs but then reduced so it doesn't burn anyone.'

Phyllis broke in here, 'Calm down Harry, calm down. We have to do it if we want to remain open and that's that. Let's get back to the staff salaries. I'm sure you can see now Matron, why it is going to be difficult to raise salaries much more.'

Neither she nor Harry had ever indicated how much they were making at the home but the profit margin had definitely narrowed since all the changes in care standards had had to be implemented. Ruth was sure they had been making a good profit but she knew there were a lot of expenses and trying to cope with all the new regulations was making it hard for homes to survive. Two in the surrounding area had closed in the last eighteen months. She had to make them see that advertising wasn't the answer.

'The way I see it is that the supermarkets, fast food outlets, even call centres, are a more attractive option.'

'I don't believe it! Those places pay peanuts. We do a lot better than that.' Harry was quite belligerent but Phyllis understood,

'Aah. But they don't have to think in those jobs. Caring for people takes a special kind of person, if you're going to do it right. We need to make sure it is right, or we'll be closed down anyway. Enough staff but of the wrong kind could be as bad as not enough staff. This is one of my objections to paying more. We don't want to get people coming to work here just for the money.'

Ruth felt this was greatly exaggerating the pay rise she'd suggested.

'Oh, you'd have to increase the wages by a couple of pounds an hour to attract people just for the money. I wouldn't suggest that for one moment. No. I was thinking more in terms of fifteen or twenty pence an hour. It might stand a chance of at least getting more people to apply.'

'Do you mean, "across the board?" The same for everyone? We've over fifty staff; it can't be done. We'd have to put the fees up so much we wouldn't get any clients.'

'No, it needn't be everyone, just the care staff, say, twenty-five pence an hour and about half that on the domestic staff wages. The senior staff are quite well paid now, the kitchen staff would be unaffected and as long as we don't alter the differentials by much there shouldn't be any trouble. We have to do something and I don't know what else to suggest.'

'Phyllis and I'll have a think about it and let you know.

We've only recently told people there is to be an increase in the fees so we can't do that again this year.' Ruth took this to mean the meeting was at an end and as the Baileys got up to leave she hoped they wouldn't take too long to make up their minds. More staff were needed now.

Harry was at the door when he said, 'What about school kids? Have you tried them? Ones who want to go on and do caring, or nurse training when they leave school? We could pay them less but they would benefit by learning something about the job.'

'No I haven't specifically tried to recruit them but I could let the two Sixth Form colleges know we're looking for people. We do occasionally get one or two enquires from individuals, the ones with more about them, ones with the initiative to come and ask for a job. Even if we got some of them they would only be very part time, probably only at weekends and holidays.'

'Well that's the time you say it's difficult to get people so I'm sure it would be a help. You get on with that while we're considering a more permanent solution.'

Ruth felt she had achieved something but she wasn't convinced that the Baileys would hurry themselves about increasing the wages and this business about the hot water was an added irritant. How many more regulations were going to be enforced? Now the Baileys had come up with the idea of school kids they just might wait and see how many materialised before they did anything else. Putting their requirements on the website was the best she could do until she heard back from them. That didn't cost anything. Problems, problems. Sometimes she wondered why she just didn't retire and have an easy life.

Chapter Thirty Five

Several months, including another Christmas, passed without any major crisis in Lakeside. Evelyn had come to them for the holiday weekend and enjoyed playing with Luke for short periods and of course, chatting to Ralph about his job in the City and trying to find out if he had any nice girlfriends. He was now earning good money and showered everyone with expensive presents although his father warned him that the good times might not last and he hoped he was putting money aside for a pension. Ralph just laughed and said that was all taken care of. He managed to avoid any discussion of his social life other than saying he was having a ball.

Nancy had her off days and these always affected Evelyn who became depressed and more demanding of Kristine and Derek. As Nancy had just turned eighty, to Evelyn's eighty-five, Evelyn expected her to be as bright and on the ball as she considered herself to be. Then there were the inevitable deaths amongst the residents that reminded the rest of their vulnerability. However, it was worse if any of them had to go into hospital as they had invariably deteriorated when they came out. It wasn't only the local hospital either.

There were horror stories in the paper every week about the filthy state of some of the country's hospitals. Kristine had her own theories as to how things could be improved without costing much money; one person in charge over all, everyone to wash their hands between patients, and nobody to wear their hospital clothes outside the hospital. She saw a nurse in uniform in the supermarket on one occasion and once she'd seen two of them trying on clothes over their uniforms. But who was going to listen to her?

They'd recently had a letter about reducing the temperature of the hot water in the hand basins; no wonder the germs weren't killed if they were only using lukewarm water in the hospitals too. Everyone said you could never go backwards, you had to move with the times but cross infection was much worse now than when she was nursing. It was ironic; she had been worrying about putting Evelyn into an old peoples' home because they used to be so awful. Now, many of them were better than the major hospitals that had always had an enviable reputation.

Several new girls had started at the home over the last few weeks. Some only stayed two or three weeks but one or two looked to be permanent. There were a couple of young lads and a girl who were only there at the weekends and Evelyn said they were still at school. Apparently they had thought about nursing as a career and were coming to see if they liked the idea. Kristine supposed it helped the staffing situation without costing too much. Besides, it was sensible to have some idea of what you were going into if you wished to be a nurse.

In Kristine's training days, nurses were on probation for three to six months and if they weren't up to scratch they could be asked to leave. By the same token, they could go if they didn't like it. Now they did a degree course before they faced the challenges of dirty beds and bottoms, foul smelling wounds or bloody bandages. Kristine felt it was a waste of your three-year degree course if you then found you couldn't stand the sight of blood. There was another problem as she saw it. Those who had a degree were not so keen on doing the menial tasks of giving bedpans and bed baths. Nurses today didn't know what hard work was. At least they didn't have to boil and scrub the bedpans and bowls as they were all disposable. She must be getting old if she thought things were better in the old days. Oh well, she'd just have to hope Evelyn didn't need to go to hospital. She was safer where she was, even if the home was sometimes short of staff.

It wasn't Evelyn who went to hospital in February, but Nancy. She got up in the night to go to the lavatory and tripped over her book that she'd let drop on the floor when she fell asleep. She tried to save herself but struck her head on the bedside table and ended up in a heap with her right arm folded under her body. She lay there for some time before she came to enough to call out. She was fortunate that night in that there was a conscientious nurse on duty who did her rounds every hour and heard Nancy calling from along the passage. An ambulance was called and Nancy was taken to hospital. The nurse notified Nancy's relatives and filed her accident report. It was not until the morning that Evelyn heard the news and she was dreadfully upset. She was on the phone to Kristine before eight o'clock.

'What am I going to do without Nancy? I haven't any other friends in this place. How can I possibly stay here on my own?'

Kristine longed to say that it served her right for considering herself superior to the other residents and not trying to make friends. Instead, she said,

'Of course you're not on your own Evelyn. There are plenty of other people there and all the staff are there to look after you. It's their job. I'll go into the hospital to see Nancy this afternoon before coming to see you, then I can tell you how she is.'

When she finally found Nancy, Kristine was relieved to see her daughter Jocelyn was there too. She was so pleased to see Kristine and was effusive in her thanks for all the visits and outings given to her mother. Nancy's right eye was black and blue and there were three or four stitches just visible under a small dressing on her temple. Her right arm was in a sling as her wrist was broken.

'Fortunately, it's a simple break but Mother is still quite shocked.'

'I'm sure she is and she will be for a few days.'

Kristine went closer to the bed and patted Nancy's hand.

'I'm sure they'll send you back to Lakeside very soon. Evelyn will be lost without you. It will be quieter there and less chance of you catching anything else. Evelyn instructed me to come and find out how you are and I must go and report back to her.'

'Very bossy she is, Evelyn. You tell her to behave herself while I'm gone or I'll tick her off when I get back.'

'Mother! That's not very nice. I'm sure she's only concerned for your welfare.'

Kristine defended Nancy. 'That's all right. Evelyn is bossy. She bosses me too. I'll come and see you tomorrow if you're still here as I don't expect you'll get back again will you, Jocelyn?'

'That is kind of you. No I won't make tomorrow, Mother, but I should get here on Thursday and I'll try to be there when you go back to Lakeside.'

Evelyn was relieved to hear that Nancy was not too badly injured and would soon be back. Kristine suspected that it was Evelyn's own comfort that she was so concerned about, rather than Nancy's. She almost expected Evelyn to say it wasn't good enough that Nancy was injured, leaving her there to fend for herself. Instead, she took to ringing Kristine two or three times a day to tell her of the goings on at the home and the iniquities of the staff, events she normally shared with Nancy. Kristine was ashamed she sometimes ignored the phone when she saw who was ringing but she did try to visit more often while Nancy remained in the hospital, rather than her usual once or twice a week.

Contrary to expectation, it was six days before Nancy was discharged and Kristine was shocked at the change in her. Jocelyn was so relieved her mother had been returned to the home as she felt she would have died had she stayed in hospital. She had seldom been washed and only had her hair combed when Jocelyn or Kristine visited. Her nails were dirty and she appeared to have lost weight, which wasn't surprising considering nobody checked to see if patients could reach the meals put before them. While her arm had been in plaster, Nancy would not have been able to cut up her food and unless it had been readily available she probably wouldn't have bothered. She was of the breed that wouldn't ask for help unless she absolutely had to. This is where she could have done with some of Evelyn's arrogant belief that everyone should wait on her as a matter of course.

Nancy's arm was now out of plaster and in a removable splint so there was no excuse for her not having a bath. Matron promised Jocelyn that her mother would have a bath and her hair washed that afternoon. Most of the bruising on Nancy's face had faded but she was pale and depressed. Evelyn promised to do her best to cheer her up so Jocelyn and Kristine left them together with a tray of tea and biscuits.

'Eat as many of those scrumptious chocolate biscuits as you like, Mother. They might fatten you up a bit.' Jocelyn kissed her mother goodbye, saying she would be back in a day or two but would ring her tomorrow.

'I don't think just one of those biscuits will hurt you, Evelyn. We thought you both deserved a treat.' Nancy gradually recovered her strength over the next few weeks but her mental health was making only slow progress. Whether or not the two were connected, Evelyn was also showing signs of decline. She wasn't quite so interested in what Kristine had to say and twice lately, The Times did not look as if it had been opened. Her hearing was not what it was either but she refused to accept that she would benefit from hearing aids. Still, Derek could always get a response and he often read the previous day's paper to her, which she seemed to enjoy. It made her day too, when Ralph came home for a visit.

There was nothing specifically wrong with Evelyn but she had lost her spark. Kristine mused that it was funny that now Evelyn was more docile, she rather wished she had some of her old aggression back. A docile Evelyn was not really the same person. Kristine came to the conclusion that she was becoming institutionalised.

Matron reported that Evelyn 'helped' around the home by watering the pot plants and spending some time with one or two residents who were confined to bed. She was, however, inclined to be bossy and tried to make people get up, even when they didn't feel well enough. Matron had had to give her a sharp word, which didn't go down well.

'Here am I trying to lend a hand and encourage some of these people to get up and about and Matron tells me off for interfering.'

'I think Matron knows you're trying to help, Evelyn, but perhaps the residents concerned would rather be left alone with their thoughts.'

'Well, they won't improve if they lie about all day.' Evelyn seemed oblivious of her own stubborn attitude when people tried to persuade her to do something for her own good. Kristine knew it was no good arguing with her but she was resolved to try harder to keep Evelyn interested in the outside world and her family. Perhaps Rebecca would bring Luke over one afternoon. All the residents would like to see him; he was such a happy, cheerful little chap.

Gradually Kristine's life settled back into a routine with a weekly visit to her mother-in-law. She managed to get to her monthly meetings of NADFAS and went on some interesting day trips and lectures. She took photos of the houses she visited, in an effort to have more to share with Evelyn. Sometimes she was interested and sometimes she couldn't be bothered, although Derek had more success. Evelyn was very proud of Luke when Rebecca or Tom brought him in to see her. She insisted on walking him around the home and introducing him to all the residents. All the old people loved him of course, although half of them couldn't figure out who he was or why he was there.

It was early July when disaster struck. Kristine was making the beds when the phone rang. It was Evelyn.

'Kristine, are you there? Something awful has happened – Matron's gone off sick – one of the staff says she's died – and if she has, who's going to look after us – what will we do?'

Evelyn was so agitated Kristine had a struggle to break in and get her to listen.

'It's all right, Evelyn, I'm here. Now what's the matter? I'm sure if Matron's sick she will be better soon and they always have a deputy, you'll be well looked after.'

'But what if she really has died? Only one person says she has but the others haven't denied it.' Evelyn was not to be pacified.

'Well if she has, I'm very, very sorry but you will still be cared for so don't worry. I expect someone will notify us of the situation as soon as it's clear what has happened. You really mustn't worry. I'll be in tomorrow anyway. What does Nancy say?'

'She's as worried as I am and says we'll have to get another Matron and that won't happen overnight and we might wait ages and who knows what kind of chaos there'll be with nobody in charge. What about our medicines and what about meals…'

Kristine managed with difficulty to break into this stream of anxiety but she fully understood how unsettled they all must be, especially with the rumours, true or otherwise, of Matron's demise.

'I'll give the office a ring and see what I can find out and then I'll call you back but it might take me a while. Don't expect me to call back straight away – and don't worry, you will be looked after.'

Kristine called the office and managed to speak to the sister on duty.

'I'm afraid I don't know all the facts yet, Mrs Arnold. We do know Matron was suddenly taken ill and went by ambulance to the hospital but at the moment I don't know any more than that. As soon as we know we shall tell all the residents and inform their relatives. Please be assured we will see that they are all looked after.'

'I'm sure you will and I shall reassure my mother-in-law.'

Kristine hoped she'd be able to calm Evelyn down. She'd ring Nancy's daughter too as she might not have heard. Nancy was less alarmist than Evelyn and had probably not phoned Jocelyn. It was early evening before Sister rang to say that Matron had indeed died, a heart attack they thought, although this was not confirmed. Sister Phillips would be in charge until a new Matron could be appointed which might take some time. Then, whoever was selected would have to be approved by the Inspectorate and that could take several months. Kristine knew it was going to be a long process and there would be inevitable uncertainty with consequent anxiety amongst the staff, the residents and the relatives.

In this, Kristine was proved correct. Rumour was that Sister Phillips had applied for the permanent position as Matron but according to Evelyn, half the staff did not want this outcome. Kristine thought half was probably an exaggeration. It was more like one or two. They felt that Jane Phillips was not strong enough to stand up to the Baileys, who they believed were trying to cut corners in the running of the Home to make more profit for themselves.

However, the most serious rumour was that the Home would have to close. Kristine felt, and fervently hoped, that this was not the case. Given that there were fifty vulnerable people in care there, she was sure every effort would be made to keep the place open. After all, they had had no trouble keeping Lakeside full and the residents well cared for until now. She could see no reason why this would not continue to be the case. Derek was of the same view.

'I can't see the Inspectorate letting such a large and viable home go to the wall. What would they do with all those dependent people? It's not as if places are easy to find. Look at the trouble we had in finding anywhere for mother.'

'Well, the advertisement is going out this week, applications close in three weeks and I believe interviews are the first week in September. Let's hope they get a good selection of applicants and can make an appointment soon. Things are rather fragile there at the moment with rumour and counter-rumour flying around.'

'Helped, no doubt, by mother's fertile imagination. She's getting her medication all right isn't she and she hasn't complained about the meals or anything, or not to me.'

'No, I think she's fine and Nancy keeps her on an even keel most of the time but she is getting very frail. It's just that the home doesn't seem as well kept and as organised as it was. It is developing a rather scruffy air about it. You're going tomorrow, aren't you? See what you think.'

Derek had thought Kristine was imagining things but he had to admit that there was a subtle change in the ambiance of Lakeside although he couldn't point to any one thing that had changed. The residents looked clean and happy. The floors had been swept and mopped. The sherry still appeared before lunch and the meals smelt as appetising as usual. He finally came to the conclusion that it was the staff that appeared different, but how? Perhaps aimless was the word, not quite focused on the job in hand? Yes that was it. They were drifting about, doing what they had to do but with no real enthusiasm. It was probably the uncertainty that was affecting them. Kristine and he agreed they would have to keep a close eye on the situation, although he felt that was the role of the Inspectorate and the owners. Hell, they were paying enough.

They made a big effort to have Evelyn out for lunch most Sundays and Nancy too when she felt up to it, but this was seldom. Kristine took them for a drive occasionally when the weather was fine and they would find somewhere nice to have tea. Back at Lakeside they felt uneasy, anxious, not sure what was going to happen next. Nancy had become very frail and spent much of the time in her room and some of that in bed. Evelyn sat with her most days and when Nancy was asleep she read the newspaper or more often, dozed in the chair. It was a worrying time for them as there were still persistent rumours that the home might close although Kristine and Derek constantly assured them that it wouldn't.

Applications for a new Matron had closed and interviews were to take place the following week. Sister Phillips had applied and although Nancy and Evelyn quite liked her and thought she knew her job, they didn't really want her to be appointed. In their view her style was divisive and they didn't feel there would be peace amongst the staff if she got the job. On the other hand, any new person would take a while to get to know everyone –perhaps the devil you knew? Oh well it wasn't up to them. They would just have to put up with whomever they got and hope for the best.

Derek and Kristine were of the opposite view. They felt that Sister Phillips knew the home and the residents as she had been there for seven years. She was also familiar with the Baileys' working practices and did not seem to be hesitant about voicing her opinion. Kristine tried not to worry about Evelyn or the home. She was being looked after and Dr. Nicholls visited her regularly. He would notice if she wasn't receiving the correct treatment.

Chapter Thirty Six

'Kristine, is that you? I'm so glad because I don't know what's going to happen to us now, they've appointed that Sister Phillips and I know there will be trouble, I just know it and so does Nancy.' As if bringing Nancy into it would lend Evelyn's opinion more weight.

'Have they told you officially, or is it rumour?'

If true, Kristine was hopeful that things would now get back to normal. Once the uncertainty about the future of the home was removed the staff would accept the decision and things would settle down.

'Of course we haven't had a letter or anything but all the residents were called to a meeting, all those that weren't confined to their beds, and Sister Phillips addressed us. She told us everything was going to be back to normal but I don't see how it can. Some of the staff are not pleased.'

Kristine made an effort to curb her irritation. Evelyn had wanted the home to appoint a Care Manager and now they had, she didn't approve. Was her mother-in-law never going to be satisfied?

'Please don't worry, Evelyn. I'm really quite pleased that they have made a decision and the staff will soon settle down. If they don't like Sister Phillips then they will have to go and work somewhere else, but you'll see, they will soon forget about their objections, especially if she handles them right.'

'That's just it, she won't. She's more likely to provoke them than otherwise.'

'I do think you are worrying unnecessarily, Evelyn. You

relax and wait and see. I shall be in to see you on Thursday and we'll see how things are then. Bye for now.'

It was a relief to get off the phone. Couldn't Evelyn see that Kristine knew no more about the situation than she did and they would just have to wait and see?

Word got out that Sister Phillips had had a staff meeting and had been very candid about the position. She'd told them that she was well aware that some of them had not wanted her to be appointed. Although she was sorry that was the case, she was now the person in charge and they would have to work together or seek other employment. She believed that Ruth Stevens had run a very efficient and happy home and it was her intention to carry on that tradition. There were many challenges ahead with the constant flow of new regulations but she hoped to make as few changes as possible.

Following the staff meeting she had then spoken to the residents in a similar vein. Kristine had judged it correctly. Once Sister Phillips's appointment was a fait accompli, those members of staff who would have preferred someone else just got on with the job. Both Evelyn and Nancy, though, continued to report undercurrents of dissatisfaction.

Rather than complaining about the Care Manager, several of the care staff were angling for a pay rise. Evelyn said she'd heard two of them suggesting they might go on strike. Kristine tried to ignore these rumours. If the staff were to be given more money then the fees would go up. If the fees went up too much, some residents would move to cheaper homes. If too many did that Lakeside might close, then what would they do? When Kristine voiced her concerns to Derek he became irritated.

'Why do you always have to imagine the worst-case scenario? Just because one or two of the staff want more money it doesn't mean they'll get it or that they'll go on strike. Staff always want more money but unless they all get together and threaten strike action, nothing will happen. I don't know why you take so much notice of Mother and her scaremongering.'

'Well, she's bound to be worried when she hears these things, surely you can understand how she feels? Lakeside is her home and she doesn't want it to collapse under her.'

'Now you're being melodramatic, Kristine. You know that won't happen. The Inspectorate wouldn't allow it for one thing. It's up to us to jolly Mother out of her fears, not encourage them.'

'What do you take me for, an idiot? I don't encourage her and I do try to reassure her, but I am concerned and I imagined you would be too. I'm sorry I spoke, but it is your mother and if Lakeside was to close it would be a problem for us, and a big one.' God, why couldn't men have a bit of imagination? In Kristine's view, if you prepared for the worst then it was unlikely to happen but at least you were ready if it did.

Derek could see Kristine was upset. She worried too much about what might happen instead of waiting until it did.

'OK, I'm sorry but we have to take things as they come. I don't imagine for a minute that Lakeside will close but if it does or is likely to, then we cross that bridge when we come to it. As to Mother's fears, I don't believe she worries about it all the time but she knows it gets our attention and she just wants reassurance.'

At Lakeside, Jane Phillips was preparing for a meeting with the Baileys. She had heard rumours of a strike circulating among the staff and she knew it was about pay. They couldn't afford to lose the staff they had. Ruth Stevens had told her about her efforts to get the Baileys to agree an increase for the care staff but so far, nothing had come of it. They probably thought they could forget it now Ruth had died. Well they couldn't. Something had to be done.

'Morning, Jane, how's things? Everything seems to be

running very smoothly since you took over, well done.' Phyllis was charm itself this morning.

'And I echo that,' boomed Harry as he planted a kiss on Jane's check, something he'd never done before. Trying to soften her up, she imagined, but it wouldn't work. They needed more staff and they would have to get them somehow, and keep the ones they had. She didn't beat about the bush.

'I know Ruth spoke to you about a pay rise for the care staff back in September and you were thinking about it. Have you come to any conclusions because I'm afraid it is now critical. The Inspectorate are due this month and I regret to tell you that I've heard rumours of strike action, admittedly from only two or three at the moment but we don't want that to grow, or for them to complain to the inspectors.'

'STRIKE! I'll give them bloody strike! We don't want people here who are fomenting a strike. They can leave and just see if they can get another job somewhere else. Nobody wants people in this line of business who are prepared to strike.'

'Keep your voice down, Harry, or the whole place will hear you. I imagine it's still about money, Miss Phillips?' The initial informality of the meeting had disappeared. Phyllis was all business now.

'Yes it is. If we could manage fifteen or twenty pence for the care staff it might make all the difference. There are thirty-six of them but some are part time so that won't make it quite so expensive. I regret to say that if we don't do it, we'll lose some of our staff.'

Harry and Phyllis went into a huddle over the files they had brought with them.

'Do you think we can get away with starting any increase on the 1st January rather than December? Christmas is a very expensive time.' The pair were clutching at anything that would delay the evil day.

'I'm sure I could sell that to them. Just knowing they are

going to have an increase should ward off any rebellion. I am most grateful.' Jane Phillips was relieved she now had some concrete proposal to take to the staff before Christmas.

'We'll not say exactly how much an hour it will be. We have to do our sums, but it will be across the board for care staff and will start on the 1st January.' With that they packed up their papers and left the office.

The following week a team of inspectors (four instead of the usual three) turned up and began poking into every nook and cranny. It was Miss Phillips's belief that they would be even more thorough than usual because she was a new face at the top and it was their job to confirm her appointment. She just hoped she came up to scratch.

The building work to comply with the fire regulations had been completed, refurbishment of several rooms was now finished and the upstairs corridor was in the process of being repainted. November wasn't an ideal time for painting, having to leave the windows open, but most of the residents were downstairs by 11am and now the bedroom doors had to be shut, the smell wasn't too bad. Residents were interviewed, as were any visitors unfortunate enough to be there that day.

Evelyn was disappointed they never asked for her views this time. When she volunteered them, the senior inspector said that as she had contributed last time, they would be interviewing different people on this occasion. She'd wanted to tell them that some of the staff were threatening strike action but Nancy had warned her strongly against any mention of that.

'If they think the staff are going on strike then they will assume the home is not being run properly and then they might close it, so you mustn't say anything. Please Evelyn, don't interfere. If it happens, they'll find out soon enough.'

'You may be right, Nancy, but we may be sorry.' If they weren't going to interview her she'd go and have a rest on her bed. Perhaps there would be a nice play on the radio but most of them were not worth listening to.

When Kristine went in to visit the next day, she heard that the inspection had gone off well and that the home was expecting a good report. They were making the improvements asked for in the last report and the new manager appeared to have control of the home. Jane Phillips told her that they would be doing an in-depth report on her competence at the next review in March, when she hoped they would confirm her appointment. Kristine was greatly reassured by this news and reported it to Evelyn. Her mother-in-law was unconvinced.

'There are still plenty of mutterings amongst the staff. They say they don't get paid very much and have to work long hours. One of them told me that the owners are making plenty of money and they should be giving more of it to the staff.' Bearing in mind Derek's views on the subject, Kristine attempted to stop these negative views of Evelyn's. She should try to look at it from the owners' point of view.

'Mr and Mrs Bailey have had a huge expense bringing the fire precautions up to the standard of the new regulations. Then they had to fix the water temperature in the baths and basins, which was an expensive business and of course they always have to do repairs and painting. It can't be easy to balance the books.'

'Well if they can't afford to pay the staff properly, then perhaps they shouldn't be running a home, they should sell it.'

'That's hardly a sensible option, Evelyn. The Baileys have been running a home of some sort for years and if they can't make it work, most others would be unable to do so. The last thing we want is for the home to close.'

This was obviously one of Evelyn's more cantankerous days so Kristine didn't argue with her. Over the last year Evelyn had become noticeably more debilitated which probably added to her frustration. She could still walk about the home but she seldom used the stairs, unless encouraged to do so by the physiotherapist. She refused to do it unaccompanied. Her diabetes was under control but she was now also having tablets for her blood pressure. Kristine knew she would never have been able to manage her at Elmbrook Manor.

Two weeks before Christmas, Derek and Kristine received a letter from the Baileys informing them that the care staff would be receiving a pay increase as from the 1st January. They understood that rumours had been circulating about staff dissatisfaction and they hoped this would address the issue. It was not their intention to increase the fees at this stage.

'Thank God for that. It's the last thing we need before Christmas. Let's hope it's sufficient to placate the staff.' Derek was gloomily aware that it was only a matter of time before the fees went up. Although he had disagreed with his mother when she had complained the fees were exorbitant, if they went up much more he might change his views.

Evelyn came out to Elmbrook Manor for three nights over Christmas and seemed to enjoy herself but they all noticed a great change in her. She had given up using a walking stick as she felt safer with a zimmer frame and some days her memory was particularly bad. She drove Ralph mad, continually asking him the same questions. When Kristine went to make the coffee on Christmas Day, Ralph followed her into the kitchen.

'I've told Granny about three times what I do all day. Doesn't she listen or doesn't she hear?'

'I know. It drives me mad too but you have to remember she's old now, Ralph, and her short-term memory is not what it was. Just tell her again and try to guide her onto another subject. She's also quite deaf, although she refuses to admit it so you must speak up. It'll happen to me one day soon and I'll expect you to show some patience.'

'Well, I'm not going to let that happen to me. When I feel it coming on, I'll get in a canoe and sail off into the sunset.'

Kristine laughed and patted him on the shoulder.

'You won't know you're doing it and you'll expect your wife, if you have one, to wait on you hand and foot. You might even be cantankerous with it.'

When she went back with the coffee she found Evelyn had dozed off, oblivious to Luke playing an exuberant game of piggy-back with his father.

'Shall we wake her for the Queen's Speech?'

'Too late, Mum, she's missed it.'

'Oh Rebecca, that was a bit mean. You know how much she likes to listen.'

'We told her it was coming on any minute but she went to sleep anyway. Didn't you say she has a sleep most afternoons? With champagne before lunch and a couple of glasses of wine, I had trouble staying awake myself. She can watch the repeat when it's on later.'

Perhaps Evelyn had needed the nap as she was quite cheerful and sociable at teatime. She watched the Queen's Speech later; seemingly unaware that it was a repeat. Boxing Day passed peaceably enough although it was never quiet with a small child in the house. Evelyn seemed quite relieved when everyone decided to go for a walk after lunch. She went to her room with the paper but was soon asleep on the bed. Nancy had returned to Lakeside on the evening of Boxing Day so for once Evelyn did not protest about going back. They would have plenty to talk about.

Chapter Thirty Seven

Kristine and Derek were enjoying a leisurely breakfast one Sunday in February when Kristine spotted an article about care homes in The Times.

'Listen to this, "As of the first of April all care staff in residential and nursing homes will be required to take National Vocational Qualifications…" I wonder if that will affect Lakeside?'

'It probably will, but surely not those who've been there for years and years?'

'Let me see… "this will apply to all carers and domestic staff, regardless of length of service…" 'that's ridiculous! Staff who've been working in homes for fifteen, sometimes twenty years won't want to start studying and taking exams.'

'I'm sure they won't. Are they going to phase it in? Perhaps they'll have two or three years to get staff to comply.'

' "It is important that care homes staff is properly qualified to look after the elderly. Homes will be given a three year period to bring their staff up to the required standard." I would think some of the Staff at Lakeside would leave rather than comply with this, wouldn't you? Oh. Hang on, here is something else tucked away near the end of the article. "The cost for each course will be approximately £300." But that's terrible. How on earth are owners of these homes expected to pay yet more costs?'

'By putting up the fees of course. There's no other way to do it.' Derek sounded very glum. 'It does seem very short-sighted. I would have thought the older ones, the ones with the most experience, would call it a day, especially if they are near retirement age. This won't help the staffing levels and I can't see how the average person can go on meeting ever higher fees.'

Kristine was sure it could be the straw that broke the camel's back. The staff had just been given a pay rise but if they were now asked to study and sit exams, how many of them would stay? Maybe it wouldn't happen. Often these things were floated in the paper to gauge reaction and if that proved unfavourable, the idea was quietly shelved. It would be interesting to see if anyone mentioned it when she next went to see Evelyn.

Evelyn broached the subject some weeks later. She had it slightly muddled but the gist of it was correct.

'Many of the older girls here are very upset. They've got to go on courses and sit exams. If they fail they won't be able to continue working here. Nancy and I won't stay here if the older ones leave because they're the nicest. Much better than some of these flibberty-gibbets who are only interested in their appearance.' Evelyn regarded most young people as shallow and vain, not sensible and serious as in her day.

'I don't think that's quite right Evelyn. All the staff can't be on courses at once and I'm sure they will do the new ones first. I'll have a word with Miss Phillips before I go and see if it will have any impact on the home. You must look on the positive side of this, Evelyn. If all the staff have proper training it will improve the overall quality of care at Lakeside, the home will always be full and they will be able to recruit good staff more easily.'

'I expect it will be an excuse to raise the fees again. You did say they were going up, didn't you?'

'No, I hope not. They went up last year. It was the staff wages that went up in January, don't you remember?'

'I can't remember everything, Kristine. Besides, I'm more worried about Nancy at the moment.'

'Oh. Is she ill? Why didn't you say? We could pop along and see her now. Does her daughter know?' Evelyn was inclined to exaggerate any problems so Kristine wanted to see for herself how ill Nancy was.

Kristine knocked gently and then peeped around the door of Nancy's room. She was propped up on the pillows and appeared to be asleep but her cheeks were flushed and her breathing rather laboured.

She backed out and explained to Evelyn that she didn't think they should wake her. She would ask Miss Phillips how she was. As they walked back down the passage Evelyn started to cry quietly.

'I don't know what I shall do if Nancy dies. I have no other friends here. I may as well die too.'

She rummaged around to find a handkerchief in the large handbag she took everywhere with her, and blew her nose loudly.

'There, there, Evelyn.' Kristine put her arm round Evelyn's shoulders. For the first time, she seemed shrunken and old to Kristine. 'Nancy's probably just got a bad cold and will be better in a day or two. You mustn't think the worst. As to other friends, because you've always had Nancy you probably haven't bothered with anyone else. Now, while Nancy's ill, you could perhaps chat to some of the other residents. You might find some kindred spirits that could be friends to both of you.'

Kristine was annoyed with herself for not encouraging Evelyn to make more friends before but she'd been so dismissive of the other residents they'd not pressed it. Both she and Derek had been happy in the knowledge that she and Nancy had each other and their Bridge friends so there hadn't been a problem. Come to think of it, she hadn't heard if Julia or Fiona had been in to visit lately. The Bridge had gone by the board as Rose could no longer concentrate enough to play but to Kristine's knowledge, they had continued to visit. Now she felt she and Derek had been short-sighted, and the staff too. They should have foreseen the problem and encouraged Evelyn and Nancy to socialise more. Still, she couldn't blame the staff. They may have tried but they were very busy and she knew how stubborn her mother-in-law was to change. There was no way Evelyn would socialise with others if she didn't want to.

'I'll go and get us some tea and I'll have a word with Miss Phillips about Nancy at the same time. I'll be back in a minute.'

'I'm afraid Mrs Jackson has a chest infection and is not at all well. Her daughter does know and came to see her yesterday. It has hit your mother-in-law hard, Mrs Arnold. Nancy doesn't really want to be bothered with visitors, and that includes her.'

Jane Phillips explained that they had tried to tell Evelyn this but she thought they were being difficult and trying to keep her away from her friend. They were also anxious that Evelyn did not go down with the infection.

'Thank you for telling me. We certainly don't want her ill too. I'm just having a cup of tea with Evelyn and I shall try to explain the situation to her again but she's now very forgetful. I'm also trying to encourage her to make other friends in the home.'

'A good idea. We have tried, but she and Nancy seemed very happy with their own company. Good luck.'

As Kristine was leaving she remembered the article she'd read. 'Oh, I nearly forgot. Will this new legislation requiring NVQs have any implications for the home. I saw it in the paper at the weekend.'

'It certainly will, although I don't know the details yet. Some of the new regulations are very expensive and are killing many of the homes, especially the smaller ones. Try not to worry Mrs Arnold, I'm sure the Baileys will send out a letter if there are likely to be any problems.'

Kristine visited Evelyn more frequently while Nancy was ill and when Derek went in on the Sunday he asked one of the nurses to introduce him to one or two of the other residents. He then persuaded his mother to chat to them over their glass of sherry. She was reluctant and would have preferred to keep Derek to herself but he persevered with some success. Nancy was still confined to bed and showed little interest in the activities of the home.

It was nearly two weeks later when a letter arrived from the Baileys. As it was addressed to them both, Kristine opened it and wished she hadn't. By the time Derek arrived home in the evening she had worked herself up into a highly agitated state.

'I told you, and you said it wouldn't happen. What are we going to do?' she wailed. 'They're saying if they have to comply with these latest regulations they might have to close Lakeside. You were so sure they wouldn't close. Where will Evelyn go? Can we be sure she's being properly looked after while all this is going on?'

'Calm down, Kristine, and don't blame me. Getting in a state won't help anyone. First of all, they haven't said they will close, just that they might have to. Secondly, there are other homes, there's Field View for a start. It was one of our options, remember? Thirdly, who knows what things will be like in three years time? That's how long they have to phase this in. Some of the staff might decide to leave but they won't go until they have to and of course the younger ones will decide to do the courses. They'd be silly not to…'

'That's the problem, don't you see? If the majority decide to do the courses then it will cost the Baileys a lot of money and that's why they could decide it's not worth their while to carry on. They have had one thing after another and it's probably not the end of new legislation.'

Derek was determined to be positive. 'They can always put the fees up and even if they go to six or seven hundred pounds a week we could still meet them. Don't tell the Baileys that though! Seriously, when we sold the house we got a good price for it and we knew we might have to use all the money looking after mother.'

Kristine was not convinced. She was sure the money would run out. 'We must be paying about thirty thousand a year already. We can't go on at that rate, especially if it goes up even more.' She poured herself a glass of wine and sat disconsolately at the table, any thought of making the supper gone from her mind. 'Do you want a drink?'

'Yes, but I'm having a G&T. I need something stronger than wine. I agree it is a worry but it's not as bad as you imagine. We pay out about twenty three thousand now because mother has her pension too don't forget, and we did get five hundred grand for her house. It'll last quite a few years yet. I hate to say it… but at 85, Mother may not live that much longer'

'Regrettably, that's true and with Nancy being so ill, it's making Evelyn very low too. It's not just the money; it's so unsettling for your mother. Perhaps you could get Ralph to come down this weekend? He always cheers her up. I'd better give Jocelyn a ring and see what she and Richard think about the possible closure and find out the latest on Nancy's condition.'

Jocelyn said the prognosis on her mother was not good. She had pneumonia now and was very weak. She was full of praise though, for Lakeside. 'The staff are wonderful. Whenever possible, someone sits in with her so she doesn't feel abandoned and did you know they've allowed Evelyn to sit with her now too? The dangers of her getting a chest infection were pointed out to her but she said she would take that risk to support her friend. I think that's really lovely of her.'

'No, I didn't know but I'm so glad. It must be a comfort to you to know she is not alone.'

Kristine's eyes filled with tears she was glad Jocelyn couldn't see. Evelyn wasn't such an old bat after all.

'Yes it is. It's half term this week and Richard and I are taking the children to see Mother on Saturday afternoon. She did ask to see them but they won't stay long. Richard will take them off to the park while I sit with her. It's important that they see her, as it might be the last time. The girls go back to school on Monday and the boys on Tuesday.'

Kristine assured Jocelyn that she would visit her mother when she went to see Evelyn and she knew Derek would too. She decided not to mention the Baileys's letter. Jocelyn had enough to worry about and Derek was right, it might not come to anything.

The following week, Kristine was out in the garden picking the first daffodils to take to Evelyn and Nancy, when the phone rang. It was Evelyn and she was in tears.

'She's gone. My dear friend has gone. I don't want to be here without her.'

'I'm so sorry Evelyn. When did she go?' Kristine found herself copying Evelyn by avoiding the word "dying". 'You must be very sad. I'll come over this afternoon to be with you for a bit.'

'That would be kind but I thought you weren't able to come until Friday, or was it Thursday?' All the days seemed the same to Evelyn now.

'Well I do have something else to do but I think it is more important that I come over to you so I'll be there after lunch. Why don't you go and talk to some of the others and keep your mind off it. Nancy is out of pain now so we must be thankful for that. I'll see you later.'

Kristine rang Derek with the sad news. They had all become very fond of Nancy. He said he'd call and see his mother after work so he'd be late home. She also rang Jocelyn and left a message of sympathy on her answer-phone and an offer of help if it were needed. Armed with a bunch of daffodils, Kristine went to see Evelyn. She was shocked by her appearance. She seemed to have shrunk into herself during the three days since she'd last seen her. Sitting hunched in her chair with a blanket around her shoulders and another across her knees, Evelyn was tearful and very unhappy.

'I've nobody now, I'm all alone, I might as well die too.'

Kristine took her hand and squeezed it gently. 'I know this is a very sad time for you but you mustn't think you're alone. You have Derek and me and you've got Ralph and Rebecca and dear little Luke. Then there's Tom, who's very fond of you too. We all come to visit and you can still come out to us when you want to.'

Evelyn wiped her eyes and blew her nose but she still sounded tearful.

'I know what you're saying is true, Kristine, and you're all very kind but being here is not the same as being in your own home. The staff are lovely, well most of them, but the rumours about Lakeside closing are still going about and if it does, what shall I do then? Honestly, Kristine, I really will die if I have to move to another home and I'm sure I won't be the only one.' She was working herself up to another bout of tears when there was a knock at the door. Jane Phillips had bought a tray of tea and some of Evelyn's favourite chocolate biscuits.

'I know you shouldn't have them, Mrs Arnold, but you never ate any lunch and you need something to eat. It's been a sad day for you but when your daughter-in-law goes, I'll come along and have a chat. Perhaps you'll tell me how you and Nancy met and what you both got up to in your young days. I believe you've known her since school days haven't you?'

'Yes, that's where we met. Thank you, I'd like that. She was the adventurous one, I was always more cautious.'

Jane Philips had developed into a very efficient and caring Manager in Kristine's opinion. Even Evelyn agreed that she had turned out much better than expected and there were no more complaints from the staff. Thanking her for the tea, Kristine poured a cup for them both before arranging the daffodils in a vase by Evelyn's bed. They added a splash of colour to the dull and gloomy day. Kristine had never got used to the need for lights most of the day during the winter months. She was sure that was why she was more grumpy and despondent at this time of year. Evelyn was more cheerful by the time she left and perked up when Kristine told her Derek would be calling in after work. With Miss Phillips going in for a chat too she would have company for the rest of the afternoon, which was a good thing.

The rest of the family made a special effort to visit Evelyn more often over the next few weeks. Kristine went to Nancy's funeral and offered to take Evelyn but she didn't feel she could cope with the distress of it. Jocelyn went in the next day and took her some of the flowers, most of which were arranged in baskets. Evelyn was quite touched and said it made her feel that Nancy was still with her.

Life went on much as before but there had been a definite decline in Evelyn's condition. Miss Phillips reported that she was eating better than she had been while Nancy was ill but she was losing interest in her surroundings and her walking had deteriorated. Derek felt that some of it was due to her anxiety over the future of Lakeside and he was determined to try and find out just what was happening. On Sunday, he would 'chat up' the sister who was pouring out the sherry.

'You're looking lovely today, Sister. You brighten up a dreary morning.'

Sister Patterson, unlike Derek's mother, was immune to this sort of flattery. 'If you're looking for an extra glass of sherry, Mr Arnold, you're out of luck. We've got to watch the pennies these days.' Unwittingly, Sister had raised the subject he wanted to discuss. He decided to broach the matter head on as his mother was in conversation with another lady over by the window and was unlikely to hear them.

'I wanted to ask you about that. My wife is still hearing rumours about the home closing and I know it is worrying my mother very much. It is so unsettling.'

'I do realise that and I wish I knew more myself. Naturally, the staff are all worried about their jobs too. To be honest, I wish we'd hear, straight out. If we're going to get closed down we'd rather know, so we could apply for other places and move on. As it is, one or two people have already moved their relatives, as you may have heard, which doesn't improve the cash flow situation. I can't blame them. If we do close, everyone will be scrabbling for places in other homes. Several have closed in the last two years, it's all these bloody regulations; excuse my language.'

Derek was alarmed to hear residents were already moving. That little snippet had not filtered through. Perhaps they should be getting Evelyn's name down somewhere else.

'Well, who makes the decision? Can the Baileys just sell up? Surely you can't be closed down by the Inspectorate. Your last report was excellent in most areas and we hear nothing but praise about the treatment and care here.'

'That's very kind, I know where to come for a reference. No, seriously, it will be the Baileys who close us down, if they decide it is no longer a paying proposition. I shouldn't think they would even try to sell it as a going concern. They've had years of experience and if they can't make it work, I doubt anyone else will be able to. Here's your sherry, Mr Arnold, and here you are, Mrs Arnold, one for you. Did you think your son had forgotten to bring it?'

Sister Patterson had skilfully changed the conversation when she'd spotted Evelyn approaching. They didn't want to upset her again but Derek was disappointed not to have found out more. It was unlikely Sister knew any more anyway.

Unless he was prepared to ask the Baileys, who were no doubt doing their sums and would make their decision as soon as they could, he would have to be patient. In the meantime, he would put his mother's name down for Oakhurst whether they had any vacancies or not, just in case. He wouldn't mention it to Kristine or she would think he knew more then he did. He would tell her what he'd been able to find out from Sister Patterson, no more, no less.

The hammer blow came on Friday the 6th May. Kristine had been with Sue in Bath all day and was rushing around getting the supper ready. She didn't open the mail until shortly before Derek came home. She was sitting at the kitchen table with the letter in her hand when he walked through the door.

'Hello love, what news?'

'"Dear Mr and Mrs Arnold, It is with profound regret that we are writing to inform you that Lakeside will cease trading as a Care Home as of 31st July, 2006. We have been operating Residential Homes and Nursing Homes for the last twenty-two years, with what we can honestly say, has been considerable success. Our Inspections at Lakeside in recent years have been excellent, which makes it particularly distressing that we are now, having to close down. In our view, this is entirely due to the excessive regulations imposed on us by Government. Admittedly, some of them have been necessary but many have not and most could have been advisory rather than compulsory"... And they go on to cite examples, you know, about the water being too hot, devices on the bedroom doors if you want to keep them open, that sort of thing, oh and one I'd forgotten about, police checks on every member of staff at £48 a time. I remember them telling me that they have to get these checks done on all new staff and if they leave after a couple of months it will have been a waste of money. Then when the person starts work somewhere else they have to get another check done. The Government's raking in the money on that one. They go on to say they will be available any time over the next few weeks for queries about other homes, fees, moving arrangements etc. What on earth are we going to do? What can we do? Your mother says she'll die if she moves to another home and what if there are no places?'

Kristine was beside herself with anxiety. She couldn't see a way out of the dilemma, without volunteering to have Evelyn back with them but she knew she wouldn't be able to cope. She also felt she should be able to and it was her duty. She got up to check the vegetables on the stove and lay the table, the letter still in her hand. Distractedly, she sat down again. What if they did move Evelyn and she did die? It would be her fault. She would feel responsible. Surely Derek wouldn't blame her? Don't be an idiot she told herself, of course he wouldn't.

While Kristine was reading the letter, Derek had removed his coat and moved round to read over her shoulder. He could feel her trembling and knew she would be imagining the worst-case scenario, as she always did. For once, he was not particularly optimistic but they needed to find a solution and wringing one's hands in despair was not an option. He planted a kiss on the top of her head and poured them both a glass of wine, before joining her at the table.

'OK, love. Let's think about our choices. We can move mother to another home…'

'But what if there are no vacancies and…'

'Hang on a minute, wait 'till I've finished. Because I thought this might happen, I rang Oakhurst two weeks ago and put mother's name down. All right, all right, before you complain, I didn't tell you because I knew you'd worry and think I knew more than I did. I wanted to be on the safe side, that's all. They didn't have a vacancy then but I think we should move mother as soon as a room is free, even if it's next week. We don't owe the Baileys anything and under the circumstances they can hardly ask for payment in lieu of notice.'

'But your mother said she'd die if she had to go to another home.'

'Kristine, why do you believe everything mother says? You know how she exaggerates. Surely you remember, she said she would die if she didn't live with us? She's been in Lakeside for two years now and has been quite happy so you have to take what she says with a pinch of salt.'

'Well, you must admit that she was only really happy there because she had Nancy for company. Now she's gone, your mother is very lonely and miserable.'

'That's true, but I hope you're not suggesting she comes back here? You know that's out of the question. She can do a lot less for herself now than when she was here before. She's now on insulin injections. It would be full time nursing for you and if it all got too much, she would end up in hospital, which is the last place anyone wants to go these days. I'm going to ring Oakhurst this minute and see if they have a vacancy. If they have we can pop over and see it tomorrow.'

Kristine went on sitting at the table, deep in thought. She wasn't looking forward to breaking the news to Evelyn. 'Have they got a room?'

'I'm afraid not. Just as well I put mother's name down though. Sister said they'd had loads of enquiries. Everyone's trying to leave the sinking ship I expect.'

'Shall we warn your mother she'll be moving, or wait until there's a room?'

'I don't know what you think but I'm sure it would be best if we both go and see her on Sunday and tell her about the letter. She is frail but she has got all her marbles and if we don't tell her plenty of others will – the staff for instance, as they will all be looking for new jobs.'

Kristine tried to think of the best option. They could have

her out to lunch but then she may refuse to go back. Anyway, she hadn't wanted to come out much lately.

'I think you're right; we'll both go in on Sunday. We could have lunch with her there. Come on, I know you're not keen, but it wouldn't hurt us, just this once. It is important for her. I know! Why don't I see if Rebecca and Tom can come too, with Luke, which would really cheer her up? I'll ring Rebecca and then Lakeside and see if we can have lunch in the Visitors' room.'

Kristine went off to ring up before Derek could find an excuse. He disliked having lunch at the home, mainly because the portions were too small. They might be OK if you were in your eighties and doing nothing but he liked a more substantial meal. He knew he wouldn't win this time. Kristine was positive his mother liked having him there and she was going to be very upset at the news. Derek cheered up at the prospect of having Tom for moral support. Kristine had noticed over the years that most men hated visiting the sick whether in hospitals, nursing homes or even in their own homes.

Evelyn was expecting them. She had heard the news via the grapevine and was not surprised they'd both turned up but seeing them all made it a special occasion. A united front and all that, she supposed. She hadn't seen Luke for several months and was astonished how big he'd grown.

Although she said she wouldn't move, she knew there was no option. When Lakeside closed she would have to go somewhere, unless she died first. Feeling as miserable as she did, she was convinced this was a distinct possibility. What did she have to live for? Contrary to her expectations, she had been quite happy at Lakeside, especially while she had Nancy for company. It was different now Nancy had gone. Her own life had effectively come to an end. She didn't feel up to making new friends at her age. She was fortunate her family came to see her often but she didn't think they'd miss her too much if she wasn't around. Still, she resolved to make an effort today and agree to whatever proposal they were suggesting.

The table in the Visitors' room had been set for five and Tom had brought the high chair for Luke. Derek had brought some wine although Kristine hadn't been sure that was a good idea.

'Why ever not? We want to cheer mother up, don't we?'

'Yes, but we don't want it to look like a celebratory party, do we? Are you sure you don't want paper hats and crackers? Won't your mother think it's a farewell party?'

Derek laughed at her. 'Kristine, you are a ninny sometimes and you do exaggerate. We always have a glass of wine with Sunday lunch when mother comes here, so why not there? I agree, crackers would be over the top.'

While they were waiting for lunch, Derek explained the position to his mother and told her they would move her to Oakhurst as soon as they had a vacancy.

'At least you've seen it, Mother, and if it hadn't been for Nancy being here you would probably have gone there in the first instance. I'm sure you'll soon settle in once you've made the move. You'll be able to have all your furniture and pictures just the same as here. In no time at all you won't remember Lakeside.'

'If you say so, Derek. Now we know what's been decided, I'd rather not talk about it any more today. Where is Ralph? Why didn't he come with you? I haven't seen him for ages.'

Kristine reminded Evelyn that Ralph was now working in London and he didn't come home every weekend. 'He was here two weeks ago and he's coming back next week. Perhaps you'd like to come out to us then, but if you don't feel like it he'll come and see you, I know.'

'I'd like that. Luke, you come and see Great-Granny and cheer me up.'

And so the lunch passed off fairly successfully. Evelyn seemed to enjoy the attention and being part of the family. Rebecca had had the foresight to bring the camera and managed to get several charming photos of Luke with his great-grandmother. Before they left they saw Evelyn to her room, Kristine and Rebecca making her comfortable on the bed for her belated afternoon nap. They kissed her goodbye, promising to come again later in the week.

Kristine found she had tears in her eyes as she walked down the drive to the car. Evelyn had seemed so small and frail when they left her, a shadow of her previous dominating and organising self. She had been so compliant when told of her move to Oakhurst. No objection. No argument. It was no wonder staff in these homes had no idea of the previous character of their residents and tended to treat them all like children. She had found herself doing it, yet she knew what Evelyn had been like. In her case, it was a relief she no longer had to gather her courage to stand up to Evelyn. Because she no longer criticised her or judged her, Kristine could view her in a more kindly light. Even so, Evelyn seemed less of a person and she found herself almost preferring the old Evelyn. The sooner a room became available at Oakhurst the better.

When Evelyn woke from her nap she still felt incredibly tired. It had been lovely seeing the family but she was exhausted and had missed seeing Ralph. Why hadn't he come? Kristine did say but she couldn't remember. That was the worst thing. She couldn't remember anything these days. Perhaps he would come soon but she would write him a letter in case she was asleep when he turned up. She'd eaten such a large tea, she was going to have an early night. One of the nurses helped her undress, gave her all her tablets and settled her for the night.

Evelyn didn't wait for a vacancy at Oakhurst. She had a massive stroke at 5am the next morning and died an hour later without regaining consciousness. She had left a note on the bedside table addressed to Ralph. 'Dear Ralph, I'm very sorry I am so very tired I can't stay awake to see you today. Will you tell your father not to worry about Oakhurst as I shall be staying here. I can't move again you see. You've all been very kind but I've had enough moving about. Your loving Grandmother.'

Chapter Thirty Eight

New Zealand

'I'll get it.' Maxine picked up the phone. 'Hi, Jack How are ya? I didn't know she was going away. When did she go? But she'd never leave Jess. She'd rather not go than leave her and besides, she always says people are mad, or mean, if they don't like dogs.'

Maxine's stomach was cramping up as a horrible premonition was dawning on her.

'Ken and I'll be up right away. See ya.' Maxine ran out the door and waved to Ken. He'd never hear her over the noise of the mower. He switched off the machine. 'What's up, you look like you've seen a ghost?'

'Mum's gone missing. She went off on Friday, supposedly to go and stay with a friend on the West Coast. She said she'd be back on Wednesday and now it's Thursday and she hasn't come back yet and she was supposed to be back on Wednesday and the friend... '

Ken cut in, 'Hold on a minute. Don't get so agitated. It's only a day over and the West Coast is a long way off. She could have broken down, had a puncture in a remote spot, anything. She'll be OK with Jess. She'll look after her.'

'No, No. You don't understand. Let me finish. She told Jack the friend she was going to stay with didn't like dogs and could Jess stay with him until Wednesday. So Jess is not with her and she has got a mobile and she hasn't rung. I just know something's happened to her. Oh come on. I told Jack we'd go straight up. She might've left an address in the house somewhere.'

Half an hour later they were getting the story from Jack. He'd heard nothing from Angela since she'd roared away from him on Friday morning. He did think she'd been a bit evasive when he'd asked her about having a friend who didn't like dogs.

'Said it was someone she'd known years ago who'd just moved to the West Coast. She did have a small suitcase and a flask and sandwiches sitting on the seat. I suppose she might have decided to stay another day but she could've rung. I did say I'd send out a search party if she wasn't back by Wednesday. Hello, who's coming up the track.'

Maxine felt her chest tighten and her heartbeat quicken as the police car came into view. The officer pulled over when he saw them outside. 'I'm looking for Mrs Brook. Does she live here?'

Maxine was shaking. She'd gone all-cold inside. She just knew it was bad news.

'That's my mother. She lives further up the track. What's the matter, where is she?'

'Does she drive a Holden pick-up?'

'Yes. Yes. Please what's the matter? She was going to the West Coast for the weekend and was due back yesterday.'

'Are these people relations? I'm afraid I've got some bad news.'

Jack led them all inside and left Ken and Maxine with the policeman while he put the kettle on. He also got the whisky out in the belief it was always necessary in a crisis. The policeman introduced himself as Bruce Fletcher. He was rather slow and ponderous, pausing interminably between sentences. Based on the West Coast, he had been patrolling the Arthur's Pass area checking on the road as there'd been a few complaints about the slippery surface and he'd wanted to see for himself. Just before the summit on the West Coast side, he'd noticed the plastic netting covering a break in the crash barrier had been torn aside and was blowing in the wind. It had been secure last week when he'd travelled the same road. On closer inspection there was evidence that a vehicle had gone over the edge, cutting a trail through the scrub and shale to the valley below.

A recovery team had managed to get to the bottom and found the wreckage of a burnt out Holden with the remains of a Christchurch number plate, with only the numbers seven and three still decipherable. Bruce hesitated even longer now and coughed before carefully continuing.

'I'm afraid we found the partially burnt body of a woman who unfortunately might be your mother.'

Chapter Thirty Nine

Maxine stood in the kitchen and gazed at the view her mother would have seen every time she washed the dishes. She wasn't seeing the sloping paddocks, native bush or snow-covered peaks. She was trying desperately to understand why her mother had done it. She had been a relatively healthy woman, who could still drive, could still look after herself; the house was spotlessly clean, she had a loving daughter who'd volunteered to look after her when, and if, she wished.

It had been a week since the policeman had called. A week, since she and Ken had accepted that the remains found in the burnt out Ute, had to be those of her mother. Maxine had come up to the house alone, hoping she might find some clue as to the state of her mother's mind. She was convinced it wasn't an accident. She just knew her mother had committed suicide. Oh, she'd not said as much to the police, but the fact that she'd said she'd never die in her bed and that she'd been drinking when she crashed, convinced Maxine that her mother had driven over the cliff deliberately.

Maxine moved away from the sink and began to systematically look through all the drawers and cupboards, starting with the kitchen. It didn't take long. Most of the drawers were empty and what was there was neat and tidy; a few pots of homemade jam, a half used pot of honey, some Marmite and three tins of tuna. The only cupboard, well stocked, held twenty tins of dog food and a large, unopened packet of dog biscuit. Ken always said she looked after Jess better than herself, which was her saving grace in his eyes.

It wasn't until she came to Angela's bedroom that she found anything of interest. Neatly arranged in the drawer by the bed were various documents: deeds of the house, bank details, and an insurance policy for $40,000 on her life. Bloody hell! She'd have to make damn sure nobody got an inkling that she'd committed suicide or the insurance wouldn't pay out, or so she'd heard. She wasn't about to ask anybody, just in case it was true. Not that she wanted to profit from her mother's death but why should the insurance company benefit? Her mother would have paid for it. She had taken it out years ago; yes 1963 it says. A copy of Angela's will was at the bottom of the pile. Maxine was relieved to see that it had been properly drawn up and signed by a solicitor. She was astonished her mother had managed to save so much money, but living up here she never spent anything, except for food and petrol. Everything had been left to her, including the house, which sometimes Maxine hated and had always been determined to sell if it was ever hers. At other times she loved it, for much the same reasons as her mother had. The beauty of the surroundings, the clear air and the solitude.

When Maxine tried to push the drawer back she met with some resistance. Something must have fallen behind it. Pulling the drawer right out, she felt inside the cavity and, sure enough, she found a sheet of old newspaper. She could see that it was brittle with age and the date in the top corner was 14th September, 1953. Curious to see what exciting news had caused her mother to save an old paper for so many years, Maxine unfolded it carefully.

'WERE THEY MURDERED' ran the banner headlines.

As she began to read the article, Maxine's heart contracted. A coldness ran through her and she carried the paper out into the sun where she could sit on the veranda.

"Mystery surrounds the deaths over a period of six months of five people in the Mountain View Residential Home for the Elderly in New Plymouth. Several residents and a niece of one of them have made a formal complaint against a nursing auxiliary working at the Home. They have claimed that nurse Angela Thornley maltreated some of the patients and may even have been responsible for their deaths. Substance has been given to their claim with the sudden departure of Miss Thornley, hours after the last death of a relatively young woman of 59. This person, who cannot be named for legal reasons, had voiced her anxiety and fear of nurse Thornley to other patients. Results of a post mortem will be available later this week."

There was more but Maxine's hands were trembling and she was feeling very cold. She was afraid to read on yet she had to know what her mother was supposed to have done. She couldn't have done it, surely? Or could she? It would explain why Angela had such a dislike of old people and her determination never to go into an old peoples' home. Maxine fetched her cardigan from the car and returned to the veranda to finish the article.

"Police were called and spent several days interviewing the patients and their friends and relatives. Angela Thornley was traced to her home in Masterton and interviewed by police. Asked why she had left so abruptly Miss Thornley said she had been exhausted and depressed by the work load and by the knowledge that patients were there until the end of their days. She wanted to work in a different environment, where people actually recovered and went home. Isobel Gardiner, Matron of the Home said that it was an unfortunate fact that in any such establishment there was sometimes a spate of deaths in a short space of time. Patients could be assured of the best possible care at all times. Subject to the results of the post mortem the police believed there was insufficient evidence of wrongdoing to charge anyone. However, Mountain View would receive close inspection in the future."

Maxine sat for some time with the paper in her hand. She would never know what had happened at the home and even if her mother had been alive she couldn't have asked her. It was true she didn't like old people and it was possible she didn't have much patience with them, but harm them, could she believe that? It was possible she slapped them about a bit. She'd certainly belted Maxine on several occasions without much provocation. But murder? Never. She couldn't believe it. Perhaps she had helped them on their way, although Maxine couldn't imagine how. Maybe she had believed in euthanasia, lots of people did. It would still have been murder though and that was terrible. Maxine sighed. The authorities cannot have been convinced by the accusations; there hadn't been a trial or anything, the post mortem obviously hadn't turned up any evidence. She wished she hadn't found the paper but she was profoundly grateful it was she and nobody else who had. It did answer many puzzling aspects of her mother's attitude to old people, her aversion to crowds and living in built up areas. She must always have been afraid she would meet someone from her past; why she had shied away from talking to the Norwegian lady they had met in Palmerston North. Maxine was glad too, that she'd come up to the house alone. She took a box of matches from the shelf and, standing in the yard, she set fire to the paper and scattered the ashes with her foot. In spite of everything, Maxine loved her mother in her own way and nobody else need ever know her secret.

Conclusion

England

Kristine sat at the table, deep in thought. There had to be a better way to treat the elderly. She was convinced Evelyn had died because she had given up. The anxiety and stress of moving again was too much for her. So what was different about the people in Mountain View? Did they give up because of neglect and abuse? There was never any proof that they were helped or pushed out of this world. The point is that they shouldn't have to give up on life. They should be able to just wind down and fade away gently and peacefully.

There was nothing very much wrong with the care at Lakeside. It was a model of excellence compared with Mountain View forty odd years ago, but it wasn't like home. People went from looking after themselves entirely, to almost total dependency, overnight. Of course there were warden-controlled complexes in some areas but they were few and far between. In New Zealand, there were retirement villages but she hadn't heard of any here. However, they did not solve the problem of going from almost total control to total dependency. A halfway house would be the answer.

Why couldn't people dust and Hoover their own rooms, do some hand washing, or even use the machine if they were able? They had been struggling with these things in their own home, sometimes without adequate facilities. They go into a home and suddenly they don't do anything. They are redundant, overnight. If the carers could be facilitators, not necessarily doing things for them but helping them do things for themselves, they might feel life was that much more worthwhile. They could eat in a central dining room if they wanted to but if not, cook something for themselves in a specially equipped kitchen, supervised if required. Slowly, gradually, people would be less inclined to do things for themselves and carers could take over. Yes, it would take much more organisation because everyone would want to do different things and eat different food. Funding would be a problem too as there would have to be an overall basic charge to cover heating, light, water etc. but then people could be charged for the level of service they needed. It would give the elderly more dignity, more control over their lives and make them feel less dependent on others.

Kristine sighed. It was a nice ideal but she doubted it would happen. If someone tried it, Government would come along and impose all sorts of restrictions, inspectors, and licences and make the whole thing impossible. She had come to the conclusion that families looking after their own relatives, with regular respite and other support when necessary, was the best solution for a dignified and peaceful end to one's life.